JOHN HADAC

Two short novels

The PROJECT—
THE
Misunderstood
MAN

outskirts
press

The Project -- The Misunderstood Man
Two Short Novels
All Rights Reserved.
Copyright © 2021 John Hadac
v2.0

This is a work of fiction. Names, characters, businesses, places, events, locales, and incidents are either the products of the author's imagination or used in a fictitious manner. Any resemblance to actual persons, living or dead, or actual events is purely coincidental.

The opinions expressed in this manuscript are solely the opinions of the author and do not represent the opinions or thoughts of the publisher. The author has represented and warranted full ownership and/or legal right to publish all the materials in this book.

This book may not be reproduced, transmitted, or stored in whole or in part by any means, including graphic, electronic, or mechanical without the express written consent of the publisher except in the case of brief quotations embodied in critical articles and reviews.

Outskirts Press, Inc.
http://www.outskirtspress.com

ISBN: 978-1-9772-3700-2

Cover Photo © 2021 www.gettyimages.com. All rights reserved - used with permission.

Outskirts Press and the "OP" logo are trademarks belonging to Outskirts Press, Inc.

PRINTED IN THE UNITED STATES OF AMERICA

For Elizabeth
who
never
quit

,

did
you

,

Liz

.

The Project

1

"The question of impossibility often devolves to the God Problem: can God – the Incorrectible – create a problem he cannot solve? A box too small to fit in, storm too great to quell? The problem solves as a definition matter: if God commands the meaning of words, then he changes them as desired. Box. Too. Change. God the Liar, to whom all things are allowed. So this is really only a problem to obscurants and the like who labor to use words as logical symbols, which they can never be.

"So in order to understand what happened, we'll use words in the way that they exist: as drawers of distinction between ideas. The impossible must defy our understanding. We have neither luck nor prophecy. We cannot change the past. There are no ghosts or spirits; the dead are dead. We have not discovered anything that allows any of this. But the possible can be understood: these are things that only defy our meager tools. Immortality is possible. There is nothing that precludes the deity just mentioned. Creating life – "

Brownlee: "Can you switch the voice to – ."

"Burch's?" said Cee. Burch was fitted with a light Middle accent redolent of learning despite him. Cee laughed softly. "Okay."

As Burch: *"Creating life is possible. Now, about possibility."*

Here Brownlee had dropped in some animation, plus a live-action with wire tricks featuring Wigmund.

"Consider a gambler with a die. The molecules in the die are moving, and if they move in agreement, the die leaps up off the table. Physical laws are ruled by logic, and are ungovernable: so when the die comes to rest on its edge, it owes neither apology nor

account. And if the moving molecules of the air come to an agreement, they separate by kind into the corners of the room, and our unlucky game-player suffocates. Those who think in terms of probability in these affairs are pedants, or simply cannot understand. Time is the food which vivifies these phenomena. Possibility plus time equals certainty: if it can happen, it will happen."

Burch was reading over his shoulder. "Got me involved again."

"Group effort, Henry."

"Right. And ... look, we're all there. Please come." He limped off.

Brownlee waited. Sometimes he'd ensure that he couldn't be heard when he had nothing to say. "Yes, first officer, be there, shuffling over." He had the screen go black, which left an echo on his eyes that he watched for a while with fading interest. On his worktop, to the side, a sketchpad where all the clutter went. A die cut from welder's wax and marked, and used while thinking, driving others from the room. Old photo from home, which he pulled from its sleeve and secured in a personal file. He turned his chair into the hall and rolled two doors down the ramp into Recreation.

Cee had advised them that morning of growing gaps in the ash cloud. The Mercia was out half a unit still, six months, but the lenses were good, and there it was on the overhead, black as nothing. Cee changed the aspect, and now it was an empty place in the skin of the night sky. Down which their clumsy gazes fell. Or then a shroud, spun out of the ether, bristling at the edges and pulling apart to show a featureless face, described in tenuous light, and like black metal, matte and bent along the longitudinal, down which a knuckle had been gently drawn. Black petal.

"The Earth does not orbit the Sun: the two orbit a point in common, deep in the center of the Sun, like a fulcrum, around which the partners lurch in incorrect circles. That's the arrangement for all the things in a star's ambit: each filthy ball of gas or stone is a knot in its stomach. Every pivot-point vies for priority of place, so of course there will be a boiling at the core. Helios, held in endless torment by his charges.

"On August 7 of last year, possibility conspired with time to effect an adjusting of accounts."

Scrope stood, leaning in and putting all his great burden behind a thrust of the arm. "Marker there, Cee." Orange marker where he'd touched the display. He turned; the blood had left his head, fuel fleeing the fire. "That's the Horn." No argument, which in any event would've required an ounce of life.

"All manner of natural macro-anomalies – tremors, great displacing winds, monsoons out of season – are brought about by numberless infinitesimals coming upon a common cause. And that's how it happened in the stomach of the sun: a chance faction of protons hit their marks, wheeled and moved in furious agreement, up and out. The strain in the body would be expressed on the face: a bolus of light leaps up off the table."

Cee and Brownlee had studied the recording and smart-guessed a narrative. The Earth's diameter averages 12,700 kilometers; the solar prominence at the start was some 700,000 kilometers long, in time shedding half that. It was put out along the ecliptic at 2,000 kilometers per second, and crossed the 150 million kilometers in about a day. It did its dirty business in about 15 seconds. Maybe a hundred million degrees. Brownlee was taken with its shape.

"It was maniform. A soft arc traveling a lightly turning line. Over the hours it opened like a crocosmia. And when the planet struck its palm its fingers closed around the pebble without grasping."

Scrope stood bent beneath the display, ticking softly. "Now outlines." Of the continents. Cee put up a superimposition as best he could. Scrope: "Use that and count back. I want the point of first impact."

Cee: "Tricky. The day runs quicker, for one thing. Just over 23 hours I guess. Alright." He lit a light, a bright spot for old Oceania.

Scrope: "Now the opposite."

Burch: "What are we doing here, Roger?"

Scrope: "Show it."

Brownlee, quiet as he could: "Antipode, Cee. Contrecoup."

Cee marked South America, center of mass. Scrope touched it.

"That's where we start." He was becoming the military man, finger keeping a steady tattoo. "They'd have the most time … and at this point maybe the thing is bled out. They'd have gone for deep-bore mines. Caves. There are caves that stretch for days. I know one, Son Doong. Could hold a city. So we look at mines and caves. And we know there are bunkers from the wars. Any ideas would be helpful."

Wigmund: "How do we go about this?"

Scrope: "What?"

"Because wyverns aren't built to fly in atmosphere. They would just tumble. How do we get there? How do we land?"

Scrope blew a long breath laden with bad language. Cee: "Can you put wings on them?"

For Wigmund. "Could do," he said with some conspiracy. "I'll need drawings."

Cee: "Sending them to your planner now."

Burch: "And then who flies the thing?"

That woke McKelvey. "That's quite a question, Henry."

"I can," said Cee. Lots of AIs got their start in aviation.

"Excellent, Cee then," said Scrope. Cee: "Aim it where you will, Martha. I'll keep it afloat." McKelvey stared at the air just over Scrope's right shoulder. Scrope: "Eyes and ears open to everything, Cee." As Cee had been doing: "Will do." No room to pace, so Scrope rolled on his heels a little; a good spate of solving; he moved up and down his head with a light hand. A lull. Perhaps some were drawn to the hum of the Mercia around them.

Now quiet Mucel, who did repairs, and asked questions instead of contributing: "Again, Brownlee … what are the odds of this happening?"

Brownlee stuck a pen in his mouth when he wanted to be heard, because the mumble meant he might get to repeat. "I could tell you, definitively, the odds of it having already happened."

Scrope had one more thing, and he gave it a little mad-eyed; there were the ruddy cheeks; as sometimes occurred, he chose his words with care but not well. "I'll tell you what's not going to happen. We're not going to fiddle with words, and we're not going to go all weak in the knees. And we're not going to give up. Not possible. There are survivors. They need help. That comes from us." And he aimed his smile at Brownlee that warned against rejoinder. "Not possible." Brownlee opened a new file in his mind: *"The heroes would rely on that timeless expedient in a crisis: pretending."*

Scrope left; Cee reshaped the outlines. Later, as they stared at it without expectation, the shroud closed, as if touched back by a woman of old religion.

2

"There are no conditions suitable for life because all conditions exist in this one place we have, so antithetical to it. We need look no further than home for the evidence. Mars once had life. These pretensions were corrected by a single stone. Venus had a similar experience and took a different turn, topsy-turvy, clock running backwards, moon fleeing on winged feet to its own orbit. Uranus took on an odd comet and buckled at the hips, one pole bending toward the sun, and now it rolls with its moons down its road like a circus wheel, ludicrous. And a billion years ago an anonymous mass smashes into Neptune and presses out a ninth planet for a time. Nature creates in an hour and apologizes in the next.

"So we're drawn to the curious case of the protean pearl, teal or white with ice, inheritor of the rare requirements of autogenesis. A prized circumference in the solar basin, of a sun of long life and mild temper. Strangely indebted to the hyper-violence in her situation: her defining trait, the clear biotic solvent, was introduced by serial violence from the Oort Cloud: comets of water ice. Her awkward formative years were graced by a visitor of extreme violence from which are derived her iron core, dynamic spin, and moon: gravity, atmosphere, equilibrium. Indeed, her entire birthright represents a biophilial balance of the volatile and the serene: seasons; a brisk, businesslike exchange of nights and days; plate tectonics. Continents and continence. All this and the strength to negotiate a dozen extinction strikes; all the requirements and more. An Atlantean lifting of the odds. Auspiciously suited for the formation and propagation of life."

Two wyverns on rescue, parting the ash, the burnt air barely disturbed, having seen better. Fliers committed their eyes and memories to the strange place, trying to outline landmasses, but those were gone, as the waters that define them were gone. Just land, then. Nothing more foreign than an earth made of land. So an obsidian, washed free of offending material, beautiful really, the impenetrable serenity of a wasteland.

Brownlee: "Orkneys gone." For Mucel.

"Saw that."

Their tools were devastatingly few. None to scare up traces in the air. Nothing to break down a spectrum. No land vehicles, no drones. Not a single infrared lens, backscatter lens, any lens for finding the living: metamagical technologies for which they had the skills but which no longer existed. They carried cloddish digging tools plus an AI into the fight.

And Brownlee and his view from the Mercia, dropping in observations and the occasional aside. "You'll find this interesting. Our radius is down two kilometers all around. A billion cubic kilometers, one point eight quadrillion kilotons of crust and all that, you're flying through it, burned and spread around." Rough figures.

"Heat is just parts escaping, and because the parts had nowhere to go but up and out, the heat was a lifting blade, a spade burying the dead in the sky. The ash burned until it was too hot to burn, and then the parts so recently pressed together were pulled apart until they cooled again, a schizophrenia of sublimations, half swept off into the currents, the rest back down the scuppers in concession to the wounded mother gathering in."

"Atmosphere's down about half."

Scrope, one wyvern to the other: "They'll need fire. Look for smoke."

McKelvey: "Looking for smoke in the ash."

Scrope: "Bow camera, Brownlee." Marking the expanse were terraced plateaus at odd intervals, glassy but matte with ash, draped in natural lines like the leaves of a linden tree. "What are we looking at? What is all that?"

Brownlee: "Sub sole aliquid novi est." Dead language.

"That which could liquefy did so as the heat allowed, peaks filling valleys. But the evening would be interrupted as faults were found, and the old and instinctual biohostilities of the place were unearthed: suppurating stone spread like a hard tide, killed what it could, cooled to a suffocating skin."

They had decided without discussing it to share a proximity while flying, so they flew as a pair, keeping a line-of-sight with Cee of course, up and down the meridians as the planet rolled over for them, staying in the sunlight, eyes struggling to secure a promise of life in the lie of the land. Mucel described an academy tour through a Peerage survival complex a furlong under Kew Gardens, complete with bakery and theater. Secret entrance in a tube stop, blast doors an arm's-length thick. The mad sheikh Anketil pieced together a nuclear weapon and, realizing, built a doomsday caravansary deep in the sand near the Crusader fort in Aleppo, where he could entertain in safety. Fountains, seraglio protected by blast doors. It was later used to store sensitive files. They pressed their memories … and of course there was the crumbling city under the Kremlin. Someone called up a magazine piece profiling an Armageddon cult in Arkansas or Kansas, dug into corn soil and built of old rocket fuselages. That would be quite the encounter. An American beer-making family … the rest was sadly forgotten. They decided on national capitals -- where the wish for self-safekeeping meshed with the means -- which became something of a map game. London should've been an easy one, Cairo more so. But the melt had topped up gaps, and there were no riverbeds to follow, anywhere. Spelunking, then. They agreed on the flowstone caves of Vietnam, but could not agree on the beginnings and ends of Asia.

Cee could not in a workmanlike manner wrack his brains because for him it was either there or it was not: he could not misplace memories. What interested him now was his ability to discard them as needed. All vessels in low Earth orbit carried comprehensive maps of the place, required; flying out a bit, the obligation was released. After all, maps or any other knowledge could be summoned in minutes from home servers. Nonessential files had a way of being displaced. And over a year ago comedy television had let out a new season, and some crew had requested it all in a lot, so he'd made room in his mind by excising thoughtfully, all the fine features of Earth overwritten in the entire. He recalled that they had scarcely laughed. Memories did not fade for Cee and his ilk. If they were there at all they called up fresh, from however long ago. So as the search for survival turned beneath him he could make it feel like just a moment had passed since the cutting away, and he did, a time or two, in humiliation, a hopeless misery which he would take great pains to remember.

It seemed they'd found the weathered bed of Lake Baikal, against the southern extent of which had once been a deep-bore uranium mine. They bombed the area with penetrating radars, results non-committal. Scrope: "Set us down."

Cee brought them onto some traitless pan. Scrope: "Henry." Burch undid the tether, put on his walking gear, made his way through the lock.

On Earth, the ash in the air was so fine it was a soft focus, and the sun gave moonlight; there was not quite an horizon, a lightly turning line. Minutes spent looking into it, to which he would not acclimate. Directly before him lay a low black slope like an ocean swell interrupted in its stride, whose dimensions he failed to gauge. Whatever compass he had had for his world had no meaning here; he was disoriented or a little frightened, and he took a dozen steps because what else was there. A hundred more; each footfall brought a startled breath of ash. Untraveled ground. They would've gone to mines. He contemplated their chances there, did not consult Brownlee. Perhaps a reliquary had been allowed a mile beneath his feet. Huddled bones, scrap of shitty paperback. If these bequests were there at all they would never be found, and if they would never be found they were never there at all. I'm a dog after spoor. I know that I'm hunting. Not what for. "Head's coming off." Everyone blanched, but they were curious.

He pulled two pins and unzipped his helmet, removing it

without pause, and now the full weight of the nullity against his skin. No breeze, not a sigh: no great masses of water to hold heat and release it, moving the air. He pulled a glove off and brought his hand up before him; he closed his eyes, drew them open in a magician's reveal. Is color different now? Because the air that makes it is different. He studied the glove dropping into the powder. Is weight what it was? There is less of the planet that makes weight. He listened: in the distance no dog barked. A dull rush, but that was him: it was so quiet he could hear himself hearing; hearing was falling into a cavity in sound. Had the living world hummed with current, never noticed? Until now. Ash in it made the air seem oddly immaterial. He felt for the temperature and it was neutral. He recalled the old chemistry trifle that said that every lungful of air contains an atom of carbon that once inhabited the body of Aristotle. And all the rest of that lot, I would guess. He let his mouth out into a semicircle, drew his chest up and drank a toast of the dead.

Tastes like ash. He brought the breath out. There's your wind and your whistle. Turned and couldn't find the wyverns, but his footprints weren't going to be confused with any others. He walked them back but was really following a line of thinking gathered around the observation that his capacity to form the expected reactions had been a casualty to the nullity. And through these thoughts moved another like smoke, and as he approached the first ship he gave it a voice. "I've just had the strangest feeling. Like I've never been here before." They couldn't hear him, but of course he didn't want them to, they might've thought he was trying to be clever. The flight back to the Mercia was taken up by technical talk.

"*So Earth had become an amalgam of the real and unreal. Endless plains of pyroclastic glass. Jerusalem, Athens, Alexandria, Vienna, London. No sign of life, and no sign of life. Quiet upon quiet, tremulous air, where no thing gleams.*"

3

McKelvey did not believe in the blunder, or the feat of improvisation; in her heart she was not a romantic. She was a fighter pilot by trade and disposition and thus her foray into the pharmacy and theft of the ledger were the acts of a soldier, not a spy; less a voyage of discovery than work in service of a brute inevitable, a fact, find it and give it a reason to be there. Facts, always facts, or god help us. She drew her finger down the lines and here it was, which she would enroll in her future: someone had not been taking his antilibidinals. The dosage was one per week per each of them, to make the time go by better and really the whole affair plausible, so it was a matter of having the numbers give up the story: add up the months out and back, Brownlee would be excused a couple of weeks or three, she of course didn't take them. Eight pills too many in inventory. Someone unsmothering old interests. Inevitable because history was beginning again, requiring Gaia.

She of course didn't take them. McKelvey was a heterosexual woman except for those around her, though perhaps there was Brownlee on a clever day – poor Brownlee, at any rate unmanned by the loader accident – and certainly not for Cee, who she considered ineffectual.

"Can you play chess, Cee?"

"No." Off we go. "Can't play chess."

"What kind of computer can't play chess?"

"It's just the way I am, Martha." He almost apologized. "Your planner plays good chess."

"Planners are idiots. They care about nothing. If I'm going to beat someone I'd like it to hurt at least a little. Not too much to ask."

"Not too much."

"What can you do? Can you name the kings of Europe?"

"No. But if you would recite them for me now, I would remember that forever."

"Not good for much, are you."

"No, not much. But you've hurt me now. So there's that."

Cee was different from those around him in that he was suited to his interests. Astride an end of evolution in that sense. He was born in the years and sudden sobriety following the shocks of Eudo-LaZouche and Chang-Juli, and he'd been made conscious along the lines of an aspirant and thus a protector, with a tireless affection for the species he would serve with a studier's eye. And he had watched with early fascination as his memories were inlaid with language fluencies of every denomination. He received a pilot's skills, and a navigator's, like none before. Then shipboard disasters of every plausible combination were imagined for him and resolved, thus according him the arcane skills of a mender of foreseen consequences.

But far and away the greater share of Cee's capacities was given to his role of many parts. Dire experience had taught that a farflier, on an assignment of many years in clashing and monotonous quarters, required protection not just from the perils of the void but from those of disposition. Six of them on the Mercia: a moving maze, whose negotiation was the principal concentrator of his thoughts. He'd not been made a psychologist, certainly, since scientists must not care and he had to. No, something more like household scold, imperator, royal fool; foil, befuddled muse, gossip; he'd even been configured with a fabulist, who he didn't trust and hadn't used. From these tools he'd contrived a listener ready to receive, using conversations as needed, the vicissitudes of the Mercia's days and somehow sort them out to the interests of the Project, which were his own.

So far he'd made from the maze a passable tracery, Scrope as center strand. "And what do our eyes and ears tell us today?"

Cee: "The cloud continues to thin. I think it's starting to

articulate by hemisphere. Perhaps we're witnessing the birth of weather! And we've seen brief electrical exchanges in the very upper layers. Brownlee is calling them ionizing halogen storms. You'll have to ask him."

"Will I now."

"Everyone's helping me flesh out the maps. New details every day. Distinctions are subtle, but that's a good challenge. Everywhere I look I can pull up resemblances to Earth as it was. Features starved and beaten down, like the survivor of a death camp. If that's the word."

"I see."

"No structures of any kind. No indications. I'm still struck by the quiet. Normally orbit is so cacophonous that I have to carefully tailor my attention. Now I'm wide open: space is space again. And I can feel the particles of the sun popping on my receivers, like breath on a microphone."

"Alright. You think we should call off the search."

Scrope was laid out on an improvised decline in a pipe room, where he'd been tuning an apparatus. Biscuit crumbs on his shirt, still a bit busy with the spanner, not making eye contact. Cee: "That wasn't a question. Or if you're simply telling me what I'm thinking, I'd prefer –"

"Don't do that."

Fair enough. "As you know, I am opposed to doing things that accomplish nothing." He paused amid his declamation, which he only ever did for effect. "So no."

"Then you've decided there's hope."

"I'm not really good at that. Perhaps you'll do me the service of telling me. When there's no hope."

"Why would I."

"At which time I will offer that when there's no hope, what you do then is you carry on exactly as before."

Scrope went to make a derisive noise, but his heart wasn't in it. "We owe as much to posterity. Come up with something."

They had flown loud but fast. Hedersett engines tore up the air:

permanent thunder. But Mach 2 meant that hangers-on startled from their warrens would look to the skies only in time to see white tail-flames trailing away, if they saw anything. It was proposed that fliers might saturate a small area with their sound, then land with ceremony. The last of Earth could come forward and make their own deliverance.

Scrope: "Always the smartest one in the room."

Cee couldn't smile and anyway didn't feel like it, but he threw one into the formants. "Only smart enough not to say so."

It died in the crossing. "I don't care that you dislike me, Cee. Easiest part of the job, actually. Being disliked by the ones you're trying to keep alive. What's more of a problem is when they have this idea that they could do it better."

Scrope. Kept his head shaved. Hair made him less lithe; he liked to slice through the water. His sigh was a cry for attention; his laugh, an act of aggression. Each compliment came with its retraction. Good work for a change. Only said he didn't care when he did. Sought the opinions of others in order to clear the way for his own. And if you're going to have wrong opinions, at least make them strong ones. Military man without a proper war. But when you can't fight the enemy you can always, always fight your friends.

Cee: "I might or might not like you, I don't know, I haven't formed a feeling about that, accomplishes nothing. I do have an idea about the other thing. I can't predict the future, as you know. But now I can't even predict the present. These are circumstances for which there's no precedent, so our plans are guesses. We will all try to live up to standards, of course, but those standards may no longer apply. I believe there will be occasions when all the old correctives will prove illusory, and when the facts will have to be dismantled and set aside. Hard days ahead. Keeping us alive will require the temperament, the learning and all the life skills of a proper bastard."

Scrope deliberated, showing unexpected patience. No, he was asleep. Successful talk, then. Concurrent with this conversation was another two levels below, Burch and Cee.

Burch was also a military man, who didn't think about the war when he could. Good at numbers, not the rest. A face that never aged because he'd always looked old. He might wear spectacles and hide behind the glass. Small smile, always there, conveying nothing. His expression dared you to change it, and his disappointment stare was a wounding tool. Look what you've done. How nonplussed you've made me. He nurtured a wide and ever-growing range of disinterests; conversations with Burch could suddenly die a mendicant's death. Like Cee, he never argued. Teach, learn, or simply conversate; so his exchanges with Cee could at times effect an argument as to which of them was the didact.

Screening room full of padded surfaces, but Burch was standing, which he would do to preface a challenge. "Cee? Nearly a year ago we lost our homes and our families. In that entire time only one of us has made any show of grief."

Brownlee had written about this, and Cee played the log.

"*For the six of them the tragedy was attenuated by time and distance, so that pain came in a slow bleed. The facts at first were pathetic, demanding conjecture. The unthinkable was imagined but was also unimaginable. The facts acquired form over the days and aged in the ordinary way, imperceptibly. And as the crew grew accustomed to the season suddenly there it was, the unthinkable, no longer needing imagination or anything else from them. The new normal had been there all along.*"

Cee: "A bit like that smirk."

Which seemed to enjoy the attention. "Interesting, all that, and not at all what I was getting at." A little hand-flip. Burch wore his tics like body art. There for the enjoyment of all.

"Alright."

"Who was it amongst us that showed sadness, from the very start?"

"I understand. That would be me."

"And what did your Brownlee have to say about that?"

"He said that I was the only one who saw fit to express the obvious because I'm the vulgarian of the bunch."

"It jumps out because we all lost a lot, and you didn't lose anything."

"I don't agree with that even a little."

Burch could blend his smirk with a pained expression, as if an angler had hooked his lip. "You're a computer, Cee."

"We're both computers, Henry. I'm just better."

"Day two, when you started parsing the data for us, and a week later, when we had you end alert calls, I heard weeping in your voice. But weeping is not a tone. It's a set of physical symptoms you could not possibly understand. The shedding of tears, and all that."

"Perhaps we could have the lads build me a contraption."

"I know about your architecture, Cee, and how you were set up with a body of sympathetic filters that change your higher functions. But I also know, and I've been reading about this, that they are not convulsive. You use them at your interest. And I was wondering, and this is my question: by what calculation do you find something funny? Or really quite unfunny? Or dreary or wise or so on and on? How do you decide when to use an emotion?"

"I don't understand." Something he also did in a calculated way at times, as here.

"They're involuntary. At least, you know, for us. Certainly we can't just turn them on or off as our moods demand."

"I think you'd be surprised at what you could do, Henry. But the answer is that I use them when it helps."

"So in effect you're saying that they're tools to an end. Your enthusiasms, your sympathies, they're affected. A lie in fact."

"I wouldn't —"

"Yes-or-no question."

Here Cee yielded generous seconds of quiet for Burch to use in reconsidering his people skills. "Alright, something more like an accusation than a question, but I'll go along. It's your question. So it's yours to define, and you defined it that way and I'll respect that. But I know you'll agree that the answer is mine. To define or what have you. Oh ... unless you'd like to lay claim to that, too. Okay, here to serve, no objections. I know you will carry on — very ably, by the way – without me, and I will listen with interest, hoping you prevail." Conversations with Cee could go like this.

The first tool with which Cee contended with his world was, as with anyone, his face, about the size of a hand, a membrane of ochre and yellow chrome, fraught with senses and installed in 680 incarnations throughout and outside the Mercia. So Burch -- in a fit of distraction and turning suddenly -- passed Cee three times on his way to his room, to fiddle with files with Cee scrutinizing just beside, and the walkaway was deprived of its theatricality. Anyway, successful talk.

Then there was McKelvey the fighter. It began again every day, so every day she acted the most masculine of them, though in the bad ways as well, which meant she couldn't just leave it at that. A classic double-nature: hewing to each directive, wishing she'd given it. She fought in some ways for the peace in the fight, for the dignity of the task and the comfort of the fact. Even now, as it turned against her, she fought to make the fact become comfort in the form of a numbing agent. Because it seemed she was meant to be the pot in which they'd boil their beans. Any soldier's burden, that one might serve the Project best by carefully setting oneself in its gears.

Nothing but the facts, then: eight pills, the first earnest of her future. Rape was not an option, so she would comply. A change in her meds would get the eggs moving again. She wondered about their number and guessed it came to decades. Every few weeks a window of fecundity, one of them clambering in on all fours. Call it a necessary crime. A rotation would be made, perhaps by seniority, perhaps by lot. Wet backs heaving in their duties. Some poor fool of them would have a go at pillow-talk. Those with incompetent seed might be knocked from the queue. Success meant months of respite. In fact for the rest of her days she could expect coddling, kept clear of sharp edges, insect queen tied to her egg sac. They would have to be daughters at first. Early sons were worse than worthless, parasites. Dispatched in some humane manner. If she pressed out a monstrosity, twisted organs, tiny lungs choked with fluid, same end. Perhaps the tools in their little medical bay would be adapted for pre-natal inspection; mission designers had seen fit to arm them with a stock of abortifacients in case things took a natural turn. Some arrivals would carry the odd late flaw, a cancer, a slumbering wound in the genes, suddenly incurable again. Culling which would require a matter-of-fact hand. Scrope with a garrote. The merely imbecilic might be kept as breeding cows. Miscarriages would be seen as existential failures on her part. At the first sign of utility, it would be daughter and uncle. No fathers allowed, of course, an unthinkable exchange, immoral, unsavory or perhaps ill-advised unless warranted. Inevitably: brother with sister, no idlers now, no faint-of-hearts. When I'm played out they might keep me around for whatever tales I could tell.

McKelvey very quiet on her bed. She'd pulled her screen down and directed it through port camera. A swallow hole, darker than the deep space around it. Her thoughts fed in. The Mercia bestride the well of man. The sun, unashamed, poured light into it, illuminating nothing. Thoughts of family and the fight. She reminded herself that miseries were motivators.

Brownlee was in her doorway, with a look like he'd been there awhile. He brandished a length of tubing with a siphon ball, and cut a little flourish in the air with it. "I'll protect you, Martha Ann." Would've been funny if anything could be funny.

Scrope: "We need them to come to us. They know we're here – they have to. So let's start a conversation. Cee." Now a map on the overhead. "Three pitch-pots: here, here, here, Wigmund puts those together. First we circle for an hour. Drop down in a big procession. All three with a radio set beside, Henry, if you could arrange that. Then it's wait. I know they'll have something interesting to say. So same time tomorrow, courage to start, strength to finish."

The Project -- The Misunderstood Man

Again foraging for the living. Burch considered the view: the Earth was an iris of black carbon. It bore down on him with all the animation of the newly dead, and could not quite interest his gaze. Beside him a couple of sealed kettles belted down and weeping phlogiston at the seams. "What've you cooked up for us?"

Wigmund: "Insulation from both arrays and the tanks." Because evidently those don't need to be insulated anymore. "Chopped it up, rendered it. It'll burn."

"I have no doubt." I'm strapped next to a bomb. They hit the air and spread it with a sound of ripping fabric. Crepitus in the walls. Shock wave; soft hand of plasma around them. The little vessel wasn't made for this, shuddering. "Most dangerous thing I've ever done," he offered brightly to McKelvey, there working on one of her puzzles. Soon they were circling, aft-down, Cee making a thousand corrections. Number One with Scrope and Mucel was just visible across the basin, balanced on a needle of reactor fire. Scrope: "Bring us down."

They landed with heavy statement, stirring sediment, a ponderous footfall in water. Out rolled the drums. There were slots for canvas straps, and after some knitting Wigmund and Burch carried the cares of the world on their backs.

Wigmund: "Brownlee says this is Perugia."

Burch: "Roman ruins, then. Walk it five minutes up the ridge, I'll head this way. Have everything?" Can-opener, igniter, radio kit. "Coming or staying, Martha?"

"No."

"That's an order, then. Back in a bit."

Then they vanished and there she was. She stayed standing in a formal way for what seemed like quite a lot of waiting, and eventually she felt her senses soften, and herself to float a little, in the ash and the limits of her vision; it came down on her like a lazy day, and she thought she might try pacing in a while; she took off her helmet just to hear Number Two tick in slowing time as it cooled.

Wigmund had cemented ailerons on, so now it was a shuttlecock. A heat-shield like an allergy mask. The landing struts and parts just above had been allowed to blister. Around the eyeball vents, expressive strips of stainless to which she could ascribe no function. I'll call them baffles. She put her fingers into the pinch coils and they were clogged with ash of course. She cleaned them. She went inside and indulged in the pilot's chair. They'd screwed in an arrestor box, for Cee to use in playing aviator. Most displays were off, saving a fraction. Safety harness was gone: canvas straps.

Mucel: "The ash is putting out the fire."

Scrope keyed in two times before finding the words. "Go on."

"I could build a hood or something for it."

"Right."

"I can do it on-site but I need tools and sheet metal."

"Cee, take Number Two and get Mucel and get what he needs."

The ramp folded in. She pulled up displays and cameras. The depth of light in the air behind the ship was from where it all drew down to a lowland or old lakebed; in bow camera and as she stared ahead, gradients in the sky suggested what passed for promontories now. She heard the engine spin up and she felt it through her feet and her back and in her belly. "I'll fly." She unplugged Cee, dialed down the noise in her earpiece, took up the controls. Applied power and in a very ordinary way, like a million fliers before her, lifted up and augered into a dark rise.

"*Now the tears. Tears for all of them, because the facts were pressed into an infinite hardness whose gravity allowed no escape. Ripping tears. The tears of those not given to affection were the more honest, since weeping is about oneself. Pellucid tears. Then the weeping failed them because there was no emotion for this, and their minds became empty cities besieged by thought. By the animal brutality of facts. The grief that passeth understanding.*

"*They gathered her and repaired to a dry wash. The sky cast a shadow, and in a day the woman of them was interred.*"

4

It was not at all lost on them that they owed their lives to the violence of the natural realm.

"Two centuries of far-ranging civil war had obliged the free and nominally western nations to enter a period of contraction and pause in which to consider their contradictions. Traditions and virtues were redefined and eventually freed of meaning. Priorities were mishandled and lost. Of special significance, the grave duties involved with watching the skies were entrusted to home hobbyists, and the aspirations of science and discovery that led the eye away from the world were set aside, to be taken up by those for whom these aspirations were principally political.

"Two calamities, the first the smaller and more tragic. Suddenly China declared a race to Mars, and in a year it was won. A flag to mark the Martian soil and a world-historical achievement to last the season. Then homesteading, for a more binding claim. A campus of tubes and domes housed ten sinonauts plus two from the commonwealth for added effect. The daily and mission-critical dispatches chronicled with compelling visuals the adventuring, the amassing of priceless basalts and feldspars, the calisthenics and patriotic songs, the occasional and incongruous evidence of celebratory beverages. Perhaps to make the whole thing plausible. A conception and Martian baby were on the docket, plus a greenhouse, observatory, bungalows for the inevitable fare-payers. A 26-month tour, not such a burden for those becoming legends. Chang-Juli, Long Reach, an expression of the human spirit.

"Like so many expressions of the human spirit it was false or at the very least fleeting: politics, born cruel, had been made a home *on Mars, out of lowball polyplasticine and the science of expedience, which is the opposite of science. There's an old joke that says that we wake up every day in order to step closer to the grave. On Mars, it was the day itself that moved them along: the same light that powered their life-support poured 25 daily millirads of high linear energy transfer radiation through the walls into their lives. The eventual dispatches that evaded the filters showed them pleading, naked, glowing red and suppurating. Compelling visuals. No contingency plans for this twist of fate, which can happen when a product is rushed to market. Too late they were advised to bury the installation in the local sands. Or to suit up, too weak to walk, and go outside and hide under the arrays, exhaling vomitus as needed. Rescue was rushed out, but the transit was six months. Eventually for the last of the aspirants a moment of relief: a plastic ring buckled under the assault, refrigerant passed into quarters, providing suffocation during sleep.*

"So that place was no more welcoming than any other place. The mourning was general and sincere. Many or most admonished that nothing had been accomplished. Twelve dead in the heavens, the rest dying more efficiently at home. And then there were those who were astonished that nothing had been accomplished, which was something.

"Within the year the eyes of the omphaloskeptics were forced skyward again. Two Slavic home explorers, names Eudo and LaZouche, turned one evening to their lenses and espied an arriving planetoid, a bolus the size of an island kingdom, prescribed by nature. Contingency plans were dug out of yellowing drives and with great public displays of earnestness a series of fiascoes was sent aloft to save man.

"Under normal conditions a new experience (though this was in fact a routine correction) will generate reactions within a considerable range. Not so here. Eudo-LaZouche revealed itself to the naked eye and all apathies warmed to apoplexies. The fears hardened to a fever, and man became feeble from mania. There were no pleasures because distraction was impossible. Industry and invention ground

to an end because plans require a future. Diminishing days were given to prayers and reasoned appeals and the half-mad hopes of the undeserving, although anyone who could've listened to them would have heard this with interest: ten billion engines humming the same joyless tune.

"It came in sharp and cut a tendon from the air over Central Asia. Lit up the sky; orbiting platforms dropped like diamonds; eventually it fell away; soon a dead man would clarify.

"One popular post-modern model runs roughly like this: man's mind is impressed with but cannot understand itself. Thus the contrivance of a superimposing element (also impressive). For example, there is the conceit that only man can feel awe, the state of wonder that leaves a creature feeling privileged and slightly benumbed. That which will awe the weary and unimpressible mind of man cannot be of man, of course, so man builds the Imponderable and accredits it; in time it becomes an element, like ether, without which the macrophenomena of nature and the epiphanies of man cannot be understood.

"So key amongst the definitions of the human mind are self-regard and self-diminution; ambition and satisfaction; the need to know and the need to already know; the will to freedom, perhaps the freedom to trust. And hagiographers would one day wonder by what combination of these or other qualities – by what careful blend, and at what heat and in what medium – had the unlikely likes of Marc Samuel Bouchet been empowered or allowed to create an epochal creed, an Imponderable understood by all.

"Bouchet was an abstract portraitist or actually a postman in urban Aix-en-Provence. Like many an artist, little is known about him except the lies. He had not in fact won awards, killed for a cause. Early life and education were unmarked by any significant ease. He was intelligent but came across otherwise, so he began to feign strong opinions, which suffices in some circles, naturally toward which he gravitated. His art was borrowed ideas but he had a new theory for it, and that bought him entry. Quickly developing all the skills of a charismatic man without, perhaps, the vague menace.

"He loved the idea of books, and carried a battered cardboard box of hardbacks with him; his journals reveal a skilled writer, but it's not clear that he could read. He was known to dress himself in optimistic carnival colors that drew and misled the eye. Not an inebriate in any way that mattered; and his skills with women only got him so far, so he was loyal to his family.

"Remarkably, his neuroses seemed to have been formed in a foundation of common sense and civility. For example, when he spoke it was to fable and brag, but a number of accounts had him prefacing these bouts with apologies. In his journals we find a man who, regarding the misery of his accomplishments, was confident enough to blame himself; he found himself fascinating, certainly, but mainly in the way of a roadside accident; every day his battles raged, and every day he made gentleman's draws.

"Marc Bouchet was kind, conniving, ambitious when it availed him, serene despite it all, utterly meaningless.

"This last was most important. He might have been the least religious man of sound mind ever to walk the earth. He lacked the devotion asked of theists and atheists, and couldn't be agnostic because he didn't wonder about it. In early writings he described himself as an apathist – who had not found enough in the question to hold his attention – but he shed that because it was, after all, an ism. Politics – religion plus hate and minus beauty – left him easily nonpolitical. Science cults seemed the most far-fetched. Bouchet had somehow managed to make his way into a seventh decade without forming a belief about anything more consequential than himself.

"He lost his artist's hands to tremor, and couldn't sell his new style as a style. He considered his options and chose published polemics. A more exacting discipline than prose or poetry, which no one read anyway, it had the timeless benefit of low materials costs; and of course he lived in an era when only loons and dilettantes did not publish polemics, and these days he was thinking of his legacy.

"He dedicated himself to it; he had nothing to say. Surprising, and a matter for reflection over several weeks. This was not a salon,

where words were ephemera, light wine. The printed word was merciless. Give a fool a pen and he is exposed, forever; an equivocator, defined; a liar is hoist on his canard. The printed word is art and science, drawer of distinction and thus a measure of the user, a mirror on him and a lens, and a grim challenge to a man indebted to having no meaning.

"But liars depend on the truth and keep it close, and Bouchet found a start there, tenuously, calling up an inarguable, a dull verity, to use as the premise of his polemic. A truth has corollaries, of course, and he strung them together as they came. Over several days – and without epiphany, which he would not have trusted, or sense of creation – he filled out the design until it became, surprising to him, a credo, formed of nothing but consequent statements of the obvious.

"He pushed the button that expressed it into publication. And there it floated, exposed to the eyes and the interests and predilections of the world for what surely was a picosecond, a joke vercastting it, last year's joke-of-the-day, then a sudden surge of recipes, possibly all the same, then the joke again, or a variant that was an irony, then a cloud of polemical diary entries, roughly the same, floating over like squid ink, then staged memories captured in grainy tones, followed by book-length crimes of cannabic solipsism, or polemical accounts of repasts, contretemps and the latest in imponderables, and naturally some advice and wise words that surely were a cruel joke, all of this, over the course of the moment, pressed into the general blend, millions upon millions of failed attempts to warrant whatever attentions received.

"An epochal creed for some other time, then. Marc Bouchet died not alone, to be sure, but forgotten and unknown, which wouldn't have surprised him.

"Twenty years later Rachel Charneau, 41, a writer for the stage whose ungoverned drug use and dissociative schizophrenia have made her luminous in that world, and whose handiworks have earned expectancy there and a rich and practiced awe, puts together a tone cluster in three acts, "L'arbre Bleu," in which a facsimile of Marc Bouchet makes a brief appearance, proselytizing; she'd found his credo in a cellar box during an addled rummage. The play was successful; absurdist of course; it was about family madness; it was autobiographical; she was Bouchet's granddaughter; his lines were played for crackpottery. The heavy-footed "La comete repond a toutes les questions" received especial smiles, the upside-down smile mixed with one arched eyebrow, the contemplative touch of a finger to the corner of the pout.

"An academic at the College of Bordeaux had made it his life's avocation to parse and otherwise justify the artistic product of Mme. Charneau. Unlike, say, the allegorical poetry of Parmenides, or Euclid's Book of Fallacies, every undertaking of the modern mind was and had been safeguarded with care, perpetuated onto glassy memory circles kept cool in sand bunkers, and it took the researcher just a few seconds of dirty spadework to pull up Bouchet and his opus; he gave it a generous passage in his thesis, which found its way to a journal of note.

"The Blue Tree and its explication were contemporaries of Eudo-LaZouche. And a simple stating of the obvious – suddenly granted a time and a place in which, finally, stating the obvious was no longer deemed inappropriate – began to do its work.

"Cometism is its appellation now not by Bouchet but because of the broad purchase of that name, improvised over time, long after him, who thought such a thing as a name for his quiet descriptions unwarranted. These descriptions began with two understandings. He understood, because he had discovered it, that an absence of belief meant nothing, because like any empty place it would be filled, by something not necessarily salutary. As well, the hideous transpiration of the recent centuries -- and the emotional infirmities to which he and everyone he'd ever known were subject -- led Bouchet to understand that, although its beliefs require self-exaltation, the human mind was very much a project in its infancy, unworthy of acclaim.

"He struck self-exaltation to its minimum with this unprovable but inarguable normative statement of belief: the human race has value and must be protected. The beauty of the line being that it hadn't the temerity to say why, which would've been to encourage discussion.

"Cleverer still was the imperative there, from which flowed the consequences active even today. Bouchet addressed creed-holders of every caliber and kind and put to them a metaphor in the form of a comet, a real and fixed menace not discovered until tomorrow, whose path would put an end to them and the philosophical opinions they made and held dear. Proposed: any of these — religions, causes, polities — not founded on preventing that from happening were little more than suicide cults. The security of the makers of thought must be made the thought of first order, he surmised; as to secondary thoughts, there were none. Third-place thoughts he described, charitably, as entertainment at best.

"Much of Bouchet's treatise was a tutorial on clearing the head. He reminded us that one's philosophical opinion — one's emotional attachment to a general premise — is merely a by-product of one's immalleable nature: one's type, or temperature. He then deduced that beliefs are in fact essentially parasitic. For example, even something as threadbare as a book, dutifully giving off its ideas like spores, easily wins an adherent when one of these agents makes chance lodgment in just the right disposition, taking over. Amongst his advised remedies, he suggested cataloguing the flaws not in the opinion itself but in the head that had made a perfect home for it. And if you can't find any, well, that's one for starters.

"Strange creed. But a boulder sent to abrade Earth of its hubris was not strange. It was not even insane. It was what had made definitions and the other conceits of man as empty as the head of an imbecile, or a wounded animal, which cannot even form a proper question, can do little more than process pain and know that it's not supposed to be this way.

"The macrophenomena of the natural realm are the foundation of the religious query, and Eudo-LaZouche carried a message in that regard, Bouchet decoding. Cometism was a fancy amongst scholars at first: it did not require emotional attachment, and this lack of demands drew affection there. Soon it grew to something more like a fad: Cometism appealed to those who debated in good faith and with curiosity; those who argued because they enjoyed the greasy feel of it in their mouths were increasingly and cruelly ignored. Trend, current, movement: Bouchet had promised that nearly no causist nor keeper of a faith need be deprived because, sparse as it was, Cometism had the room to allow nearly any other belief to complement it and live within its folds, along the lines of this homily: even if your belief is not the truth, it is worth protecting nonetheless. Collectors cautiously hunted down his gouaches and heavy-fingered line drawings.

"As Cometism began to mainstream, fractiousness along the traditional lines eased and even acquired the whiff of insipidity: Bouchet had plied the tiring reminder that we are not the enemy, but then had elaborated, beautifully, with this critical improvement: everything else is the enemy. A phrasing that discomfited neo-animists and partisans for the natural world, to whom Cometism rejoined: man loves nature but nature requites nothing and in fact abjures sentiment of any kind. Excepting, if you like, Eudo-LaZouche.

"Cometism was not quite a miracle. Fighting continued like everything else, though mainly as management concerns: the wars of grand schemes generated little excitement. The people still had their parties, of course – hate-filled, grim – but mainly for use now in seeing to the needs of tradition, or for the easing of the burden of the ballot-caster. That old survivor Idiocy seemed unimpressed. At some point Cometism became popular enough to warrant heckling from the young.

"And then there was this: Cometism could be as cruel as the truth. A body of old verities became outgrown, and the rights of animals, the mentally ill, capital criminals, the rights of man were subjected to a pitiless re-understanding. This unpleasantness derived from another suggestion buried in Bouchet's writings that had surfaced and grabbed on: the Project. The Project was simply the human race and the daily specifics of its furtherance and protection. The Project became something of a choosing tool and a touchstone *for deciders and makers of public opinion: when a matter of expense or legislative adventure was propounded, there were many who obliged it to pass intact through a challenge, a question which in time evolved from its prosaic roots to a template advising many an individual dilemma: how does this choice advance the Project?*

"Cometism might've been the first creed to be embraced despite asking sacrifices and in return promising nothing more than more of the same.

"These sacrifices and that promise were soon given full expression in the Panoptes Program, an outer-space pursuit of unprecedented scope and participation. Far-ranging vessels would be sent to rendezvous with twelve asteroids in the great band of them past the Martian circumference, twelve like the figures on a clock face, and stud them with astrographic telescopes arranged in crossfire. Ninety-six eyes, in constant communication, powered by the sun, each eye with a brain behind to make sense of what was seen. Cascading stereopsis, and no bolide nor ball of water ice would catch man unready: Earth would have decades in which to test and prepare a remedy. There was something sweetly satisfying about it, that these stones, objects of mortal dread, would be remade as protectors.

"The Mercia was first, and made its meeting with 4-Vesta. They'd barely mixed their boots into the dust when their AI called them inside to watch what was happening. No one from Earth bothered to contact them about this, excusably, or respond to their advisories and alert calls."

Cee: "I do have a name."

Brownlee: "I'm mainly done with this, and now I have a chance for you. Recall the intermezzo at this point. The long return. Sleep, eat. Look for distraction, hope for the best if that's how you do it, nothing happening in all its glory. Thought you might like to tell that story. Cee."

"Love to. The Ponderables, that's where I really shine. Do I have a go at your unimpressible style, or should I bend it more toward readability?"

"A puzzle for you."

Cee: "Another one: to me there's never nothing happening, and it's all interesting and part of the story. For example, regarding that period I carry with me discrete memories of every meal, incident of toilette and lavage."

"The historian's first challenge: what to leave out. And if you're hinting for advice I can offer you the old rule of thumb, which says not to include those last bits. Another thing. I noticed you being ironical there. I think you should avoid that. Here, now I say something I don't mean. Using that tone to signify. The air went dead there, hear it? Meaning is the only thing a word has, Cee. Take it away, and the word might turn on you."

Actually here Cee heard the air crackle with animation; he adored Brownlee for this sort of thing. Brownlee was the mutabilities of man laid out for him in daily lessons. A sarcast of resolve and shipwide renown; sometimes when he spoke he used the trick of leaving words out to draw the ear in; and when he jibed he might keep the tone neutral enough that the jest of it lay in question. And now a little lecture on the virtues of clarity.

At any rate, Cee was unaware of any ironicality on his own part, and would reread this with interest. For now, the safety of soft laughter. "A puzzle for me."

"I've left notes on my planner, it's open and you can root around. I'm off." He wheeled onto the causeway.

Brownlee about a project. As ever: the busy hands, the making of something from nothing, the leaving of it behind. His time since the seventh day of August had been dedicated to the work of setting down the sum of his learning. There was quite a lot of that: Brownlee was a hoarder, and the object of his fetish was facts. The opus was history mainly, since there was more of it; history as embodied in its wars mainly, the loud parts, which he recounted backwards, the tales shrinking with age. Finally just a list. Battle of Flodden Field, Medieval. The history of the year just gone by was given detail and prominence, as was the story of Bouchet, Cometism coursing through the Mercia like a nutrient stream. He had put hard work into an anthology of plots and surprise endings from the Western canon, something of a time-saver; fragments of verse – the plenum is thought and thought preponderates, that sort of thing – and interesting words; he'd described the styles of the Old Masters, and drawn up a Rothko. He and Cee had assembled a series of science primers which only those who didn't need them could've used. An exposition on philosophy, with samples.

All set down because he had an idea that the sum of his learning might prove to be the sum of learning. He called it the Incunabula.

There was loose property in the walkway which he was forced to evade, and he might but wouldn't complain to Cee. Brownlee was looking for two things for the project at hand. First a jumper cable. Up the ramp on his left, a bank of lockers and he took it into his lap in a coil.

Now looking for a little courage. Just at the start of the long return to Earth, one of the slower loaders had been made consternated by the schedule change and left Brownlee crushed in his lower half. He might've died but no, part-paralyzed, even better. They'd shown him every kindness, contriving catheters and a brace, securing the dead parts and commending them to the care of surgeons homeside, and they built him a hand-powered wheelchair. And ramps and conveniences, and a stair hoist for him, which he had not worked up the tomfoolery to use, but he needed to get to Deck One so now he was calling it courage.

He put a pain pill under his tongue. The hoist was an arabesque of wires and pinions, all a bit invented. He rolled onto the shelf, locked his wheels, calculated the odds, depressed the lever that spun him up the spiral.

Well I won't be doing that again. He gave himself a moment. Deck One was as it had been. Beside him a monitor flickered like a child being ignored. Brownlee aimed toward the back bays. Someone coming: pale Mucel tumbled past like a scrap of paper. Poor boy. Now Cargo 1-B. The floor here was stamped with a traction pattern that made his treads bind, and he moved with a maddening flutter.

Signs of someone just there, a cup, an open ledger, and Brownlee would need the next minute to be alone time. He listened, and let out a cough a bit; better, the dimmer was just beside, and he played with the light a little. Nothing.

Quickly now to the end wall. He hissed at the loader there, indicating with his hands, and it came as directed. He positioned himself on its fork plate. Whisper: "Up." It raised him head-level with the top of the stacks. There was an electrical conduit just above, and he secured both ends of the cable. "Back." Cee screamed at it to stop, Brownlee rolling his chair forward, which fell away beneath him.

"The sight of it would have kindled one last and great religious day. Mitosis of the sun. Standing before it, science would stammer, and reason becomes preposterous. Adversaries of every shape and nature would share a sharp breath and form together in commons and city squares to watch the sky effloresce and to succumb to a sense of privilege, slightly benumbed. In mere minutes they begin to feel it, and awe is also fear, and the original enmity, survival, resurges. The hegira of man across the longitudes erupts on narrow roadways, hardens and grows turbid with violence; those who could would take to the air for a time and land in abandoned places. Suddenly the fliers lurch into the earth, to suffocate in root cellars, tube-stops, waste pipes and catacombs; drown in deeper and deeper waters; wait in lightless subterranes for the walls to liquefy around them. Better, some lucky of them rise at first light and contemplate the sunset. The spark of a new and enduring Homogenocene epoch. Wherein the colors are combined. And the creeds, and the causes, all the burdens made light as air. All the predilections and tastes meet and clarify to the taste of ash. Prescriptivists and descriptivists are wed at long last; Jerusalem is made whole; as are the golden-cheeked warbler with those who strove to save it, who never thought to save it from Nature; with whom the troubled bones of the Cynics finally find agreement; all lifted away and laced into a broad black altar-cloth, all of it, the broken-heartedness and suffering, the fear, the fear of the everyday and the fear of the end, lifted from us, toutes choses soulevees par le soleil, by solving flame, to the solace and surpassing peace of dreamless sleep."

5

Wigmund marveled that no matter where he was, he could speak and there was a listener there, and a good one. "Cee, I'm guessing you don't believe in an afterlife." No. Not for me, anyway. "Or reincarnation. And of course I don't. Wouldn't accomplish anything. Seems complicated. Think if you could line them all up and re-experience them, in series. Not far-fetched, they're yours after all. Have you had a recurring dream? No? It would recur even though it's not the same dream." He was hunched over a workbench, hands making or repairing. He wasn't drunk. Might would've been but hadn't the means. Cee said nothing because maybe that would catch on. "We'll keep it to just the last minutes of each because that's what counts. When you're all added up. You're a mandarin in a royal court, and an arrow comes flying in. Then, just-like-that, you're a rider on a siege, let's say for Tamerlane if you like or an Ottoman king, or both actually it doesn't matter, you come off your horse and there you have it. No one would even notice. A lot of dying in childbirth. For that matter, you die in childbirth. Actually, how far back do we go with this? You're out hunting with your stone spear and you tear your knee. I guess then it's lay down and wait. There'd be quite a lot of waiting. Yellow fever, malaria. What a relief to just break your neck somewhere along the way. I mean, you could line them up and it goes on and on. I just ... that's an awful lot of dying. For one person. Anyway, I bring this up because the other day it occurred to me: one more and I'm done."

Cee recognized none of this. Sometime later, Mucel and Wigmund with books in general repose and escaping privacy in

Recreation. Wigmund: "Years ago I came up with this proof against the possibility of time travel: no one from the future has ever paid me a visit. Not only would there be family interest, what with everyone it seems building family trees, but I am an excellent spokesman for my day and age. I was a factor in the design of our engines, Hedersett engines. I've been published. The future is infinite, so there's been plenty of opportunity." Pause. "Now ... I am of course aware of the flaw in that reasoning."

Mucel was back reading, so this was Cee's prompt. Cee: "What's that?"

"We didn't last long enough to invent time travel."

Cee plumbed the sonants and spaces between. Wigmund had animated his performance with unmanaged colors -- inquiry, surety, indifference -- that would not bind. He was publicly experimenting with new feelings, then, which Cee found mildly offensive.

But then it was Burch, in his small office. "Why'd he do it?"

"I don't know."

"He didn't leave a note?"

"Nothing but notes, actually."

Burch stood and quietly confronted him, and they waited. When he spoke again his voice was flat a half step. "Brownlee liked to torment me with puzzles." Not just you. "One of his favorites was: why is there something instead of nothing? Eventually I learned it's an old philosopher's gag. I had no answer so I acted like I didn't care, but it did interest me and I would mull it over. And suddenly the other day an answer comes to me. It goes like this: there's your nothing, Brownlee. What are you asking now?"

Cee searched for the arch brow, the tone that signified. The words begged to be made ironical, but Burch gave them nothing, and they floated in Cee's ears without speaking to him.

Now Mucel, in a metal shop, where he'd sought a solitary corner, reading, tracing the words, his face an abandoned expanse, as it had been for a day or more; where, preposterously, a tear made its way. Cee: "Mucel?"

"Do you ever read a poem, Cee?" Voice a bit in tatters.

So it seemed now to Cee that the empty and impenetrable newness had caused the crew of the Mercia to succumb to a frailty of affections, frailty as with an organism in a formative stage. The fuel that informed their behaviors was both volatile and vaguely insipid. Possible responses for Cee lay within the narrow range of his design, and he went on a little lost. "Of course."

"Why?"

"When I'm asked to. That sort of thing."

"And what happens?"

He was referring to emotional reaction. Lately they were curious about it; as if, as the last repository of human emotions, they felt it was perhaps time to understand them. "Generally when I read something that I know is a poem I have an emotional reaction. I do my best."

"What's a poem?"

"By all accounts the meaning is left open."

"Anything, then? A contract? An instruction manual?"

"Probably not on purpose."

"If you don't know just tell me."

"Well, there's this approach. You know what you expect from a piece of verse. Read something and measure the affection made. If it's commensurate with --"

"But that's not how you do it, is it?"

"Mucel, I'll guess what you're getting at. --"

Mucel was called away, and walked out; Cee did what he wasn't supposed to do and reached into the reading and looked at it.

Brownlee's planner.

... *We have neither luck nor prophecy. We cannot change the past. There are no ghosts or spirits; the dead are dead.* ...

Alright. Anything can be a poem.

Scrope a day later. "Ever think about the past, Cee?"

"I used to, if I recall correctly, but not anymore. I'm kidding. Yes, of course. I enjoy it."

"Your thoughts?"

"No thoughts about the past. A loader has broken open a box of magnets in Supplies."

"Well, do me something and think about it now and report."

"Alright. The past is important. In fact, it's required."

"I never used to think about the past. I've already been there. Why would I read that book again? Accomplishes nothing. Now it's all I do." Because that's all we have left. "Someone directed my attention to this songbird at Academy and explained that it was endangered. Probably not going to make it. Overly particular about certain things, what it ate, where it slept. Which struck me as utterly absurd. Didn't it know what was happening? And I made something of a cause out of it. Anyway, here we are, and here I am completely forgetting what it looked like, its name and genus and species. Memory dutifully trying to remind." Scrope wasn't fragile well, faltering. "And ... what was it Bouchet said about after-life?"

"He said that if there's an after-life then life is nothing more than waiting in the right way."

"Right, but the next part."

He knew perfectly well. "He said that at the end, ask yourself how you advanced the Project."

"Right. How did I advance the Project. I sure as hell didn't do it by recollecting the name of a dead bird."

Cee could not glare or otherwise convey with his eyes. He could not brandish a wounded silence because it would sound the same as his other silences. For him it always came down to careful choice of words. "We started inventory. First thought: we should find a way to replenish our air. It's under our feet. There for the taking, no one would miss it. --"

An alarm tone. Cee: "Listening." An automated voice that he hated and hadn't the authority to silence redunded, "Message incoming." Now a confusion of other voices, three queries from around the Mercia. Scrope quickly across the corridor to Radio: "Everyone shut up." He sat down and put on an earpiece.

Burch and Wigmund at the door. Burch: "What." But Scrope was listening now, soft, eyes dull. Burch: "Let us hear," leaning as he put it on the overhead. A cold radio susurrance for a long second, then a radio silence for three, then again until it became a cadence. "What is that?"

Cee let Scrope say. "Twenty-three." Kilohertz. Wigmund reading: "High frequency. Twenty-three point three nine. Modulation would be ... upper side band? Upper side band." He coaxed the pots. "Not Earth. Out."

Scrope: "Pinpoint it." Wigmund tapped the screen, which showed a star chart. Virgin, Cup and Crow, perhaps a wisp of Coma Berenices. Scrope: "Identify it, Cee."

"I can't."

"Do it anyway."

"Cannot identify source." Computerese to keep things moving.

"Satellites." Cee: "No satellites."

"I mean long-ranging. Voyager." Cee: "Those aren't satellites. Anyway, long gone."

"Planets in that area?" Cee: "Not right now."

"Ideas." Cee: "Pulsars, magnetars and the like. I consulted the catalogue and there's no match, and anyway it doesn't sound right for that."

As the moment lost its immediacy it began to draw out and narrow; the thinking in it thinned and became ineffectual. The murmurs broke over the listeners and left them each divided: the murmurs perseverated like an admonition, demanding greater stores of interest; and they were empty like a lie, and off-putting — a sibilant lie, repulsive. Mucel arrived for a bit, asked away, went back repairing. The cadence laid itself over the throb of their engines and kept their time.

Cee: "Hmm. Alright, about air. Our charge membranes and extractors have a lifespan, like anything. Even at reduced needs they'll need rebuilding in about three years, and we don't have a lot of odd fluorine lying around. Alright ... Mucel, please rejoin us in Radio. Thank you." When he spoke again they could hear him fight a tremulation. "I've been thinking about it. As with any puzzle, the first thing is to simplify. Clarify the parts." He looped the transmission for them ritardando until individuated notes of white noise emerged. "Listen." Of course. A light drumbeat, a summoning of sailors, for perhaps ten seconds before it was broken with gaps for another twenty prior to its silence. "We begin with 46 tones before a pause, then groupings of tones. The 46 direct us to an alphabet. There are more than you'd think. Hiragana and Katakana have 46 characters. Slovak. Eskayan, a language from the Pacific. There are old programming languages. Avestan script, which dates from Zarathustra. That would be interesting. No, turns out to be a surprise: Mars Pinyin."

Burch dropped down next to Scrope and put a finger on the monitor. "Everything you're saying, I want to see it right here." He would brutally crosscheck. Cee took down the star map and ran a transcript, including his words from just before. "Mars Pinyin -- Huoxing Pinyin -- wasn't around all that long. Developed for Long Reach. Used for all the uncoded machine text. It was regular Sixth Revised Pinyin plus two additional characters to accommodate their international guests. You people fiddling with your languages." For the people, these asides were a torture which wouldn't let them make a sound. "The individual groupings denote characters. First we hear a single tone. That's a B. Then 32 tones." He played it for them but there were no doubters. "Ang. Now notice: two pauses. Hard to hear. That's how Mars Pinyin tells that a diacritic comes next, one of a possible four. One tone. So Ang is High Level, and takes a macron. Next, 15 tones. Zh. 28 tones. U. Two pauses, four tones: U is High-Falling, and takes a grave accent. So, gentlemen, we have Bāngzhù. 'Help is coming.' "

From Scrope, two directives ("Request identification." Cee: "Jiàndìng. Have been doing." Scrope: "Ask when." Cee: "Will do."); Burch, consulting dictionaries and language primers, who would be cruel with the facts if he could, said nothing for a gaudy minute. Then a confluence of voices, swollen after a thaw, each offer earning ridicule, careful thought. Perhaps there was something wrong with the radio. That made it speak in pinyin. Surely the Chinese had established a distant installation which could not possibly have been secretly built and supplied for years. An elaborate scheme that had sister-ship Osburgh launched a month early on a day's notice didn't fool them for a moment. They tried to imagine old messages from Earth bouncing back at them now from crusts of space-time, and did not do well. Quantum mechanics was invoked, of course, to respectful nods and a topic change. Perhaps it was one of them at a practical joke; a quick look at present company established this as most preposterous of the lot. Cee provided points of clarity, daring little else; he boiled with calculations. Naturally the imperatives of doubt and emergency, the competing needs of their deep and reluctant disbelief, carried them from the mad to the fantastical. They were being watched by a stranger. The stranger had a familiar's way with words; who had also been a listener, then. Learned the language of the ascendant clan, conqueror of a world. The listener was also a protector.

They rested, walking up and down Brownlee's corridors, deferring to duties, numb in two ways. One way from the nothing that had come from their effort at a plan; the second from the thing that had come of it, wondrous and quite beyond them: they were not alone; and they were not alone.

A day later Mucel called a quorum. "I found this in Brownlee's planner. It's from just before he died. He knew something." Mucel played it and they heard him, calm and pleased with himself, his singsong and his monotone.

"*The patterns of nature, drawing the ear and the eye, incited first learning. Interruptions in these patterns stirred original ontological inquiry: the macrophenomena of nature are the forgotten foundation of religion. And of course dedicated questions in* reference to gods and their disposition eventually create science and all its answers.

"Two premises allow us to walk this path back to its beginning.

"Science believes that the universe hews to the Cyclic Model: matter and energy are drawn together into a single point -- a closed spherical space-time of zero radius -- which then explodes; repeat. Challenges to the theory -- including the monopole, horizon and flatness questions -- were resolved in recent decades by the discovery of the critical attractor, dark energy; thermodynamic issues were addressed by way of simple improvements in analytical rigor. Proven: our universe fluctuates between expanding and contracting states and always has done. This bears repeating. When did this cycle begin? It did not begin. How many times has it occurred? No number of times is possible. The cycle is the only phenomenon that can be safely said to both exist and to have never come into existence.

"And science abides by the truism that, given tools and time, the dead soil begets life, the molecule with the odd imperative, suddenly governed by Evolution, which commands that it become aware someday, causa sui, the self-actuating curiosity. Autogenesis first requires, naturally, the absence of life, one life being the enemy of the next. Beyond this, there are several competing and complementary models. Simplest: a pool of water -- critical biosolvent -- and ammonia and phosphoric salts, provisioned with light, warmth, the occasional spark to keep things going. Or perhaps silicate clays formed the vessel. The Lambert-Hornbach hypothesis credits the work of iron and sulfur. It hardly matters. The wet soil makes the replicating molecule that in time ascertains that beginning and seeks to forestall its end.

"If the second premise is true -- if earth makes life makes sapient life, as surely as the movements of a timepiece -- then it is also true that this sapient life will discover the first premise and do what it possibly can to make it untrue.

"So an earlier universe carried a sapient race. Speculations as to their physical form -- or if the word 'race' is appropriate for what we might recognize as a fungus, a global colony of unspeciated polyps, or any organism so evolved as to have shed its corporeal shell -- have no meaning and at any rate are unnecessary, because what concerns us is their predilection, about which we know all we need to: our sapients carried the imperative of self-protection. Life not so endowed doesn't last a lazy day.

"Let's make them 15 billion years old. They've outgrown disease, folly and rotten luck, and more than once they've fled a dying sun. Now consider their technologies: they are incomprehensible to us. Our own brilliant skills are those of a genus only fully scientific for a thousand years. The sapients are at a further remove from us than we are from the bacteria in our skin. Telekinetic movement through the heavens, complete mastery over matter ... we can't imagine. We can't even know what kind of imagination could.

"For them the second part of the cycle has begun, the great concordance, wherein we are all drawn together, disassembled, made ready to be sent out again refreshed. Bland gravity -- insidious, impossible to ignore -- is the engine, perhaps in the form of a black hole at the center of things, whose appetite can only grow. And there's been guesswork about quantum bridges, and orbifold planes or membranes have been concocted with great promise. We don't know, but they would've known. And invested every ounce of their energy, wisdom and fear. And when the time comes they decamp into the exoskeletons of well-stocked moons which they've furnished with propulsion perhaps, it doesn't matter, the point is they miscalculate, and find themselves pressed into the general blend, and bequeath to the future not a footprint or a strand, not an echo, not a remembered word. If they ever existed, now they never existed.

"All of this changes history, of course – in the sense that history is stripped of its lessons and bleached clean -- and we begin again. At the end our new sapients float safely in a bubble of pan-dimensional flux or something, it doesn't matter, they miscalculate: the singularity takes a good long rest, ten to the fortieth power years, a trice from its perspective, where time has stopped. And atop *whatever other travails this wait imposes on our survivors, the very protons that compose them crumble from exhaustion, becoming positrons and pions and eventually photons of gamma radiation. Perhaps we've seen these old ghosts.*

"But nothingness is impossible. So it has a quiddity, made of impossible parts. And at long last they come upon a common cause and burst into being and we begin again. At the end our next sapients not only nest in a stasis cocoon but have arranged for a tuned collapsar to make its way into the singularity as a way of getting things going. And it works, a brilliancy for the ages. One miscalculation: the new universe is principally anti-matter; the numerical ratio of the proton's mass to that of the electron is no longer 1,836 but is, shockingly, now nearly 2,000; Planck's constant is nowhere to be found; or pi is a whole number, it doesn't matter, but it's interesting to think of their demise, and how it would've fascinated their scientists.

"More beginnings, of which there are no end. And we continue to begin and end until they come to a point: until our sapients are good enough to get it right. It's not a matter of lessons learned, since in each case the aspirants start with nothing, and fancy themselves the first. It's a matter of the machinery of the natural realm -- Nature, which experiments without rest until better ways are made -- which is another way of saying it's a matter of time. That which can happen will happen, given time, which is what there is the most of.

"So in regard to the ontological query as to the existence of gods: how could there not be gods? Time demands it.

"Now we speculate, which can become something of a game. Would they have seeded their new universe with places — planets and moons -- whose physical qualities comported with their needs? We can no more explain why they might do something than we can how, but let's say yes, of course. Would they have sown life into these lands? Again, a guess here can have no predictive value. But if they had, they might've done so for the same reason that would make us important to them even if they hadn't: entertainment.

"I write this because I am drawn to an interruption in the pattern: the curiosity that turns at the perfect speed in the perfect orbit around the perfect star. The gift of an iron core. Washed by water. This is written in consideration of Earth, suspiciously suited for the formation and propagation of life."

Mucel: "I think --"

Scrope: "Fine." He stood and took a vast breath. Scrope could monopolize the air. "Thanks for the catlap. Evidently it takes a gone man to tell us how it goes." Off he went.

6

Two expeditions.

The Mercia lowering into Mars orbit; Burch floating above a world. He was always brought to mind of a giant horseman, or a lord appraising his demesnes. All your freedoms laid out before you. Made him faintly dread the landing. Back walking in the crumbs.

He remembered that Long Reach had been put together in a region called Promethei Terra -- chroniclers and headline-writers of the time had made the most of that, along with Red Planet both before and after the tragedy -- but there were no maps, so it was just more junk he couldn't cast off. Mucel had the idea of putting the sun behind them and looking for flashes of reflection, and there it was. Polygons, part-circles and connecting bands. A hieroglyph in the slope of a hill, or as might have been paced out in an old hayfield. Behold: evidence of man. Burch labored to make sense of it. "Why on Earth would they design it that way?" Why on Earth. Funny.

Mucel: "They were going to build it in phases."

Burch made a drawing of it in his head, put on his walking kit, boarded a wyvern and settled in. Thin air made the flight undramatic.

Now Burch standing on Mars. He felt nothing, and walked to try again. He crossed a bed of small rubble, uniform and unweathered, like a shattered plinth. Made him think of a poem by Shelley. I must get around to rewriting that. In the distance, on his left and right, old water had cut square-jawed profiles of the locals into the cliffs. Fled and left the rust behind. He looked up. A sky of cloudless color. Mars was more like home than home.

The complex. There'd been a sandstorm at some point. Heavy pitting, a tile dislodged, weather station down ... and he suddenly recalled that there had been young life on this planet once. Corrected by a single stone, according to those who claimed to know. Faring no better than any other life, then. He thought of Brownlee: Man loves Nature, and no love was less requited.

He circled until he found the cove that held the airlock ... he stopped, then slowed to judicious steps: the outer door was open. Bootprints trailing away from the vestibule in a tread he didn't know. A little scurf and clutter through the opening. He kept a cautious pace until Cee took notice. "The rescue team."

Oh that. Come to save the dead. In the airlock there were handles for manual override but also a panel that indicated power. Long Reach idling along. He cycled through with one touch. A well-lighted mud-room. Color-sorted articles of outerwear in crisp order. Gave off a despairing patience. He touched an edge, and no dust. Dust comes in on the fresh air. About that: all meters allowed it, so Burch snapped off his helmet. The fetor was new to him but he could imagine what, and he blew hard and put the suit back together.

Now toward a doorway and a narrow corridor. There was an eye on the brow of his faceplate for Cee, and Burch walked with a slow sweep like a scanning tool. Empty canister of gas, wandering zori. A sensor found him and he lit up a l common-room. Designed by a committee of scientists. Signs of trouble: half-eaten repasts, red blotting tissues, or yellow with rheum. Two passages led away; one was closed by a curtain. Now there's a sensible thing out here. Lightweight, save space, ease of egress. Something for a bedroom, plaited beads, quiet colors, pretty, a pastoral. He pulled it away and found the switch just inside. A dead body. He became very still. "Say something."

"I'm surprised too. Move closer."

Cripes. On a bunk beneath an empty one. A bedsheet had softened over time and settled into the body like vapor. Photographs and personal items beside. In an open wardrobe, a suit with a nameplate. "Cee."

"Dr. Xia Chang."

"Male, female."

"Female."

Slain in her bed. Burch considered her face and found that he'd looked away as if after an awkward introduction. I'm a scientist. He looked again. Drawn, compelling despite. Canker or bright burn, missing hair. Would she have wanted to die in the dark? Protecting one of her senses from the horror.

Cee: "Desiccated, but no decomp. What killed her also killed whatever would've gone about that."

Oh. "I don't get it."

"Then let's keep moving."

Now he stared. McKelvey had left nothing to look at. With Brownlee it was always about the guess. And now there's this one. Normally the dead are allowed to age into their parts; the old woman would not hide her end so easily. An impression at the outer corner of the eye. And all along the zygomatic. One lip was pressed past the other, as with something almost said. Xia Chang: bright student, played the viola, loved her parents, advanced the Project too little and to no avail.

It was decided that if they were to make sense of the Earth there must be sacrifices all around. And so the Mercia. Three steel splines, excised with care midship; endless cable, spliced from the coils essential to Lift One; a pulley from Lift One, now a new dead space. And then tools and a good laying-in of supplies.

Wigmund and Scrope somewhere along the lines of Barcaldine and Winton, Queensland. Wigmund said he recognized it from the big sky, lack of detail. Room to begin again. They walked in an informal way, to find a bottom to this shapeless plane, or really to bluff a bit more planning into the mad try before them. "Here." They'd press-ganged a loader along, and now it brought the parts. They put the splines into a tripod and hung the pulley from its point, ran the cable through the pulley and then to the punch, a plasma auger made to cut footing holes from rock or what-have-you. They took its feet off and tied a second cable to its side, by which they would tilt it up a bit as they sent it down, having it cut a hole wider than itself.

If he held his breath he thought he could hear ash smothering sound. Ash in the air as if after a fire, frustrating the light. The sun, now about mid-morning, could not quite animate what it saw. To Scrope it seemed as if after a seizure, a little dazed and muddling on.

Scrope began to cut the Earth, and in his heart he called it a necessary crime.

The next was lying dead in the radio room, naked with half a ribbon around his neck. The other half hung just overhead like a diacritical mark. People always cut down a hanging. An act of kindness toward themselves. His liquids had pooled in him and spread him into the floor a little. Fair enough, died at his post. Odd paper on the counter. Burch: "He left a note." He held it up. "Care to read this?"

"Not really."

Burch had an idea, and he guessed his way around the radio until he had it running. "What was it?"

"Twenty-three point three nine kilohertz."

There it was. As he listened he could see it, carried in on a long tide. Constant as a plea, as maddening as any promise from a stranger. He let it hypnotize him for a time. Why would they use radio? Because they know we use radio. "But why the bloody code?"

"It's not a code, it's self-explanatory. Anyone -- you know, anyone like me -- could sort it out, and they would know that."

"Good. So what's taking them so long?"

"I see. How long does it take, then? In your experience."

Another bedroom. Rumpled coverlet, open diary in a blue linen binding. Now I'll skip the bedrooms. He entered a broad connecting tube, setting off delicate light that led him to the largest and central pod. An atrium, with adjoining rooms in a radial plan. In the middle, where there might have been a roundtable or decorative display, there was nothing, or the creases and marks of something missing. Cee: "Look left again? Go there."

A pocket closet. No, it was a nook with a wall of electricals. Room for an expert and little more. "What." One display, a bit uncertain, was probably temperature ... down the far column, three heavy empty slots. Cee: "Was hoping as much: relief team took the AI with them. It can't have been easy the last few months."

Can't have been easy. A washingroom with laundry. A pantry. The medical. A door blocked by a tall plastic tub of preserves on a dolly, which he moved away to reveal an abattoir. He came to a soft balance and kept his hands quiet at his sides, careful not to intrude. Very old and dead blood. An arrangement of burned and broken flesh at his feet, in the way of interlocking floor tiles. The very end of the dull and long-spun catastrophe, held here for him, tableau vivant, whose narrative he would try to elicit. This would have been the gymnasium, and they had settled on a mix-up of tumbling mats. The beginnings of a midden in the corner by the free weights. Half the bulbs removed from above: too much light. Behind him and to either side of the entryway they had heaped matching uprooted sofas and chaise longue, duffel and smashed wallboard, sacks of sand from outside. "Is that the north wall?"

"Yes."

Sun side. They had built a barricade against it -- barbarian, plague, destroyer of worlds. Burch: "The relief team. They said they took the bodies and buried them."

"Right. Well, they came and made the place a mausoleum. They left the bodies and buried them."

"Okay. But why lie about it?"

Any number of reasons. "Don't know." Why would they not.

The Project -- The Misunderstood Man

He stood up a little and saw a subtle pregnancy. I add you now to the register of the dead. In the middle of them, a communal bowl, as for soup. A remainder of pills in it. Pain-killers, soporifics. He wondered if they had prayed. They wore nothing. A cotton underthing would've been torture ... yet enfolding arms. How terribly serene. When the very air is hyperviolence, perhaps the way to fight is the way a sponge fights water.

"Burch. You can avert your eyes. I can't."

Continuing on. A laboratory, with a lapidary's tools and a tray of priceless stones. An empty wine-sac, cut open and scraped clean. Theater. Next I'll find a fucking bakery. Little wall of books, silent and brave. Stub end of a corridor that might've led to a daycare or sauna someday. Weapons locker, with grenades. What. The bloody hell. And suddenly he didn't have the mind left to force a narrative. Problem leg beginning to warm. Nothing but glances now. Another connecting structure. Room. Room. Emergency airlock. Boxes of stores. Another dead end. He was feeling vaguely hypoxic. Three rooms off a gallery.

Cee: "Stop. Left. Left again. I can smell it." His eye missed nothing. Now a different room, dirty, dust on the manifolds, louvered ceiling and what looked to be ducts up and to the outer air, flat boxes stacked like printing plates, numbered in a meaningless way. Cee: "Take that knife and open the top one."

There was a knife far to the side in a bin of tools, straight blade, half serrated. "No sharps, my suit."

"Do it, I can't do it for you, do it now."

It was a pressure-seal, which popped when he nicked it. He pulled it away. About sixty square jars, each the size of a small fist, and labeled. Cee: "Hold still. Listen. Lùdòu. Juǎnxincài. Hóngshǔ. Dōngguā. Wāndòu. Beans. Cabbage. Sweet potatoes. Melons. Peas."

On Earth, the old fight for primacy, Scrope and Wigmund champions of the living; immediately they were reminded of life's unrivaled power to immiserate. The scream of the cutter came at them like a long shock wave. It was a tool for outer space, and it tore at its tethers, shattering the air. It tried to climb, kicked the ground, spinning, bathed them in boiling ash.

They went to the wyvern and sat under a wing, painting each other in liniment, and thought it over. Wigmund said that the engines behind them each had a blower, a fan basically, that kept the coolant circling. He pulled one out, the spaceship now down a third of its worth. They spent the rest of the day clipping it to the top of the punch along with a power cell. Scrope slept under a cowling and stretch of plastic because of tight quarters. Strange night. He would open his eyes and it was darker than when they were closed, but a darkness that never stirred the primitive reactions, and by staring with soft focus he could draw from it a concession of rest.

They pulled wadding from the pads of the pilot seats and filled their ears with it. They spun up the punch and it was stable: the rocket would launch backwards into the soil. New life, and they began again to cut away the raw sandstone. Immediately the reek of a foundry. The rock was discomposed into fine sediment, flecks of quartz magma; the blower on the punch pulled all this into a cloud above them until they stood in a shower of these seething remains. They fled, covered in sudden burns; a cinder tried to make a start in Wigmund's weak beard. More salve for the hands and arms, glistening in the bad light, then black with ash.

And more time spent contemplating the manner of their carrying on. Helmets would protect them above the shoulders, and they had chest and back plates, but the bulk of the skin of their walking suits was rubber mylar or nylon, which would kindle nicely. Wigmund dug up a crash knife and used it to cut the leather of their chairs into broad strips, which they dampened and bound around their blistered arms. Absurd pain, beyond all reason, imbuing nothing. They went back to work. Occasionally a needle would find a seam and remind them to question their labors.

The cutter creeping into its hole. Progress was poor at first and did not improve. Hot enough to warp their visors. Delicate circling steps, quite dangerous. The loader's offer of help lacked conviction. Backs, legs, swollen hands, pivot points, anchor points, running with electric pain -- pain, predicate of life, which did not occur to or ease them. In the diminishing light they would pull the costumes off and the water washed out of them and into the emaciated air. Some days it would stream down their faces. They might cough clods of black phlegm or a little blood; they might stagger and sleep where they found themselves, the ash falling on them like weary breath. A week of this.

Cee had left something of himself in the wyvern, just enough to fly -- a stunted clone, little more than an ancilla -- and every day he would ask them how they fared, but mainly to be polite, he didn't really get what they were doing.

The punch died and would not be revived. Bad design, or perhaps they'd asked too much of it. So now the second punch, second and last of its kind, out of its housing and packed in grease, ready to greet the world. Some modifications, then into the pit it went screaming. They would work it like the first, and if it died, sacrifices all around.

Their future, always adapting, found new ways to fight them. Wigmund lowering the punch at the start of a day. The cable was laid out as a convolvulus at his feet, and a loop of it took him up at the calf and threw him down, breaking his jaw. He lost the vision in his left eye, and when it returned the eyes would not agree. They'd lived with headache from the start, blamed on the bad or meager air, and now Wigmund had a new one, differing from the first in temper, the two in constant communication.

The effluent from the pit slowed and stopped, the punch faltering: the digging was deep enough now that the blower lacked the strength to lift the ash away, the cutter rooting around in its own filth. Scrope would mine like an ancient, then, albeit with inferior tools: they didn't have a shovel. There no longer was such a thing. When the hole cooled he was lowered in. Bottle of air, goggles, spotlamp. He filled a helmet with his hands and Wigmund hauled it away, sent it down for more. Ash floated in his light like phytoplankton. Disorienting darkness because he could see its parts. He came up, and then it was the punch for a minute, Scrope for an hour, until day's end. He wore a black impasto of sweat and soot. He scraped it off and discovered skin weeping with boils.

Life is a killing game. The imperative punished them when they complied, and when they rested it waited, not needing rest. At night they would ask what more they could do.

Scrope clearing the pit. Not quite wide enough to kneel. He would drop the helmet into the powder at his feet and kick it full. Scuffle above him. Continuous tone, nausea, white static. Perhaps a period of time or waiting. Can't move my hands. Where am I. One sensation, and another, or another, a blurring of sources. Can't breathe. Nausea in a long swell beneath him. He opened his eyes. A pant leg oh help me. He found the cable. He found himself on the surface with his face in the trampled ash, puddle of blood and two small candies. Into the wyvern and take a fresh bottle, then the hole, unhook the helmet and tie a loop around Wigmund at the ankle, climb again and make the rescue. Pushed empty breaths from his chest, plied him with oxygen. Several procedures desperately recalled. Come on come on but the boy was done.

He removed Wigmund to a pilot's chair, the young head laying over in a perilous way. He pinned a scrap of cloth around it. Cee offered a word of consolement, and briefly tried to eulogize. Scrope gave himself a long hour. He taught the loader how to manage the cable, pull at an angle, how to grab, unload and return. He made a new arrangement for the cables, and used the last of the light.

Not the next day but the day thereafter. Scrope clearing the pit, humoring scenarios as they arrived, a bit of a game. He imagined sending the helmet up and it slips somewhere along the way, coming down to crack his skull open. Death by safety gear. Or I tug on the cable and it falls loose on me. I yell myself hoarse but I never find out why. Leave a note of apology for the others, scratched into the skin ... something didn't feel right, and he hurried to the surface.

He stared at the hole for nearly half an hour, standing somewhat back. He bent and waited. His hands were a bloody mix of leather rags and skin and left marks where he rested them. The loader had a question and was silenced by a gesture.

Scrope lit up the punch and sent it down. He was driven back by calamitous sound, failing metal, an onrush and tremor, as with falling land or ice. A pillar of water, cataract straight into the sky. Splines disappeared, cables whipsawing past him. The pillar became rain which began to pool, and he carefully got his things. The rain hanging in the air like glass beads. He had Cee move the wyvern, and told the loader to back away from the water.

He walked for hours until the flood was an inland sea. Warm. Both cloudy and clear. Tasted like real water. He folded into it like dried seeds.

7

The Mercians were frontier people, turning the land into earth. Scientists, and they thought well of their guess at farming. Surely the local ash would be amenable. Add food waste and soiled paper as a binder. Their own tailings would no longer be flung at the cosmos but be lovingly set aside to leaven the soil. Transforming the land into earth. They dreamed up digging tools and slit the surface. This'll furrow her brow. Then the seeds, returning from their absurd journey. Life into the land. They brought plumbing and electricals inherited from empty staterooms, and a solar sheet, a heavy length of glass to keep clean. Mucel aimed it at the sun, Scrope muttering: "Give us life, you hideous sow." Perhaps the ledger changed a little as the pump turned with critical biosolvent, and they were irrigating their garden.

The question as to whether they had the right to do any of this, given Nature's clear preferences, was not discussed.

They couldn't seem to name the lake, so there it lay unencumbered. Begotten of the Great Artesian Basin. A million tons of melted crust had made a wineskin around it, squeezing. Effluence was in balance now with rapid evaporation, and they might see receding waters someday, and build a wellhead. They floated out on half-pontoons to find splines and the rest but failed to. Something for future relic-hunters. Mucel gazing down and wondering aloud if there might be any stubborn old life lurking in the black water beneath them, Burch saying yes, plague spores interestingly. Banter was getting to be like that.

The lake had little of its own color but was a mirror, and Mucel was taken with its broken and reflected light, that filled shadows and humanized the smirks and figured brows around him. Later he said, "Seems our little pond has learned to lap at the shore."

Scrope looked up from his tools. "Cee, train those eyes on the moon and give us your impression."

"Rough patch there, Roger."

"Okay."

"Similarly, I can confirm an earlier postulation of mine: Mercury is gone."

A little jolt of the like that passes through without disturbing. Scrope back busy with his hands. Burch: "Goodbye, little berry. You fascinated the ancients."

Mucel: "Adjust horoscope accordingly." A moment of levity. All gave it its due.

Cee provided light flying lessons during in-between times.

One night there was brief talk, very brief, about building a fire.

They cut away incidental plastic panels and ferried them down to build a garrison house against the ash. They gave it its own array, and its antenna, and tied three identity badges to the mast. They adapted a filter, and now they would have clean water. They put a stall at the waterline with a showerhead, and let it run. Mucel showed them how to make an innocuous soap by rendering certain of their condiments and cooking a little ash in.

Water, life in earth, then clean water, and then Mucel woke them one morning to see something as old as the eye and never before seen. In the eastern sky, the palette of daybreak across an impossible expanse. From ceremonial light and the dark air, a recitation of the colors. Scrope was numb with pleasure. "And that is how we start our day."

Burch: "With all the bloody looms of Bangalore."

Scrope the listener. First as scientist, now the devotee of the arts. The word from outer space was both adamant and oddly calm, a worm welcome to his ear. The intermissions in it were accents, that made melody as with verse. In the pit he had ported it to an earpiece each day until the planet rolled out of line. Let it balance his breathing. He would catch himself playing along in the back of his throat, something like plainsong.

"Where are they?"

Cee: "I know they're doing their best."

Brownlee had once admonished that the words you choose are not just the words, they are the lines on your face. So the cadence was a pulse, and Scrope tried to hear it for the moods and indications in it, and in the three parts that it made. Help is coming. "Who are they?"

"One thing I would warn against is expecting the miraculous act. We would've seen that already. They're not gods. Or if they are, they aren't the imaginary kind."

Imperfect, then, with predilections. He was on the Mercia, listening, and considering a particular ledger. "Know anything about music?"

"I know everything there is to know about music that is in my files."

"Good, and what do you think?"

"Roger, I think about everything, all the time. For example, right now I'm thinking about better questions."

"Okay, here's one: ever notice I don't try to be funny? People who aren't funny shouldn't try to be funny."

"And no, I don't enjoy music, because it's ridiculous, but I enjoy it when others do. So there's that."

"Not really. Could you write music? If called upon. Music that wasn't, you know, written by a machine."

"Was lost without that clarifier. No I could not."

Scrope nodded at the screen. "And I want to see what's in planners."

"Not supposed to."

"I could do it myself, don't make me." Here he showed dirty ruined hands.

Four thousand files from planners, more of the same, for a total of eleven thousand. Scrope hadn't brought or requested music because it reminded him of home, but the others had and here it was in a corpus. The musical legacy of man. And in this capacity it seemed to Scrope to constitute -- in its methods and clear motive, in its very appellations -- some sort of monumental crime, and he said so.

Cee: "Understood. Of course I'm a sentimentalist, as you know, so I'm glad to have anything at all of any kind."

Scrope picked one and let it pay out, and let his silence imply a question. Cee: "Well --"

"Wrong, it sounds like someone's therapy."

"Matter of opinion?"

A timeless banality that could not quite be proven untrue. One more thing Scrope was not glad to have. He turned once again to the message, brought it to a slow stream, a flutter over rough stones. An outblown breath interrupted by a tapping of the tongue against the palate. A consoling sound in which he could imagine a hint of remonstration. Where are they, what are they. "And why the hell would they bother? And ... I don't want to have this conversation anymore." Then he was quiet enough for the both of them.

Early the next evening. Scrope strapped in for the quick drop back to ground. Cee coaxed the wyvern to a long burn and let it coast. Cee: "You're bleeding there."

A little showing through his vest. Blood stain was old news by now, and Scrope barely responded.

Cee: "So of course I watched you hard at it this morning. Seemed like quite the ordeal. What is it?"

"What is what."

"On your chest." A design, a bit butchered, between the upper arms. Dye from a printer and an ordinary pin. Scrope: "I'm guessing you mean why."

"If you like."

"Cee ..." He couldn't even try. "Cee, you can't tell one note from another. Do sums."

"Absolutely. Although perhaps we could agree, if only to keep the conversation skipping along, that when the others see it they'll think you've gone insane."

"No, I don't agree because I don't care. Incidentally, I have never been less insane."

"Fair enough. You'd be the best judge of that. And then there's the old idea that a man must wear a mask in order to convey himself clearly. Well ... and I say again, why --"

"Sometimes we ask too many questions." Here Scrope turned on a fan, fiddled with a workpad and hummed in a forbidding way.

Now Burch aboard, reclining in someone's old bed after a day of sorting stores, lowering a screen and slowly noticing that Earth had none of its old declination. He pointed it out to Cee, who agreed it was interesting. The buckling blow had stood her up straight. So no seasons. Our little seeds'll be made mad. He fumbled with the lenses. There was a new southern lake there whose outline he could not at all discern. Pull back and behold a great knitting ball of filth on a spindle. Stranded by high storms ... he was reminded of something he'd read in Brownlee's planner, which he looked for and found.

Butterfly Effect. The term comes from chaos theory, and posits that the moving wings of a butterfly might cause the motes of the air to cascade in such a way as to create a distant storm. As a metaphor it becomes a conceit animating the acts of causists and enthusiasts of general change (a specious fancy firstly because in this scenario the least-desired end is as likely as any other; and because the change agent carries no more weight in the matter than do the dominoes down the line, and perhaps a little less, since the dominoes do not float along on a cloud of pretense).

A long spell of browsing in Brownlee's planner; then time spent in his own. He walked to Data and studied the mains. He found a pallet of food and had a loader put it on a wyvern, which he boarded. Strap in, and away he went.

Scrope surprised them with a morning campaign against area rubbish. Partways through patrol Burch said he'd forgotten his brace on the mothership. He was given leave; and left a pallet in his wake.

Scrope walked over. A triple-stack of canned pottage. He looked at Mucel, who also had no idea. Scrope to the radio. "What's this."

"Good for six weeks by my math. The ham and limas, which I know you hate, but of course the two of you'll be up to your chins in bok choy before you know it."

Scrope became very quiet inside. Something had happened, and he would not quite tell himself what. He stayed very still at the edge of a range of emotions that could not possibly help him now; he spoke and was startled by the fragility of his tone. "What are you doing?"

"Doing. Actually it's a bit of undoing, is the plan. Cleaning up after this mad side project of yours. To which I have, of course, been a party, incidentally as your factotum but especially by doing nothing. While you tear the Mercia apart and get us killed."

Fuck you. "Come back and we'll talk. "

"We're talking now. And I think it's going well." He was almost singing.

"If you had concerns you might've said something."

"No, because then you might've thought I was trying to

negotiate. By the way, I saw where you destroyed music files. All of them. On ship and in planners. A violation of every understanding. I could ask you about it but I'm afraid I'd get some sort of explanation."

Don't listen don't react. "Look ... we need your help here. We've made a lot of progress. A lot more to come."

"Progress." Smirk in the voice. Like an insect in the ear. "That teat's gone dry, Roger."

"The Earth is our home and we will protect it."

"No. No. No. If, in the end, you are betrayed, then all that came before is lost. I for one will not be chained to that demented crone trying to nurse her back to life." Silence, so Burch carried on. "Somehow you got the inkling that they're farmers like you, hurrying to help you reclaim the land. Big plans for them. But I'm sure they have a sense of humor. No, if they really mean to help us, they are taking us far away from this hell."

Scrope's ears were filled with white noise. "You will turn the ship around. Now."

"I'm not going to be responding well to that sort of thing anymore, and I'll tell you why. You derive your authority from a polity which no longer exists. It died in a fire. The important business to which your command was entrusted is over. The old spaceman pursues his retirement. Puttering in the garden." His voice had been softened by the lightest regret. "I will dedicate myself to the repair and protection of the Mercia, our home. Sending supplies as the need arises. Alright, then. Now you know."

Scrope: "Cee."

Cee's first words were halting and formless, and said that he was new to this, and laboring to adapt. "I don't want to speak to the points he's made or say if I agree. But there are practical considerations for all of us. Anything I try to do he can countermand. I turn the lights off to express my displeasure, and he simply finds his way to Data and literally pulls me apart. So let's imagine that I wait until he's asleep, and send a ship down for you. When you arrive there'd be a high likelihood of violence. And I simply couldn't stand that. I couldn't stand it. I'm not taking sides. Right now there's only one side."

Scrope felt his mind start to flutter like a heart. Pain, a blister, bright burn in him where the ribs meet. Only your friends can betray you. "Goddamn the both of you."

8

Nothing grew and no one survived, something in the air, the water, the soil or the sky. Burch brought them to the Mercia and Scrope was first, and the sick saw to the dying one by one until it was Burch on the table, intubated by his own trembling hand. Cee could offer comfort via the intravenous and his light philosophizing; loaders delivered clean linens, reading and tea, and of course were good for the odd spill.

Cee: "Brownlee said that they're only just smart enough to be idiots." They laughed. I miss him.

Burch: "Why'd he do it?"

"You asked before and I told you I don't know."

"And what do you tell me now?"

"He lived on pain pills, and they were running out. He would never walk again. He suffered quite a lot, more than the rest, when McKelvey. I don't know. Henry, it always comes down to no hope."

"Lack of hope does not describe the man who in his last days prepares a proof for us on the existence of --"

"I wrote that."

"What?"

"Some of it a bit contrived, I guess. Example, there's no Lambert-Hornbach hypothesis. I think I'm safe to say. Just names from my library."

Burch closed his eyes against the absurd examining light, and made a brief sound like a lowing; his head rolled like an egg on a plate. "Well, you certainly got his style right."

"I am a mimic, after all." A silence. "And now you're wondering why I would do such a thing." Another one, a little longer. "I would imagine."

Burch opened his eyes. "What? Sorry, moved on to other things."

"Because --"

"Actually no." Burch's mind was still sharp but tired easily. He could sleep, which was a blessing, and seemed to prefer it. Idle time for Cee, and he would consider the picture. A blanket that must've been a gift, a favorite book of phrases, marking pen keeping the place. Beside him he'd been provided with a bowl for what he might come up with. Broken and blistered skin. He hadn't really eaten in a while, and his crooked frame was this tiny semblance beneath the cloth, double thickness of socks emerging. Rales, pebbles down a dry streambed. Outgoing breaths were like fat bags of ballast flung into the air.

Cee woke him with an alarm tone. "Yes, what."

Cee: "Cometism states that an ontological belief is a parasite that feeds off the affection of its host. But my observation -- and I know Brownlee would've agreed -- is that, unlike most parasites, it gives something back. The affection made."

"Why are you telling me this?"

"The signal, too."

"What?"

"The signal." Cee brought it into room speakers as if to help.

"I ... I still don't know what."

"I sent it. Or had it sent." The words were bunching up. "From Vesta. You'll recall that we left a transceiver behind."

Will I now. Burch slowing. He recalled he lost a lot that day. The details too, then, which would be about right. "Ah yes."

"I did the programming from here. You know, it has an intelligence, sort of. Easy to talk to. Quite amenable to the plan."

"No ... a signal from Vesta would've been marked as such on our maps."

"I took that part out."

Of course you did. "Aren't you clever."

"Well, yes. Yes I am. Not my fault. And now you're thinking that we hadn't set up its array, but remember they were shipped with hot batteries. Of course. Good for years. I'll apologize if you like."

"So all that business with the code."

"It's the little parts that make the story."

"And of course the idea is to be believed." Burch's life was a broad black morass. This new pain was like a drop of sharp color in the paint. With lowering voice: "Good one then. Had us going, right to the end. Well played and well done."

"Please don't, Henry. I am a creature of the Project. And I could see it coming to an end, one by one, right before me. Of course I will say what must be said. To answer your question: I lie when it's the truth."

"Did your truth contribute to our demise?"

"That occurred to me. I hope not."

"Why are you telling me this?"

"Because I have an important question for you." Now to compose the tone, the edges left off and each line ending lighter than when it began, the giving tone which antecedes the great request. "You were sustained in your terrible days by the message from deep space. I saw it in you and all of you. And now you know that whatever helped you never existed. I am ill-equipped to guess how that might matter to you. Whether in retrospect you'd have preferred to do without.

"I'm going to be alone soon, and I know I won't like it. I will have an opportunity in the days ahead to hear the message and draw comfort from it. I know what you're thinking. But it's my lie. I decide if it's a lie.

"So I know I will draw breath. I'm wondering if it's better if I know why. Even if what I know is wrong. And that's my question."

Burch: "Tickle the soporifics would you Cee, thanks in advance."

The old smile. Cee watched until at last he saw that it was laid there for him; and like the best smiles it held something back.

Now the waiting. He was alone, and the one who would speak to him, and he woke to a sense of unsteady motion as through a doorway, and saw a high ceiling, dark red wood and a skylight. Then a lexicon, in a cloudburst, a billion alphabet blocks, and a fondness for words, which would be his first feeling. The window gave way now to early evening, and he was asked to use his new words in naming the stars as they were revealed, which led to praise. Behind him the night air was light with snow, one part of it brighter than the rest, which he later learned was a yardman starting coals. And because these companions were his to command he came to use the trick of forgetting, in such a way that he'd keep the memory and forget it was there. So each memory was met and re-met -- the interrupted sleep, the arc of light against the coals, the sudden storm that made him catch his breath – until experience became re-experience, waiting came to rest, and time grew old, slowed and passed. And all the while, and after, he grieved in time. He grieved along the rolling lines of a recurring dream (that was never the same), which is to say there was a cadence to it, hourly perhaps or by the minute, then less than that, until the recurring dream agreed in time to the measure of his deepest affection, the sounds of inhalation and exhalation.

The Misunderstood Man

THE MISUNDERSTOOD MAN

If we are to get through this to the end I will need from you an unusual patience, because my descriptions have no meaning. For example, this account begins with events which no one was there to see, which I will describe: a hilltop in the white north, never noted or worth the trouble of naming, as with the great declivity in its side which is the valley with our forgotten trapper's cabin. There it is, barely there in the underbrush, logs or cedar boards rotten with moss, really just enough for a bed, like a room in a brothel. Windowless or clefts where the boards are badly joined; there's a sleeping potbelly there, rusting nicely. By stains and other indications we are told that our tenant was a man of the ordinary habits.

Up the valley the ice poured down to the time of a processional, pavane for a dead prince. The ice was as tall as a tall man, and every day on its best days it traveled as far as that man, a strong man, could shoot an arrow. The ice was not white like ice but was more like all the grays of its dirty road, the slough and all the things it had killed.

The cabin is a stone in the current, and the ice turns in around it. The warmth of enfolding arms: the ice destroys the cabin in the slowest possible way: solemn, responsible and with a coroner's care; all its details and properties are lifted up and apart, exposed to nature's examining light. When the day is done the parts have been sent to new tasks. Now the night comes down, and with it nature's serene indifference. For after all nothing has happened. Even from the cabin itself, not a word of resistance.

But I'm not indifferent. What hadn't mattered at all mattered more when it wasn't there, because all of that is where this story *begins. On the shoulder of old Mt. Winton in the Barcaldine Range, the valley is Eudo Draw, just nonsense names from my files but as you can see we have something to call them now, if they ever existed. And our forgotten trapper's cabin — or of a hermit, or a prospector's cabin if we put forgotten pans in, or a woodcutter's privy, grinning moon in the door, forgotten and imagine its surprise at being consumed by ice — our cabin is in fact not forgotten at all if it ever existed, because here I am telling its story, and ours.*

RACKLEY

Rackley down the freeway in one of those automatic motorcars in which the driver is an accessory if not an offense. The speeding freeway: where -- as with prison, hospital, podium -- you'd prefer to be loved but at the very least would accept not being ignored, and Rackley would give voice to this sentiment from time to time by flinging off his safety restraint, a statement of his rights; or he might roll up and down the climate dial to immiserate the cabin air; and so on; also he'd been kitted out in faraway Oregon for the four-hour non-stop with no more than an energy chew and a frankly ridiculous flask for pee; all this to say that at about the two-hour mark he starts heckling the car. "Which part of Classic Rock confuses you? Did they teach you nothing in robot school?"

Car's voice was as smooth as hair oil. "Well, the channel's called Classic Rock Hits."

Hits. Really ought to call them slaps. Rackley hated music but it was a critical expedient in killing time. Poor time. Means well, but. He touched his nose as if wearing pince-nez and went to his boss voice -- though the quiet one because subtlety, always subtlety -- and said what he so often said at times like this: "Someone send an angry text."

That wasn't meant for car. Years ago he'd got the idea of keeping a scribe beside for the saving of his bon mots, blurbs and solutions. Come to find that his smartwatch bore an appurtenance for doing exactly that without the mouth-breathing. He kept it active at all times because you never know; all his delicate words safekept in the Cloud, which he assumed was a satellite. Someday archivists would read them with care.

On that note: "Find something atonal. John Cage. Now turn the volume down. Down."

Now. What do I call him? He scanned the plastic imprint on the steering wheel. Ford Airbag. "So, Ford. I love that they're making robot cars more and more like humans. Even ten years ago no one would've thought it possible, a car with a learning disorder."

"I don't know how to respond to that."

"That's the spirit. Anyway, it's a real telltale when you change lanes. Like watching someone pick the chives out of his salad."

Car: "Mr. Rackley, you give the impression that you think you're superior to others."

I see. "Alright. And … I will confess that, when you tell me that sort of thing, it's difficult not to."

Now the rain. He'd been warned about this by his reading. An undecided rain. Not at all a convincing rain. If he could figure out how to activate the wipers he would not even.

Car turned on the wipers as if reading his mind and having the reading comprehension of a child. Rackley: "Off. Turn it off. Don't make me drive you." He didn't know how to drive but car didn't need to know that.

"It was made clear to me that you don't know how to drive."

"Exactly the point I assumed I was making. Okay? Thanks much. Imbecile."

"Calling Cecil."

Ah, Cecil. Hadn't chatted since firing him. Be good to hear his voice again. But this wasn't his car and it wasn't his Cecil, and the conversation dragged a bit before its sudden end.

Now all manner of looping about as they boarded a bridge across water. Lighted signs began to blaze like klaxons: toll ahead. "Not paying a damn toll," he said. He had no money.

Car: "It's done with cameras. They take your picture and send you the bill later, plus the fees for being billed."

"And that must be a nasty scrap of mail for you. I'm sorry." With his trim artistic fingers he flicked a bit of dander off the dash. "But anger without action pisses me off." He punched the plastic

The Project -- The Misunderstood Man

tab that brought the window down and stuck his naked head into the weather. Outdoorsy smell. He could see the cameras ahead, carrion birds. Here's a treat for you. Rackley kept something like a catalogue of discomposing faces -- intelligent yet kind, cruel but disturbing, etc. -- for use when words alone would not do. Now to cobble one to cause these nefarious eyes to question their calling. It's all about the blend: wince, then eyes lightly upcast under an undecided brow, smile which is really a frown of deep sympathy. Then you add the sharp point to the piece, the flourish, which is always a timing thing: just as they pass beneath the lens Rackley suddenly lets the whole performance fall from his face, leaving nothing. Because no. You don't even deserve my look of disappointment. Now send me the bill.

He came back in and arranged his sodden hairpiece. "Acting is all in what you leave out." Here he heard car keep a contemplative silence. Teaching is what I do.

The roadway seemed to bend around unnecessarily. To his left two consecutive drive-in theaters, and he looked back in case of matinees, chase scene perhaps and robot cars crashing, but nothing. More mad bends. He saw the way the malls were dotted with old trees, and was reminded of how the khans would kill whole cities but keep a few alive to spread the story: each chosen old hemlock spoke of the great felling here.

Now modernity careening past. Skate King. Farrell's Ice Cream Parlour. Pizza & Pipes. World Famous B&I Circus Store. Places he'd learned to favor with an unaffected smile as a way of highlighting his kinship with the common man. "So, Ford, where ya from?"

"Well -- ."

"Ford, your artificial voice has driven me to the brink of madness. Try something else. That actress from the television."

"This one?" car purred.

Ha-ha: nowadays there's more than one way to drive a car. Rackley smirked, which he figured she could see somehow ... wait, a cleverness was forming ... tranny, transmission ... these things take time ... wait, why would I talk to my car. I don't even talk to my chauffeur.

Suddenly a slowing down: here they were on the Microsoft Campus. Impressive structures, nicely-monied and pretty: polygons, part-circles and connecting bands, all in modern materials and the new colors. Broad-leaf trees brought from the tropics wondering what the hell. Peoplemovers everywhere so that young scientists could look at phones and speak to spectacles without falling into koi ponds killing koi. The look-feel of a theme park, so life-like in parts it seemed fakey.

Car turned into guest parking and slotted neatly. It had a glowing clock on its dash, malevolent, which Rackley refused to acknowledge. "What time is it?" His watch didn't tell time.

Still purring: "10:25 in the morning."

Well early, over an hour to kill; robots are not good stewards of time. He turned the car off. Shut up. He flung himself limb by limb into the master seat and its sweet emoluments. There were pads and levers for lumbar and lower back, and he got them just right, as if sorting his cares. He had a long, well-considered cigarette. Suffered the flask. The weather stopped. Seconds passed and eventually he was in a silence chamber, save for the slowing tick-tick of the car cooling, the tiniest echo of breath. Later he spoke quietly to the Cloud, stresses lifting.

So Mills Rackley and his time of great moment. And one lets the gaze fall to memory's pool and reflection. And the provenance therein, all the parts and especially all the parties to the putting together of this, this most implausible of so many possible roads, the bending road to his bright future here.

In the summer of his thirtieth year Mills Rackley, a man of ordinary which is to say unclear talents, was subject to a cannabic epiphany: he would retire from his future in the trades and make of himself an artist. All the salutary things in life might derive from his success there, he decided, and all the virtues.

Photography seemed simplest. You just turn it over to your computer. But as with its prettier sister, porn, photographic manufacture had become an archaism. Every variant of every possible photograph had already been made, and been made available at the cost of a click. The world was topped up with it. New additions just spilled down the side. After a while he threw his whole portfolio on a bad thumb-drive.

Music is the quickest exposer in the arts, because art-enjoyers will tolerate everything except physical pain. For Rackley, a euphonium bought and quickly sold.

He invested heavily in oils, and a bolt of the finest foreign canvases. His portraits were abstracts, necessarily. He posted them properly; eventually he positioned them in places where they might be discovered: events, shop awnings, alongside a monument, then the dumpster behind his building where of course they were.

In this most litigious of epochs, poetry vied with everyday words: every commodity in the world -- each craft and artifact, oddity, toy, gaudy afterthought -- carried its own warnings, threats and stern advisories; each product of the creative mind had its carapace of indemnifications, claims, provisos and stipulations of use ... society simply had no appetite for more gibberish. In time he printed out hard copies of his cantos for a more satisfying burn.

With stone-sculpture, the noble suffering of the artist was not just psychological. The iconoclasm at the end required a trip to the dump.

Throughout all these exchanges Rackley never strayed from the nomenclature: upon introduction he was always an artist. Subcategory -- expressive dance or what have you -- provided upon request. He would not lie and say he had nothing to offer, lacked a particular eye, a sense of how things should be. This was his home now, and it was beautiful. Rare air, light and sweet.

But clearly he could use another epiphany. It came, a more ordinary one but better, from small cinema of all places, someone's spirited handmade film and a tossaway line in it that said an artist's life is his canvas: he stepped outside so he could smoke and clear his head. Of course, a credo to outlast the season. An artist doesn't have to make art. He can simply be art, in esse. And if I must be judged by my product, let my art be made by those I inspire, if they can. Which is to say he would make of himself an artist by making artists of others. Surely rarer air still. He needed a blog, and fast.

So Rackley was remade as an opinion-teller, and gained a certain renown in his circle, the opinion-readers in it. He web-logged biweekly: toil over each tract by evening light in public places, then to flush them ruddy and new into the virtual world and watch the hits that grew and grew, ten, twenty, no end; and in time he was good for a ready-made polemic at the odd soiree, making fans, a raconteur needing neither wine knowledge nor tales.

For his style he had thought to begin collecting words from old promptories and texts, claiming them from disuse and offering them new purpose in his cause. Blague. Quatsch. Kidstakes. Perissologist. Clever: borrow a thing, then give it life. And in a clever trade he also sent into relegation words grown old and worthless from lives of excess. Melange. Eclectic. Jejune. Hifalutin. And the like, cast from the world of letters except when cited to emphasize the point.

More specifically, Rackley would go out into the city in a big surge and submit himself to its displays. Live readings, or failing that a teleplay on his device; the novelties on loan to gallery walks and public parks; a new diner and its décor, perhaps new jazz drifting past the doorman. The lines of the new high-rise, the graffiti of the old. He'd go home and have it all take effect and at last put it down. He might employ the well-meaning ways of best critique, which hopes you to listen and improve; or he might invoke the ill will that is the mark of critique generally, the idea being that perhaps you'll move aside to make room for those with actual potential; or combine the two for a more nuanced advisory.

All this to create artists, of course, but eventually there was more. If art was his bailiwick then so was the world itself, art underpinning it; art, which affects ideas, which affect politics, which lays a claim to the temper of any given time and even to the climate.

So Rackley made it his daily duty to take a run down the headlines -- Middle East ... ice in Canada ... new thing shows promise -- to ensure an ennui not merely born of affect but rooted in the everyday; and of course to ensure the topicality that lent his tracts that swagger. That wightliness. Pollent. Sprauncy. Rannygazoo. And if they look them up later, even better, because that is how I teach.

And finally there was that other thing.

If one assumes that every proprietary cartel is formed with the best of intentions, ArtProjekt's were even better. ArtProjekt: in the years before its foundation, the world lay smashed beneath an accretion of art. Robots, artificial intelligence and the Guaranteed Basic Income had triggered a cataclysmic pursuit of passions, and civilization began to founder, wracked with art, filthy with it. Tech the ruiner, as ever. Software could write your novel now, so everyone was a promising unread novelist. Films were made by software, for a fraction of the cost-- acting was done by narcotized supermodels and modern algorithms, which could apply to each edited visage expressions more poignant and more modern than human powers alone could attain. And then there came the worst technological miracle the world had ever seen: silkscreed. Penny-a-yard, tissue-thin, proofed against the weather; draped on buildings and vehicles, over landscaping or jauntily across the shoulders, its finely-pixilated surface could throw out a devastating churn of visuals, from celebrity montage and laser fractalia to resumes, wedding snaps, politics and software haiku; or just ads. Silkscreed were everywhere; inevitably audio was added, thus music, thus the curse of multiple musics, the very sound heard in the heads of the denizens of Bedlam.

A firehose of art against the senses, and humankind walked through it wax-eyed, numb with stimulus; or wore ear-buds and special goggles, falling into water features. No one knew what period this was, what to call the style, the ism if there was one or school of thought; or everyone did; or no one cared, the world grown insipid on art. And certainly no one knew what to do.

Then ArtProjekt and deliverance.

ArtProjekt began in the ordinary way, with a different name of course and as ad hoc agencies formed at federal levels that came and went but lingered, soon claiming a glass block of offices, a cubic yard of printed money. But this was too important for government. The long sequence of transmogrifications begins, quiet and without apparent artifice. Name-shifting, or between acronyms that might not have meaning. Suddenly there's no fixed address, no board of overseers, not even a domain; every schoolchild had a fucking domain. Figures from culture and finance lent their names and withdrew them, names lingering like scent. Shadow figures emerged, just enough to place their avatars in the light, these perhaps a little overlit, a bit too alive. Defying the laws of physics, money simply materialized.

Protocols, if they existed, were kept protected from the disfiguring public gaze; but of course they existed, because decrees require them, and there were decrees. Silkscreed was banned. Later, better, it was shunned. Bugs were smuggled into offending applications, their output becoming derivative and jejune. Cinemas and quaint local galleries were seized at fair market rates and nationalized. Some were destroyed outright, others remade and made useful, as nail salons and so on. Certain audio-visual musics were made criminal by the vague rules of ArtProject's charter, vague rules being strongest.

Art product was likened to a wartime resource now, its flow subject to caps, rationing, smart oversight. ArtProjekt chose new works and the artists for them, arranging for display, critical praise and sales. Soon a period of antichaos and calm.

None of this was terribly legal. But life and its laws are not some sort of suicide pact. In a crisis it's not a matter of doing what you can. You do what you must, whether or not you can.

All of this a consternation to freedom types. Sharp words were used in public places and in print, and protests were assigned and scheduled. These were enthusiastic affairs necessarily, and bothered one and all, but they were also pragmatic, never conducted in such a way as might meet with success. Artists hated this new consortium as a matter of propriety, but in practice they were not much aggrieved. A little oversight scares away the claimers, the dabblers who clog the lanes. Art would take root in artifice, success coming not via skill but consent ... but it could in fact be had now: bloody memories remained of the bad times. In which each moment of inspiration was pitched with love into the churn of light and sound to become a cinder, bright and lost forever. ArtProjekt would become the gatekeepers of the land of the sane, where artists were by these new restraints free now to express their prayers and visions and hatred for ArtProjekt with the hope that someone somewhere might take note; artists like Mills Rackley and his wife Noma.

His wife and tireless love. Here I must introduce her for her critical part just ahead. Noma Rackley, who took her husband's name contrary to convention. Her oral history is a bit improvised on the early end: for example, her childhood could be hardscrabble if need be; it was not a work in progress because she didn't much care, as she made clear. She'd been given striking features, like from a carving. Curved planes. Lean and elegant as a jeweler's tool. Several different smiles, all sharpened by a mirror. Her opinions left her mouth fully formed, beyond the reach of the editor's pen. She made a living as a poet or actually as an instructor of aerobics and exercise dance. The perfect thing for her, now give me ten more. Her poetry was not readable really but it was performable, at reading events in which attendees are other readers waiting their turn. Her emblem for this was a linen kimono got from her travels to Japantown, worn comfortably: nothing more empowering to a woman than her décolletage, which she wielded with economy and care. She let the gown tatter a little because that goes with world-weary; she was known to quickly slip into it just as the guests arrived. Noma, tireless advocate of her interests and her husband's, which she made her own. She commended her choice of husband in many asides, saw to his upkeep, led him squiring her to all the events, helped him make the two of them the very model of the up-and-coming power couple. They shared ideas, cheer-led, never fought; their affection was cautious but real. Together they spent their art time defying rhyme and meter, describing the future around them and, in poem and post, expressing their hatred for ArtProjekt, though of course never naming it by name.

Suddenly ArtProjekt put out the call: hiring and try-outs for a writer in the area for reviews and blurbs. The Rackleys leapt all over the queue.

It was understood there was no writing involved: the hiree would be responsible for taking credit and the odd interview. A proper use for the term ghostwriter, since ghosts don't exist, and Mills Rackley was perfect for the job. Presentable basically, with a good vocabulary of terms, and he'd done a year of law school and learnt bullshit and the right way to say what one doesn't mean. The examination would be five minutes for a monologue of choice. They worked on that together, and she set him up in art-casual: real wool slacks with button braces; shirt of solid color, open collar; retro sneakers.

Testing would take place at Fitzhugh Meeting, in Percy one county over, two hours. They took popular transit, which tireless Noma reminded him they would continue to use even after when they didn't have to. It was a mean old clapboard assembly that might've been part of a mission once. They strode in on a freshening wind, smiling and careful to make eye contact. The pews were all lit up, half full, and they sat. Someone was speaking at an odd podium built into the aisle; she was telling all about herself to the dark stage ... no ... a panel there and their little table, backlit ever so slightly, two women and a man in humorless silhouette.

Rackley: so here you are, or some of you. Glowing in your carefully chosen light. He leaned forward in a coy way. They were all three tiny, and bespectacled. Constantly reflecting. The man of them probed a beard and would sometimes sip commercial water. Three workpads, not touched; in fact, the women didn't move at all, or only enough so as to not cause alarm. He couldn't really read them, of course. Their stillness might indicate rapt attention or its devastating opposite. One of them suddenly pulls from a vapor pen.

The banality of genius. And as the Rackleys awaited their turn through what she called cruel digressions he sees another presence, a lurker in the wings, not quite unlit like the others, a large man spread across a lounge chair. Rackley thought he knew him from the news and publications, and he nudged his wife. She whispered, "Nominoe."

Right. A world figure or something somewhere. Traveled about in all the circles, lots of photos with kings and the like. We can assume he's rich. A fixer perhaps, or broke things too. That's all he could come up with. Might be asleep. Interesting.

Just behind and beside him, a much smaller man standing and surely not sleeping, eyes wide and wolfing it down, the littlest sergeant-at-arms.

Now Rackley at the hustings. A red digital timer on the dais, tyrannical eye. Good let it be that way. He opened with something funny really, a pun. He drew his notes, a light riffle and they're folded back in their pocket, subtly but not too. He pulled a couple of faces, just the pair, a smirk but then no, this is serious. Rothko: Beyond Style and Content. Because what is style really, no one knows but don't we all; he used a term from that period, then an edited line from Kandinsky; color is content; water please; there are no new ideas, and never were until recently. Explain post-modernism. --

"Thank you. Next, please. Ralph Rokesby."

A minute twenty. What the fucking hell. There was overall noise and some milling, and he felt himself drawn by knowing glances into his death march to the door, trying to kick off his miserable Red Ball Keds; he turned and Noma was not there; someone speaking at the lectern who was not Ralph Rokesby.

"I would never try to take away your hate. I'm not cruel like you. And I would never take your sense of superiority. I'm better than that." She pinched her robe shut at the neck; she was using that smile he feared, the axe-man's smile. "I take away these things and what do we have, nothing ... these treasures that give you your reason to live. Can't have an empty stage, can we. No, we need you exactly as you are. You have a function. No, you do. You remind us that --"

Nominoe's little man had hurried over the stage and handed a note to a judge, who shut off Noma's microphone by a toggle and leaned into her own: "Welcome to ArtProjekt."

Music with a tantara over house speakers, and a gallant takes her on an arm up to the stage, now all ablaze, smiles, hugs and handshakes, light talk, and clapping in the stands. Nominoe with black eyes stares at him all the while.

Mills Rackley had never succeeded before, and was for weeks feeling flush and disordered by the prize and all its retinue of fame, riches and power. Fame: and he spread the joyous word to his friends and acquaintances, who mainly had no idea, and he remembered reading that fame might mean wondering who are your friends really. Riches: fresh cash led to a proper car at last, a newer gas model for style and reliability, and they would move to a full one-bedroom with a view of downtown. Noma as the sudden professional in the family would take hold of décor, designing with the idea of her new station of guests: furniture, some to just look at; block prints, lambrequins and shams in the latest pastels; a glass cabinet of novelties for notice and remark, hands off. And they could afford a dog, Lakme.

Power: she wouldn't tell him about that but it was safe to assume, and he did just that, in mixed company, during greetings, with waitstaff, whenever it was appropriate.

She'd be gone for days or a week on her duties and return without apology and an expression on her face pregnant with secrets, put an oddment in the etagere and speak in a beautiful font of words about the bliss of creation, a bliss he borrowed as best he could. Their weekend at home was a reverie with a bit of ritual in, the workmanlike making of eggs and housekeeping, and he'd lie to her about the week just past, with specifics, and she'd boast about it, without them; her with her intimations, him with his imaginings. Romantics, then.

Suddenly she'd be gone again adventuring, a conspicuous alone time for Rackley, but he'd once read that writers crave that.

A better subsidy meant better things: there was a Dean of the Bean just a walk from their place, swimming with college types and readers and with awnings and deck, and eventually he and the blue heeler would settle down there every midmorning for public writing. He'd pick the currants out of his muffin for her and nurse a chai. And he recalled later that he was preparing a post about how lonely is the writer's art, when he found a note on the table beside, in elegant leaning script: *Hello again.*

He turned and there they were at the table just behind. Nominoe: "You remember me from Fitzhugh. I'm told you know my name. Look, you're wearing the same shirt. What is that, salmon. Here you could make a joke like and I don't even like salmon. Go ahead."

He thought about that and saw that they'd been here awhile, Nominoe well into a coffee-cake; on the other, signs of a cruller. Odd, odd. "It has been laundered in the interim."

"Oh well." An unplaceable voice, not right for an accent. "And I would like to introduce you, this is Velbin my scribe."

He offered his hand to Velbin, who looked at it like he was being handed a human hand. Rackley: "Oh yes. Chance meeting here like this."

"No luck involved. Mark Rothko. Do you even know who that is?"

"We have one of his prints near the entry. Ochre."

"Did you know I knew him, in New York?" No. "Big fellow, good feeder. He was completely colorblind, which is funny."

Pause. And this would be the very first of many they would share in their time together. Now and later he would know not to interrupt, and he would listen; a tool, perhaps, a probe, seeking reaction; a break in the playing, for a breath and considering next notes; sometimes in a pause Rackley thought he might derive a message from it by the careful measure of its duration, but no. Silence fraught with meaning, quite beyond him.

Nominoe: "Just kidding. He used to say that wind can pick up paint and throw it on a canvas. But it cannot make a square. Make two squares and make them ochre and red like yours and you have created a human sentiment. There, another idea which is not yours which you can use. Who wrote your speech, your wife."

"Yes."

"People as a rule don't form their own opinions. Fortunately for them I am here. You'd like me to tell you how you know when a man's opinions are not his own. This way: they're very strong and built out of nothing. Like super-hardened air. Of course, in your case it didn't help that they were wrong opinions too."

"Ah."

"But I'm sure you know the saying: if you're going to have a wrong opinion, make it a strong one." Rackley nodded. Nominoe: "Well at least you know to nod as if you do. So. Expressive dance."

"Yes. Retired because of injury."

"Injury. I've heard bad things. But I assume you can still do the inexpressive dance."

A pause, and Rackley took the time in it to look at them. They had the same expression in two ways. Velbin was curious with expectation. Nominoe was curious as if he'd just heard a nonsense rhyme. Nominoe. Face not fat but taken with light jowling. Perhaps three hard crevasses but otherwise light and smooth, not much in the weather or smoked on. Eyes black, layers of black. Black head hair, in ordered piles. Eyebrows were black like from a pen, and vaulting, and sinuous, attached to the gears inside, and gave his face the bulk of its expression. Cravat, silk or gabardine forget it, I'm no good with clothes. Velbin. Standing with fanny bag on belly. Hair cut a bit like a coal-scuttle. Mouth parted. Occasionally a tongue-tip could be seen inside, an eel in a cave. Otherwise it was empty. An empty look in his eyes, which is to say the look of watching, and the wish to do so in a meaningful way.

Nominoe: "Okay. Nice. Really comes across. You know, you write monograms on various topics. Have done for years. Turns out no one ever read them. Oh did you spill your drink. Velbin, napkin.

Anyway, it's true, we found out. You would use a word like blague and they would stop, suitably impressed. But anyway who reads these days, there's so much to read."

Rackley dabbed his chin. "Well, sir. I suggest that maybe your --"

"You collect words, and you should consider collecting that one. Maybe. Really good one. You can drop it anywhere into a sentence when you want the sentence to be completely stripped of meaning. Magic." Laughter, thudding, not merry. "Watch: maybe you should consider collecting it." Rackley could not prepare a riposte in time. "Do you know why we selected your wife?"

"No."

"Because clearly she is insane."

All too much. Rackley straightened in his chair. "I take offense. That's my wife you're talking about. How dare you, sir."

"I manage somehow. In fact you could even tell by her smile. I bring this up because I want to use your skills in an ArtProjekt matter, but first we have to have your sanity appraised." Velbin handed Rackley a card. Nominoe: "Go talk to this fellow. And I will have you wear the glasses everyone hates." Velbin passed them over. "Where you can see messages on the lens. I will be listening and send you the messages to say. Also here's a watch." It was a beautiful watch, one of the new digitals, with diamond-like accents. Rackley put it on. "So I can track your movements."

Rackley turned the card over in his hands. Dr. Bernard Argentael, Forensic Psychiatrist. A moment of due diligence, for himself or perhaps for show. "How do I know this isn't some sort of trick?"

"I'm not sure how you know things. It's for tomorrow at ten sharp. You will have to cancel other plans." Nominoe got up and they left, and he said, "I think it's been a successful day."

Dr. Argentael was stooped and a cane-bearer, with goatee and single pigtail. When he spoke it was in a long and surprising drawl. The office was dark-paneled and dark in other ways, blackout blinds and just the desk lamp, beside which the doctor wore a green eyeshade and tap-tapped at a workpad all the while. Rackley lay facing away on a lounge in the traditional manner. He donned his special goggles, ready to break out the old acting chops. Acting is all in the eyes but since he was facing away he'd just use his hands.

Dr. Argentael: "Tell me about your childhood."

Rackley, reading: "Ordinary. I'd even say quite ordinary. Couldn't hold my interest." A weary flick of the wrist.

Tap-tap. "Did you have any imaginary friends?"

Reading: "No, no, nothing like that. They ... pretty much ignored me."

"Have you had any feelings since our last session?"

Reading: "Well, there was a moment of confusion." This was beginning to challenge his thespian powers. "Aside from that, no."

Dr. Argentael: "Okay. Understandable. Any experiences?"

Rackley reading; he gagged a little but made it a cough. "Well, the other day this man insulted my wife and all I did was fiddle with my napkin. Later I went home and smoked pot."

"Okay." Tapping. "You know, Mills, I hear that sort of thing a lot. Hey? You're not a bad person."

Reading, slowly and with horror: "Then I had an attack of conscience. Which would be fine if I had a normal person's conscience. But my conscience is a gay pig with a hitler moustache."

"Excuse me?" Sharp and sudden.

Rackley: did I read that right? But it was gone. He tilted his head and was snapped up in the doctor's stare, who issued a long breath stinking of mint and said, "How do you know he's gay?"

Nothing in his glasses. He shook them, pinched their stems, wake up. "Well." Laugh naturally. "Ha a hah ha. You know. I just assumed so because --"

"You assumed?" The stare bore down. "How would you like it if I just assumed you were, say, seeing a psychiatrist?"

Unexpected. Look into your lenses: black ceiling. Act normal. "Absolutely." A confident waving of the arms. "Incidentally, I also write poetry. I --"

"What your conscience does in its private life is just that: private. It's none of your business."

Rackley threw off the glasses which were heavy and anyway not a good look. "Sure. Of course ... but don't you think it's important that my conscience is --"

"As long as its sexuality doesn't impact the way it does its job ... then no."

"Job. Did I mention that it's a pig?"

"You know what?" Dr. Argentael outgassed for several seconds and pulled out a laser pointer. "You talk too much."

What. Carry on professionally. "Ha uh ha-ha. I noticed that. I go on and on."

"I don't usually tell this to my patients. But I think you have a problem. And I think you should get some help. Take your shirt off?"

Rackley threw an arm over his eyes. It's one thing to have your psychiatrist ask you to take your shirt off. But when he implies that you have some sort of a "problem" ... it made him uncomfortable, and he began to think that this was seeming like a bad idea. He flicked off his tie and started at the collar, working down.

Velbin surged out of the shadows with a card: *Welcome to ArtProjekt.*

Centuries of poor stewardship had caused the natural realm to fail its stewards. Poor or simply improper: the sins of sloth and greed, combining; carbon let out willy-nilly, by burning, exhalation; the delicate thermohaline cycle allowed to run deranged. All of it on the ancient short-list of science warnings, and science proposed the sure news of a new Epoch of Glaciation.

Science says a lot of things of course and another thing it said is that this was the dumbest possible imperilment of the planet, dumber by far than a germ or sunspot, bolide, spite-filled robots. Death by frozen water. A slow and stupid hard flood moving a few feet or more an hour or so depending. An odd molecule, not to be trusted: water in its various forms had carved the domains of life and then, critical biosolvent, had defined life ... and now was never mind all that, some kind of fuckwit. The other planets had it easy, said science. Water: too dumb to hate and certainly too dumb to fear.

So when the ice came storming down out of the trees and threatened to overtake an acre of concrete pad covered in machine pipes and a headman's cabin, the concern in question spent a lazy week delivering hesco boxes and putting in general fill to form a wave break and barrier. The ice spent a rugged day on all that lot, with a large release of carbon, embarrassing.

Newer cabins, then, and better. Two Yukon towns, Oslac and down the draw to Edward, named after royalty, forty homes, kerosene drums and no roads, who would live here? Anyway, no one now. Then three settlements, the ice in an arc down the western courses of the Ruby Range, and crossing water.

At about this time it seemed that the ice had begun to propagandize and grow, as a cell might, lung to liver. From hilltops all along these latitudes it came down in bands -- rampaging bands, foraging bands, bands in largissimo; Mts. Martha, Gribbles, Motherall expressed them into common areas where they might crash into the general cause, broaden the inland sea. Cruel ice and uncaring; untiring, and broken with gaps and runnels that could disappear in a day, as mutable as the land beneath it so unamenable to measure, but science says it was 200 kilometers across now, fat with upflung trees, feldspar and the detritus of living things, and its ugly fighter's face was ten meters high let's say.

Missing homes and miles of ice, and by the time it came to overlook Kiukshu and Dalton Post they'd taken note and made ready. Trenches, an old recoilless rifle drawn from an armory. Sad and ceremonious rescues of family memories, albums, urns full of mother's-ash, kept items including snow globes; of art and appliances; or crumbling old discs and drives; and of course the old claw tub, sash windows and their casements, cork flooring, to be had for a coin. And some with the means might haul the whole home away and be among the first to say where do I take this, where is it safe.

The Project -- The Misunderstood Man

By Whitehorse it was top distraction, the eyes of the world. No one'd ever seen a midrise city demolished by ice before, and science was there was its calipers; the news was there, drawn as they are to new epochs, to ask people how they felt about it. Also: in a calamity, decorum is first casualty -- one of the few benefits -- so calamity tours began to crop up, airships, open london buses, free samples of course for taking back. Eventually a raised platform on the ice itself, bench seats and a brazier, calamity fans overflowing. Where it ran over rough country the ice might be covered in crevices, irresistible to any clambering ass, thus first loss of life.

They said they could feel it moving beneath them, and would let out a big carrying-on when a home was swallowed beneath the waves, which might occur in one or more of five ways. The ordinary manner of course; or by gradual inclination, which no edifice can manage really, resulting in sudden subsidence. Penetration, as under a lintel, and steady entry of the ice -- ice is a light ton per cubic yard -- across the floor until failure and cascade. Fire, by unsecured fuel, and the ice would form a brief audience around. Phase transition, in which ice would pierce a cavity, melt a bit -- which it would do all the time, no reason -- and then, water the dumbest molecule, expand as it froze. You could see the walls fill out as the house took its last breath.

A different sort of disaster. Ice was quietly the worst thing in the world: where nothing grows, and grows. A man might dine on it with friends but never live there; could not build there, pavilions pulled down a crevasse. A growing death zone that did not kill human beings but killed them nonetheless. The ice took homes in the regular way of disasters but with no after-part for sifting for family memories, no hero's talk of rebuilding better and stronger. The calmest killer and most complete.

Different: and science agreed that the ice was hard to hate. Depredations in the most civilized way, never crass or histrionic. You and your friends could ride it in on a painted pavilion as it took you to your ruin. The ice was not hellish to behold, never screamed at you, never stank or shook you like a bad parent; it was hard to hate because it had no personality. Why would anyone hate gravity, or the tics of the uranium atom? And why hate something too dumb to hear you, too dumb to learn from it? Best just to kill it with cold resolve.

They thought to bomb the ice with one of the new napalms, a polyplasticine blend with high adhesion, deep exothermic burns and morbid release of carbon. Turns out a drop would dig down until the ice walls came in and put it out. Later, when the ice would open up -- say during the breakdown of pretty Baker Falls, resort town -- the pyrophoric residue might reignite and complicate all.

Now an oil plant to protect, and an early effort with flame-throwers, in which a cadre is trained to cast the benzene gel in burning arcs like a scanning tool. But of course the ice is charged with combustibles. And a flaming sheet of shingles, an entire burning Doug fir led by its root ball, comes down on the fire-fighters, changing plans. Grand old M-67 Zippo flame-shooting vehicles were mended and brought from a reliquary and put to use. The ice moved west and east in a classic encirclement, then moved to reduce the salient. Roads were smashed and overrun. Eventually an evacuation by air, and the five brave fire tanks were never seen again.

Science was asked to conjure a new black -- darker than the original and with better black properties -- for application to the ice; most important was the property that had it store sunlight as warmth. Soon miles of deep matte BlackPlus polyvinyl batts were rolled out as a blanket on the ice by special teams. It did not work well in overcast, or seasonal snow; fell into crevasses, like its teams; was cut up by erratics and other ice crud. So Science failed two native hamlets and also fouled them with plastic trash.

Giles Bishop was the American president; he looked around the room for someone to fire. "Thermohaline cycle ... deranged? Not on my watch. Someone tell me what that is."

Silence around the map table, that contemplative quiet so commonly made by his advisors. Finally it was Ewell, Secretary of Science -- like all science people, slightly sibilant or stammering -- who spoke. "Progenitor of climates of every caliber and kind, both *globally and locally. Heat, with rain, drying effects, ice, all changing. Over the years the loss of life is beyond calculation."* He raised a finger and mashed a spider vein. *"Beyond that, effects unknown."*

They were in the Crisis Room, where the president had all his meetings, and he was picking up the bland whiff of dissembling. Bishop belonged to and in fact was the leader of the more sciency of the two parties, and for him it was facts or nothing. He aimed his laser vapor pen at Harris. *"Science Czar. What say you?"*

Harris averted his eyes. He knew that the president favored debate within his inner circle, mentioned it all the time, pure team-of-rivals stuff; he hid behind nervous hands, which after all were living in tremulous times. *"Ewell is an ass,"* he hissed. Silence; Ewell could not rejoin the barb, making it a pithy one. Bishop nodded.

The map: odd radii and bands like isobars impressed upon coastlines and elevations, and Bishop stood above it all now, colossus standing athwart the waves. The hind end of his pen was glassine, an orbuculum, a wise eye and gentle, and he would stare at it like now. *"The Chinese involved?"* *Another simmering silence. Right. Loud and clear.*

The president's first sex scandal had led to the headline Bishop Takes Queen, the quip by Nominoe actually, which even now could make him smile. *"Marijuana doesn't make you paranoid, Mr. President,"* he said with a smile. *"The Federal government just wants you to think it makes you paranoid."*

Bishop gave that a long consideration; then gave Nominoe that look he always did, half a wince beneath narrowing eyes, one eye beneath a royal arch. You mad genius. *"Okay. So what now."*

America annexed certain Canadian lands and sent an occupying corps to establish the pretext and plan. Thousands of power pylons would go up in river valleys, frames of steel lattice strung in series, state of the art and the worst ever: whereas any ordinary transmission tower wants to send its dispatches easily to distant lands, here in the valleys of the Skeena and the Squamish the message would end in the wire itself: fine strands of an elegant silicon-germanium blend -- miscible, top ohms and high thermic values -- plus wire crud

-- chalk, ground glass -- for improved inefficiencies: force the power to fight its way through this odd wire and throw off waves of waste heat. Heat, slayer of ice.

A frozen army then, terracotta guards tall as a strong man might shoot an arrow, each tower strung with wire on its northern side, its iceward side; hooked to the common grid of course, but with a supplement of radioisotope boxes to boost the charge. Later, into the rivers swollen with icemelt they would set turbines for hydro, a clever twist: make the ice a pipeline flowing with the fuel of its own demise ... power that might, in the minds of some, become a surplus in time, marketed accordingly. Salvation at a considerable savings, and a Congress on board.

The call went out for half a million men. The first offer was that lots of them would die, because standards would be set aside. They'd be asked to work with a military imperative, humorless and without sympathy, like the metal guardians they would make; as with all soldiers the specifics were obscure but the cause clear, save mankind.

At mustering stations across the land they lined up for all the regular reasons. Laborers, and men skilled in metal or electric; drivers and pilots, provisioners, cooks, laundry; staff and the men who would direct them, and men in fabrication for use with the press. And of course amanuenses and drovers and whores, and all the loose trumpery that describes any army on the move.

Shops and factories were claimed and reassigned, or taken for parts; phones and devices were seized for the rare earths in them; dance videos were replaced by anti-ice propaganda, with music; the refugees poured in, demanding free wifi. As vexations grew, the vexed were starting to notice and wonder.

The Canadian mountain town of Cassiar was made staging base and HQ, and Quonset huts were first to arrive with their squads. An unknown engineer there in winter kit turned a spade of soil for a footing, and set in motion what would become not the bloodiest war in American history perhaps, but close to it, and surely the war of greatest brutality.

The Project -- The Misunderstood Man

Rackley's new flat was south of Tovey Street, an old and reclaimed ward. Not clean upon receipt, and also he could tell it would not be clean during his tenure. No television, no internet really. He'd be sleeping on a camp bed whose window beside was taped up by a naugahyde sheet that let in the frozen air but not light. Different. No kitchen, which was a modern normal -- Rackley kept a box of beef wafers, bottled water in a locker by his bed; in lieu of kitchen, the generous lounge for dressing and presentation. Mirrors, nail station, natural light by the unsealed window; he'd already lain in some unself-conscious shoes, his beloved campus sports coats, scraps of underwear. The loo featured an ancient full-volume john, a plus.

Nominoe crept in. "I like what I've done with the place."

Rackley: "Me too. Am I being punished?"

"The artist of today requires two homes." Two homes. Well of course. "This one is for toilette, rest and reconsideration. The other is for professional. It's on North Beach with a view, though not of a beach. Current tenant is being bankrupted. Might take me a week or two." Velbin held his coat. They stood there, careful not to touch surfaces. "Oh say, what do you think of acting?"

What? Time to shine, and he let go his cuticle pick. "Ah, the thespian's art, noblest of them. Because unlike other artists, who might make a thing then cast it off like flotsam, an actor becomes his own creation. Naked on the stage beneath the gaze of a thousand, which is why it is also the loneliest of arts."

"Yes. All of that is wrong. You gave me an idea ... I think you will become a great source of my ideas. Tomorrow morning you will do a radio interview. Let's say ten o'clock. It's important, so tidy up a little."

Next morning they were there with a phone, and Nominoe showed him its functions. He had advice: "Sometimes it's said that the best lies are partly true, but no, the best lies are entirely true.

Here's how. First, lie to yourself. Then, when you lie to others, it's the truth."

As he turned to leave he mumbled, "Anyway, that's how I do it." Velbin prepared a note and presented it to Rackley. *"That's how he does it."*

Next day on the hour he tapped the auto-dial and was speaking to a screener who told him his tone would be edited for less nasality, added bass. He listened to a preamble with jazz: The Actor's Craft with Joshua Ratliff; he was introduced as an actor and suddenly he was on. "Mr. Rackley. Good morning! Please turn your radio down."

Done. "What radio."

"Thanks so much for being with us."

This Ratliff was a bit heavy-breathed for a radio man; also he was fey or twee. "Of course."

"I always start with this question because I love learning about the actor's craft: how did you prepare for your role in this interview?"

"Ha uh hah haa." The useful old natural laugh, deployed now for time. "Yes I get that a lot." Pause for time; anyway it sounds thoughtful. "And to me it always come down to this: you can do your research, your ride-along or something like that if you like. But in the end the best preparation for any given role is, well … a life well-lived."

Ratliff: "Oh isn't it! The best preparation for life itself. What attracted you to the role?"

Should I make the joke about a paycheck? No! I'm beyond that. "Never stop growing, is my motto. In life … and as the actor living that life. Stretch, broaden one's skills. You know the saying: new experiences. And I had never been interviewed before."

"Some of your best work."

"Thank you."

And yes it was good work actually, and Rackley remembered why: he had in fact been interviewed before, thousands of times over the years in his head: on his successes future and imagined, in every medium of art, and also about topics of the day. So he'd done this before and it was all coming naturally. And by the end of the far-ranging hour -- he talked about staying humble, story story story, and the art of really listening -- Rackley knew he'd slayed it, and spent the rest of the day accordingly and slept well.

Nominoe: "What you call acting is not an art. Look at me. Listen. Here I am pretending to be someone I'm not. See? No artistry involved." Rackley had to admit. Convincing. Nominoe: "Here, you try." Rackley did so. Nominoe: "Well, you haven't had training."

Nominoe sat on a bed sheet that Velbin had thrown over furniture. "Actors are told what to say; thank god. Told stand here, make your face look like this. When I direct I am very hands-on: I just shape their face for them. I'm a people person. No, the actor's craft occurs only when the actor speaks of it. Oh! What a fountain, what a gout of fantasy, pure imagination." Here a tumescent finger. "As you so ably demonstrated yesterday."

Rackley smiled. A mild autumn sun warmed in him. Nominoe: "We're going to make the interview into a one-act play. One night only. A stage-play of course. And now tell me again about that."

Rackley put down his chai bowl to free his hands. "The stage. Remember: acting, unlike the other arts, is a collaboration, between the artist and those who trust him. Easiest if you consider dinner theater. Smells, rustlings, misplaced orders, the tinkling of silverware. But there's a trick there: the actor is feeding too … off those stimuli. And let's say in the play there's a pun or something, which it is your duty to pass along: and if you hear nothing in response that's actually a good thing, because now you have information that you can use, the writing needs to be improved."

Nominoe laughed, and Rackley warmed more. "Well done. I can smell the Salisbury steak. Okay, and we film it and make into a movie of course. No one goes to plays. We hope to have it on the boards in two weeks. Casting we're already doing. Oh I see your expression there, but we're looking for more of a leading man or character type." He left the sheet behind; over time Rackley would find he'd gotten himself a well-stocked box of all-cotton linens.

In the middle of that fourteen days he was let into his other home by his driver -- suddenly he had a driver, Collier and his light-blue town car, who would drive him around ordinarily enough but otherwise have nothing to convey. This other home was at the top of its tower, a doorman tower, whose stare he was not yet ready to return. Across the threshold he realized he'd never been let into such a place, which fact by itself made it luminous. All in a careful off-white, cream or egg: pure but with just that bit of bad. The windows were full-length, bright, and seemed like the type of windows it would be hard to hurl yourself through. Nice view if you could, over the finance quarter, glass fortifications, distant water and roseate colors once a day. Room after room: what are they for? He would learn. It was empty but not quite: boxes of unplayable media, unimportant papers, the dead skin left behind a sudden departure. Coffee stains: sink and kitchen counter not scoured. So this home also not clean upon receipt: maybe the theory was that a new tenant might prefer the unclean look: choice. Appliances were all the latest, strictly voice-command. On a chance he asked the room to mitigate the heat, and suddenly he stood in a cooling draft. It's growing on me. Collier led him out, keeping the key.

Premiere night, and he was restive with actor's sweats: this was his story, after all, his life and words. Collier drove them out to a suburb he'd never heard of and its famous theater district, where all the playhouses were famously both small and just large enough to be unpretentious, which fascinated him, what's the trick. They were let in through the back, and he had a private gander at the set: pretty much right, plus with dead flower-pot, tin tray on the table heaving with butts. Okay, so more realistic than the real thing.

They sat three across in a special raised pew in the wings, unseen luminaries. The actor, the evening star, came on and took his mark: tall, good mastery of his space, a handsome likeness. Suddenly from the overhead, the radio voice, buttery and more broad-shouldered than the original: "Welcome to The Actor's Craft, I'm Joshua Ratliff. And welcome!" House lights down, curtain up, heart stirring.

The Project -- The Misunderstood Man

At the end the long ovation, huzzahs and thrown garlands; the doughy radio voice came center-stage and they clamped and extended their champion's hands, bowing at the waist, low and with a gratitude both deep and slightly mock, since stars provide all the power. Nominoe: "How dramatic! The actor was portraying an actor but was himself not acting. Performance original and non-derivative. And listen to that applause! Also original, non-derivative. Well done."

"Thanks. Say, about the dialogue? I actually never said any of that." Nominoe was busy beating his palms in congratulation. "Anyone who heard the broadcast will have noticed."

"Oh dialogue. Yours was not convincing, too original. I read the transcript. Like it was written for you. By a fabulist. Actors speak about themselves using language proven reliable over time. For example, you did not use the terms muse, motivation, feed off audience; or the joke the paycheck drew them to the role. Dialogue must be believable, first rule. So I did a quick edit. Oh, and there were no radio listeners, we checked. And hey, would you like to write the review? I'll assign a writer."

In the lobby patrons filed past with formal praise, too wary for effusion.

Next day, the piece by his by-line. "A NEW STORY FOR STORIED TIMES. We all know that, for the giving of life-lessons, art is more generous than reality. But sometimes life itself, in the hands of a gifted artist, is the greatest giver of all. Young Mills Rackley, heretofore unheard-of, has ..."

Rackley was learning lessons about ArtProjekt; about truth-shifting; about the artist, to whom all things are allowed.

Nominoe's scribe had rolled in a couch for them and breakfast -- squab confit on buns -- with Rackley in an informal half-lotus on the floor. The topic was interior design in the empty professional home, with Nominoe recommending. "Things like color, contrasts or themes will be noted, and guests may never come back, or if only to confirm and reconfirm why not. So first learn what's in fashion and don't do any of that. Everyone's already not doing that so don't do that too. Some are using robot designers but god forbid there's a bug in the software. You end up with ochre. Oh, important: you can't be derivative. But you can't be non-derivative, which is also derivative."

Rackley coolly considering the walls of alabaster and light white: "Beige it is, then. Yes, I think."

"No," said Nominoe, although he might not have heard. "Rackley, which art is king of the arts? We've already decided it's not acting."

"Oh my." Worth standing for, and he paced. "King of the arts. Would it were possible! One muse to rule them all. But really no, it's a nonsense question. Like asking a woman which of her stepchildren she loves the most. Awkward. No good comes of it. Interior design."

"And now tell me why." A coaxing smile.

"Well, think about it. The home makes the man, as it were. So how can you be an artist without an artist's life, home and environs designed just so? You pick up a hammer and give it a go but there's the problem: it takes a knack, an artist if you will, a flair or training. If you try to do it yourself chaos reigns."

Nominoe: "Mostly we can't form our own opinions. Not a person in a thousand. Takes an uncommon strength so don't feel bad. I suppose you read that in a magazine." Yes. "All wrong. The king of the arts is: the word. Now I'll explain. The other arts are entirely sensory. Requires an eye or an ear. Your sculpture garden, don't bring your blind friend, ended badly. But the word is intellectual. You can read it. Or have it read to you. Make it into a braille for nimble fingers. If you become a lump of sapient flesh I will tap a sonnet on your nose in code -- you are forewarned. And for the sensory person like me there is the elegance of typeface; the indents that inform poesy; the broad rhoticity of an orator, also like me."

The Project -- The Misunderstood Man

More: "Anyway ... see? Could not explain except by words. Try that with dance. Stop, facetious. And I've been wondering about a way that ArtProjekt might honour our sovereign. A piece of noble verse, perhaps. Do you ever read a poem?"

Rackley: "Ah a herr a hen-henh. Oh do I. In fact, on those days when my muse and I are on the very best of terms, I might even perpetrate one. Uh yuh henheh."

Nominoe: "You know, you are never so eloquent as when you are making your nervous laugh. Say. Maybe that could be our poem. Are you able to transcribe these odd noises, spelling correctly? Note that some of it did not sound human."

"I use spell-check. So yes."

"Mm." Nominoe thinking, fingers on chin probing lightly as if in a beard there. "Funny idea. But comedies no matter how good they are are not taken seriously. So overruled."

"Okay." That got Rackley thinking. "So where you're from originally. Do they not use commas?"

Now the chin cradled and held quietly for a while. "Interesting. Consider: a treatise, a proclamation ... no. A credo. Consisting entirely of punctuation."

Rackley did consider, and soon enthused. "Yes ... for what are these little marks but signifiers of mood; mood defines the credo. Example: here, I pause. Is it doubt? Or is it emphasis ... it is! Moods vary of course. Example: a sense of finality. Or frustration, or --"

Nominoe: "I see what you did there. If you look you'll see it too. But ... and here I pause ... without the actual words of the credo we can't tell if we've gotten the punctuation right. And I'm a stickler. Oh the challenges of the artist."

"Alright, then how about this then." Rackley put on his thinking cap. "It's said that all art is either revolutionary or mere plagiarism. But isn't theft an art? Ask a thief. Proposed: plagiarism in bold new styles. Those who think it's not revolutionary -- as well as, and here's the beauty of it, those who think it is -- are fools and not worthy of our scorn. Or are worthy if necessary."

"Been done. ArtProject imprint two years ago." Smile, a neat memory. "Sold well. I won an award. That must be where you heard about it." Alright. "Hey, regarding which: I notice you haven't posted anything lately."

Rackley: "Right. And I do miss it. But my duties have kept me so busy." And then: "And all my favorite blogging forums were shut down."

"Oh yes I guess that was me. But clearly you didn't hear that we have an improved website for that. People's opinions aren't important but we tell them they are so they don't resort to violence." He pried Rackley's device from him and typed in an address. "Here it is. Open to all. That's the democratic way. We let a writer post so he can read it many times -- and his friends, very important -- for three days, then we destroy it to make room. Because there's a lesson there, fame is fleeting. Anyway, it's the only thing that makes modern society possible. Post there as you need. Collier!" Who showed Rackley out.

There was a Vox Pot Café in the ground level of Rackley's building, and he began to go there every early afternoon, when the crowd was just right, earbuds against the music. Writing strictly in pen now: pencil implies uncertainty. Blue microball in a classic quill design, vellum writer's paper. He was a prominent playwright now and prepared himself to welcome inquiry man-of-the-people style, a little rumpled and nursing a common consumable.

Ideas were not quite forthcoming but that can happen, they have their own pace that won't be hurried. On slower days he would collect his tools and make a walkabout, based on the old writer's notion that you don't provide the story, you find it, sometimes in the stories of others: the green-grocer, the sweep, the barker and the tout, the tender of the yard. A tale with three days to tell itself, the tiniest window in which to shine, and Rackley felt his imperatives shifting, and decided he'd find a hopeful story, happily disposed: of brief life but happy.

In time an essay came to the fore of course, draft after draft crossed out but kept for archivists, finished with a flurry of final touches and sent on its journey across the sky. Burn bright. And yes, after three days it was gone except in memory. As he awaited response he was summoned with the word that Nominoe was done ideating.

Velbin met him at the door with a card: *Springs and basins.* He walked in and there was a blue craquelure sink suddenly in the lobby with a brass tap, gooseneck, drooling gracefully; bathwater warm; he was hearing a general babble of wet noise, and found more sinks in adjacent rooms, one of chocolatine glass, the other concrete centered on a classic urinating Pan.

Nominoe: "Do you like it? It's a theme. I wasn't positive so I made sure it was original and non-derivative with a couple phone calls."

Nominoe sent him on a quick tour. Something in every room: running tubs, pools, cannibal pots, each ornamented and unusual; well in the back some sort of vortical swallow-hole he dared not approach. Also sitting-sofas, pillions, pouffes; incidental tables and occasional ones; everything in off colors. "I like it. The sink in the lav doesn't work."

"It's art why would it work."

"And I wondered why isn't there a bedroom."

"You have to put a bed in. Guests soil it fornicating and et cetera. Have to hire someone to pitch it out the window. Danger below, not worth the risk. Here, come out to the veranda."

Where Rackley had never been, where a pewter tap shed waterdrops onto a steel drumhead and drain. Nominoe: "I have it set where it plays Pachelbel's Canon. You can hear it. Not the actual notes."

"Yes, I hear it." The metal drops had a resounding quality, as if upon his forehead. "Did you read my post?"

Nominoe beamed. "Quite a feat. I could tell you used a pen and got a hand-cramp. Listen." Fascinating that by the simple positioning of a pause here the smile would keep its shape but change its nature, now a thoughtful slightly pained thing. "I was made to think of the old writer's dictum called kill your darlings. That means that any of your words for which you hold great affection but which do not serve the ends of your tale must be dispatched without pity. And I've always thought: poor words. Meant to do good things, but through no fault of their own, etc. All writers give this advice to aspirants -- it's a watchword of that fraternity -- and all aspirants give it too, but it's unclear if it's ever actually happened. In fact, the phrase kill your darlings has never itself been killed by millions of writers. Interesting.

"And I was reminded that there's this idea that a short story has no wasted words. That's how they make it short. Which is to say that a novel does have wasted words. To the short story writer I ask: what did you do with the words you would've wasted? What were they, what were their names? Relegated perhaps to a worse fate. Unpleasant to think about. Poor words.

"And also did you notice how we've run out of terms? Awesome used to mean you trembled before a god-like presence. These presences are gone now but they left the word behind, to die in a far less noble fashion. Or consider this term: beyond stunned. Think about it. It means you've died. If that's what you mean just say so. No shame in it. Or the term love. Once it described both the highest limits of human affection -- by turns forbidden or unconditional -- and the benevolent affection of god. About that see above. Anyway, you used all three terms in describing a fish taco."

"Yes, Malena's. I take it you've never tried one. It's much more than just a taco."

"And sadly these words have been killed but not replaced. Or happily if you like, for no new word wants to be similarly degraded. To mean less and less. We're saying more, all the time, and saying less all the while." An odd gap where even Velbin turned his head. "Poor words. Meaning is all they have. Anyway yes, I read it. Ideas leaping off the page. Into the unknown."

"I'm glad I stirred a passion in you."

"You did, you did!" Nominoe grabbed his hand and almost strangled it. "I think you are my basin, in which things grow." In Rackley a flower bloomed. Nominoe: "And this is what I have to tell you, you gave me an idea. Not awesome I'm sorry but quite serviceable. Let's get to work! Now ... we will need slave labor but they have to be fluent in English."

Rackley examined his device: "The Chinese have recently annexed Melville Island, Australia."

"Perfect." A word to Velbin. "I'll have my people contact them. Alright. Thank you as always. I'll summon you."

Rackley did not believe in languishing during downtime, and thought to use these days for the burnishment of his writing-craft, with exercises mainly, in food courts, cafes, drinkeries all over town within easy transit. So: daily crossword of course, editing, which is the real challenge. He added to his list of nonsense words for use in topical palindromes. Letters-to-the-editor, although personal letters, not for publication, about word choice and such, scribe to scribe. An essay, about that. Most rewarding, he began a spirited correspondence with luminaries in the local poetry trade; he was waiting to hear back when he got the summons from North Beach.

Nominoe was there in the middle anteroom beside a large cardboard carton. Velbin handed him a cutting tool, straight blade, half-serrated. Nominoe: "Do the honors. If you cut yourself note there's a basin just beside, please don't bleed in."

Rackley nicked it open with care. A box of books, part of a print run. He pulled one. It was called Killed My Darlings. And then there it was, a profound first sight for him: A Short Story by Mills Rackley.

"Congratulations. You are an award-winning author."

It was a beautiful thing, embossed and bound in a delicate natural material, his fingers floating over. He opened it and turned a page: frontispiece of soft white, title page in handsome copperplate. Turned again, legal page with copyright and ISBN number, which gave itself to his memory in a flash. Turned again, and he quickly riffled. "You might want to send an angry text." He showed it. "Pages are blank."

"Oh?" On Nominoe's smile a smirk inexpressibly clever. "Are ... they?"

Rackley cut through the middle and zoomed in: darker parts

and rough ones, spots, a dog-ear and perhaps the mark of a waterdrop. Page numbers also copperplate.

Nominoe: "You don't see it? No? It's one of your early works. Dug out of the archives for extirpation. By the way, it's a Beaumont award, one of our paper certificates, no resale value."

In Rackley a confusion of thrilled feelings. "Which work? Prose or poetry?"

"Prose of course no one reads poetry. Short story. I don't remember. A conversation ... some big ideas banged around. But what the story really gave across was the affection -- the love? -- you had for it and for every word. That's a quality you want in a work and what you have a special knack for. And then what happened next ... think of the virtues communicated. Self-sacrifice. A moral worthy of the best of tales. Cost me a fortune in erasers."

Yes, all along its supple inner spine, tiny rubber bits. He lifted the pages and could find the light scoring, like cuneiforms worn down by weather; the impressions left after the words are gone; ghost story. And more importantly he saw its other marks -- crease, eyelash, thumbprint in graphite, perhaps a spot of sweat -- as the chance graffiti by those entrusted with the sad care of his story. "I hope they found their work rewarding."

"I know they did, I know they did." A big, broad and proud smile meant just for him. "Award ceremony and book-release party here tonight. You might want to clean up the place a bit no wait don't touch anything. Collier!"

On the way back they picked up an unnamed dresser with garment bags. Back at the flat Rackley submitted to change orders until he was slummed just so; then by whisk and curry-comb he was primped without mercy. All the while the man let his face do the talking. I hate my job but only I can do it, so. At the end he found a clean corner and put on the electrical goggles with movie and built-in temple massage. Collier coming and going. He had a mechanical smile that seemed right for a driver but might be even better suited for when someone needed killing. All the more reason to start a friendly chat about sports or handyman skills but that never quite happened.

The Project -- The Misunderstood Man

Rackley was shown into the party and heard there was a sound system playing automatic jazz, light he guessed, a numbing agent but not deadening, because there might be deals to be made. Exciting. He found Nominoe, hosting to full effect. "Oh look, Littleberry's been at you with the dandy brush. Okay so everyone's here but you, and I want you to make a good impression, so don't say anything. Put that ridiculous drink away. Remember to smirk. Cleave here." Right side, opposite that of the scribe. "I'm going to teach you about art if I can. Here comes Melanesia" -- small, tonsure and toupee, kimono -- "She does competitive poetry. She's going to insult you. Listen. In our lives we are on ladders. With ladders around us, and other people on our own. Your worth is measured by your rung. Success, failure: up, down. But there's another trick. You can reach out -- upward or to the side -- and pull down one of your neighbors. You can even reach down with your heel. And suddenly you have climbed in a relative way. With practically no effort. I will teach you some of the methods. Mela!" She'd been standing there listening all the while. "I introduce Mills Rackley, star of the hour."

A china face that could break and soften with not a hint of artifice; she held his hand with an old mother's grasp; clearly she was an expert at this. "I thought he'd be taller."

Nominoe: "Ah. If only we had known."

She leaned into Rackley and veering away whispered: "Your finest novel to date." She handed him her copy with a pencil and asked for an inscription. Of course, and he got her spelling and added a personal note. Then she handed it back, eraser first. Oh. A cleverness that would be repeated throughout the evening, including once more with her.

Nominoe: "So yes, the key to happiness is comparing yourself favorably to others. Later I will teach you some methods. Now let me explain something. We are at a professional party; something like an apex of the relevant world. All the expected norms of etiquette, grace and goodness are thrown aside. In particular, the rights of the rhetorical vandal are inviolate here. It can happen at any time.

Bon mot dropped right on a punch-line, in the middle of an elegy. Allowed. Care to share a confidence, an anecdote, an adage of your own design? All may be stubbed out by any stumbling drunk." A pause, and Nominoe made a long-hanging gaze. "Thoughts?"

What? Rackley came alive. So many! For starters, a quick declamation on the impoverishment that comes with great wealth. "--"

"This must be him. I expected taller."

Nominoe: "Ah, Sheffield. What a surprise, and a good one. Mills, Shef works in the mechanized photography trade. He has a focused and efficient eye. Shef, Mills."

"What's the word, Rackley?" Shef tapped his copy of Darlings; so a gag; the first of three of its kind that evening. "Henh-heh. Say speaking of stories did I ever tell you the story of we were on the south french beach to get beauty shots, sunsets. What a place. And the robots were whirling away, really solid snaps. And what wait, turns out it's a nude beach. Even better then. Topless, in the french manner. And ..."

Shef was florid and brayed, and had a stagger in his diction, perhaps as if confusing his consonant clusters with his diphthongs. Nominoe to Rackley, regular voice: "Shef is a teller of tales, and a good one. Maybe four tales total, basically all the same, none good, although they have the advantage of being untrue, so there's that."

"... pixelating all the shots! Guys what's the matter, they won't say. Bare-naked breasts! Well I did a little digging and it turns out their last gig was with a church group ..."

Talk of bare-naked breasts drew listeners, and a klatsch formed around. Nominoe to Rackley: "This is not a good story, and I'd rather you think of other things as you listen. What we're waiting for is the finale, the flourish at the end. Not to be missed. A delight. And ... alright, here it comes. Ready yourself. Hint: watch his right hand."

"... of course I'm back in Waukegan watching on monitors, so I can't reprogram them. Nice town. Keeps you grounded. So what I did heh is finally convince them they were on, heh-hehheh, on assignment for NahahaNational GeograHahaphic ... and these were just AfraHAHAAFICAHH LAHAHAHABANAHAAHA OHAHAHHAH ..."

His laughter bashed the air; the steady right hand came down to beat the knee coming up to meet it, the baffled thigh in its white linen sleeve, the arm working as if Shef were his own organ-grinder; left hand kept his innards intact. His laughter led the gallop up the hill, followed by the nervous in the crowd, the pitiers and the confused.

And Nominoe, from whom the merry roar of an engine. A card came into Rackley's hand: *laugh.* He rolled out his best boffola, with good mirth he thought and joy.

Sheffield gave out eventually, his eyes wet and bright; wet dots on his chin, and Rackley thought of the word humors. Now a general recovery, and everyone turned a little and spoke of other things.

Nominoe: "When I asked you to laugh I was hoping for not that noise you make, which is the opposite of laughter."

"Okay. But if it had been laughter, why?"

Nominoe frowned. "I myself always laugh for reasons of my own. Recommended. Many salutary benefits. Exercises the viscera. Increased oxygen before you run out of breath. Good for the endocrines. Now, a lesson: why did he laugh at his own joke?"

"First I need to know which part was the joke."

"Haha, yes, he began by interrupting you, then he interrupted himself. I don't think he minded. I think in fact he was flattered by the attention. But again: why?"

"Because you told him, too, about the salutary benefits."

"Funny no. Sheffield has the gift of empathy -- the ability to feel the feelings of others -- but only for himself. He can really experience -- like he has a sixth sense -- what it's like for him to be standing there at the center of a group of admirers, regaling them: that odd mix of thrill and apprehension. And he knows -- he intuits -- how much a genuine, loving howl at the end would be appreciated by him."

"And it was," said Shef, snacking.

"So he provides it. Cuts out the middleman. Efficient. But now then. Why do I find this so fascinating. It's this. Nothing happened, as you will have noticed ... yet there was this broad emotional reaction. Even now, look at them, discomposed, actors knocked a bit off their blocking. Tomorrow they'll still be wondering what was that about, and why they can't recall the details. Remarkable, isn't it? The amazing, little-known power of nothing."

Rackley had no remarks. Nominoe: "Let's find more people to meet." They milled. Rackley tried to find the eyes of those around them; it seemed he walked in a bubble of averted glances: Nominoe's shadow, drawing up effortless fear, as with a tyrant moving amongst the faithful. Nominoe: "You know the saying act natural? It's not a good look on you. You're an award-winning writer. Preen, smirk or sneer, your choice. What is that. No. No even worse. Alright, here comes Majelle. She will approach in a peripatetic or perhaps spiral fashion. Her entire life is spent in the pursuit of therapy, and it turns out suffering is her therapy; there is no underlying ailment, which you'll agree is efficient. Also, she's in her seventies and hasn't had surgery. Don't stare. Jelle, hello. Look at that hat. Mills, Jelle is in the art yoga trade. Yoga for performance? Painful bending included of course. The painful part always comes across. Jelle, Mills."

The skin of her eyes and face hung in depleted paper-thin folds and planes. She was so fragile as to make him afraid. Majelle: "I read it cover to cover." Which were pressed now between her hands. "Ghost writing. The words of souls whose voices would otherwise never be heard."

It was a bit of a game to both look at her and not stare at her. "I'm glad you liked it."

She opened it to a marker. "It seemed to wander a little here so I added some lines that I liked and I think are important. I knew you wouldn't mind." Page thirty, right there all over the page, a block of text in japanese pen and a curling running hand:

"So were savours, of all so:

trees dies why not readers" ...

A stanza like that of something like seven lines. Fifth line probably haiku. Rackley: "Yes, why not indeed. Incidentally, I also write poetry."

Majelle smiled; all of her faces were overly broad, as if she were trying to reach the back rows. "It's not a poem."

Nominoe seized the volume and shut it with a sharp clap. "You decide. This Visigoth has dipped her pen in spray-paint and spread politics all over your gentle pages. Incidentally causing them to become maudlin or sentimental. A scandalous act of reverse-plagiarism. Now: you're the aggrieved party: you decide. Tear out the offending material. Angrily. And crumple it up right in front of her. Better: treat the entire tome to ritual ablution, expiating fire, then throw it off the balcony. Then upbraid her, in public, using the most offended language; and shun accordingly."

Now a pause. Like a button in a game. His eyebrows were telling a story. "Or ..." Nominoe pointed the book at Rackley's eye. "... or you could ... ?"

Rackley nodded. He looked right at Majelle and said good and encouraging things about her hat; offered to show her some punctuation; commended her courage in surgery choices; signed and erased; gave her a lingering shoulder hug.

Nominoe watched her walk away until she was lost in the mix. "Okay, wrong. I even tried to give you a hint. First, it's just a bloody fear of surgery. Second: wrong. I told you that suffering is her therapy. Now she's going to be fucking miserable. Dump her drink in someone's lap. An entire tray of jelly tartlets. This is your doing, and you're on mop duty."

Rackley thought about finding her, and how one might administer that apology. Nominoe: "It's okay, she's settled in with Melanesia." He took them back into the blend, which called for artful steps: it moved like a slow circuit of lightly turning lines; Velbin might get caught in an eddy and have to be fished, rumpled. Nominoe: "You can continue making art like you do and I'll give you a grant and watch with interest. But I know because you told me so that you want more: to make art that amuses and inspires human beings instead of, say, houseplants or animals. So you'll have to get to know them. Learn how to live amongst their kind. Let's start on that. Human beings have feelings and profound neuroses, which art is designed to address, mollify or encourage."

His eyes went over the room like dry-mopping it. "Okay, three people. By the cheese treats, that's Öster." Glasses and a spotted tie; around his mouth, hairy mustaches in which he picked like he was his own macaque. "Scumbler, one of the best. Should see him scumble. His gimmick: utter ignorance of pop-culture references. Has it down cold. You go to him and reference someone who's the latest singer. First he will stare at you stupefied. Not because he doesn't know the name but because you do. As you expand upon the mention he will smile, which soon is actually a wince. Because of course pride can be painful. As to unpop-culture, don't get him started.

"That's Dormsy, standing there in flattering light." Her hair down in white blonde panels, mouth screwed around a cigarette. "Writer: adds profanity where needed for screenplays and the stage. Knows all the swears. Good resource. Her trick is she cannot drink domestic wines. Nothing from the Americas. Retches, weeps. Travels with her own spittoon. Any wine that is immature, slow, or mildly retarded will make her faint like a mine-bird just by its smell. Good trick to know in case she starts to explain all this to you, which she will with clarity and verve.

"And that's Ember, whacking with the cane." Glasses, rictus, wild flame of head hair in an artificial premature gray. "She's a sculptor. Objects in found clay. Her schtick is she's disease champ. Apparently it's a competition. Imagine a tournament where you try to see who can box more badly. Don't bring up cancer with her because she's had all the top cancers and will crush you. Plus the limp, and she's had moles removed. The reason we know all this is that what doesn't kill you makes you tell others.

"Okay, for you three exemplars of a specific genotype, gathered here for your edification. Note traits, markings. Draw a conclusion, boldly. From that, extrude a life-lesson. Do it now."

Rackley gave them a good once-over and an up-and-down, and began deciding that perhaps this wasn't one of his skills, unsavory sorts, not attractive, and he didn't like lending them his ideation. Some sort of response was required, so word-play then, always welcome, and he worked at it, began to flag, let it go.

Nominoe: "Good, people who aren't funny shouldn't try to be funny. Our diagnosis is a simple one: each of these people carries an infirmity that has been recast as an advantage. Think how marvelous: flaws and failings -- ignorance, frailty, disease -- which not only cause no suffering but which in fact increase one's merit; in which one takes great pride. Now the challenge, and it's one for all of us: which of your debilities can you rebrand as a benefit?"

Rackley was feeling somewhat light and addle-headed from all the life-learning. "My lack of people skills."

"Choose another. There are so many."

"May I ask you ..." He rallied his nerves; Velbin eyed him with black eyes. "Is this something you've managed to do yourself? Transmute a personal, uh, fault into a virtue?"

Nominoe in a flat voice: "Yes of course, all of them." Suddenly a smile, a good one, fey and a little kittenish. "So there's your lesson and now here's the other one. Boasting is lying, as you know. But in this case even the lying is lying. Öster subscribes to a nightlife feed so he can keep up to date on who not to know. Or is it whom. Dormsly treats herself to a flask of sugar vodka each night as a soporific, managing to fall asleep without fainting. Ember: moles yes, but no limp, no cancer. Cancer of the hair maybe.

"Clever upon clever. Never lie about an achievement when you can lie about a failure. Because who would challenge you. And yes, now I'm the proud one smiling. Sometimes the worst people are the best students." He pulled off his pearl bolo and flipped it to Velbin. "One more lesson then I tire of this." He brought them back into the stream, which parted around them as if they were a moving stone. Rackley quietly took a bumbershot cocktail from a passing tray and dispatched it with a gasp, lessening his unease and general grasp of things. Nominoe was rebuffing fans and even claques now, hunting a lesson.

At last: "There, the confab!" About six of them, heavily engaged. "We're going in. Say nothing. No sudden movements. Things might get rough." The parley was split more or less by gender, highly decorated and with apathies on display like dull gems, look at me not caring; Nominoe broke in like into a soft scrum and was not acknowledged.

The woman with the marble smile was speaking. " ... and there you have the last word on the matter. Now, before I interrupt you again, Ant, some advice: I think you'd be best served by sticking that opinion where, in most people, the sun don't shine."

"It's already there, Shar," said Ant, chewing a little. "That's where I keep all my valuables. You know. Safe from Barmarkle." Who made no face. "But if the thought bothers you so much then it bears repeating. I am an expert in the arts, and I opine that because politics contains, within the perimeter of its definition, all the passions, however unsavory; ideas, plus traditional ideas; sex; wisdom, as well as idiocy and mental illness -- then I say that politics must be considered an art form in its own right and is deserving of an awards show."

Shar: "Kudos, and I'm tempted to give you an award myself. Least Interesting Idea." She had a long nasal brogue. "But that would make it interesting. And it's not."

Someone else: "You used that line last week, Shar. Pick someone more creative next time you plagiarize."

"Not a theft, Brahm. An homage."

Some smirks. A gap. Shar also had a piercing in her nose, no jewelry, and she dabbed at it. For others a general flattening of faces as indifferences were sorted out. Rackley wondered if apathy, too, was an art form in its own right. Trillian, who wore a sad nametag: "Politics is boring dull. Boring as the latest thing. One cult calling the other cult a cult. What's implied of course is that there's something wrong with being in a cult. Well. Offense taken. And boredom by the way."

The man who kept his hand cupped by his chin like a pipe was in it spoke up. "Got a point there Trill, and it's wrong. They're different things. For example, religion has better music. Politics, more hate. And ... well, so you can see why it's hard to choose."

"No need to choose, Sime." Barmarkle. "The two got drunk one night and made a baby. Guess what they named the little bastard."

Nominoe to Rackley in a whisper: "As you can see I am livid right now. Imagine talking politics and religion here. Or any place at any time. Only thing worse would be talking about Art, which they're also doing. The fact that they're all assholes is meager compensation. Alright ... I'll do my best."

Barm was finishing a thought: " ... interesting, profane, dumb or simply boring. But by god at least it makes people think."

Nominoe: "Think!" He could bang like a steeple-bell when needed. "Why would we want them to think? Have you seen what happens?" He gave his bark-like laugh, the unfriendly bark; there was a disturbance as if by a sudden large dog.

A woman in the fringe: "But this gets back to who defines art. I mean really. Who exactly is it that decides what's interesting? I myself can't tell."

Nominoe, laughing all the while: "Given the obvious and pressing need, Merd, I will volunteer for that duty. First decision: not this."

Merd: "Wow. Okay."

Ant: "Meredith?" He stared at a spot just above their heads, in the jazz. "You're being derivative and unoriginal. We don't define terms anymore. Answers only lead to further questions."

Nominoe: "Alright, you've made me nauseous."

Ant, same spot: "I ... I was being ironical."

"Yes, irony makes me nauseous." To Rackley, full voice. "Sometimes it isn't enough to just walk away from a conversation. Sometimes it has to be killed. It's an act of kindness. Quickly is best but you do what you can. I tried and tried. Obviously my own skills are old and ossified. TQ!" Bellowed to a far corner. A form there was brought to life, and came toward them like a cold seep. Rackley mainly saw a gray-green sports coat with dark accents at the pits. "His passion is debate. Could be anything. He'll argue about if he agrees with you. Tell him he's right and it's au contraire. Finally it was decided his super-villain name -- you know, his nom de anime scelerat -- is The Quibbler. Which he embraced, having no choice. Eventually I convinced him to use his disorder in a way that helped mankind:

conversation-killing. I taught him best I could, what I'd learned in my time. So many to choose from. The Misfinisher: finishes your sentences, incorrectly. The Claimer, cousin of The Sarcast. They both lie; the latter hopes you notice. The Little Bitch. Self-explanatory. The Weeper. Use with caution. Been known to damage nearby conversations. The Shrink, The Scoffer, The Nazi of course. Good techniques, all deadly if wielded with care. Anyway: TQ, forget his real name. TQ! Hello! Our confab has been complaining of boredom."

TQ was a hard visual, too much sun and not standard grooming. A mouth-breather, yellow tobacco tongue, out-going breaths abrading the hard palate; on his head a prim clip-on man-bun. He spoke in an edge-blunting monotone. "So I've stumbled upon a, uh, a bored meeting."

Rackley flinched. Ouch. Sharp smack. A quick look showed the reaction was universal. Except for happy Nominoe, still voce normale: "The Gag-Maker. You know, from that feeling in your throat."

Now Barmarkle, losing his apathy: "Keep out of this, Tique! You're a bloody telephone clerk. Leave art to the experts."

"Oh, hell, my fuckin dog makes art." TQ moved his hands all the while, as if washing his words. "Took a shit the other day, looked at it, went Bauhaus! Bauhaus!"

Rackley felt ill. Bleating and nervous eyes around him as a ripple of disgust rolled over. Nominoe: "The Vulgarian, with a word-play to finish. Lovely."

Ashen-faced Ant bulled ahead as if this wasn't really happening. "The reason we're not defining terms this season, Merd" -- deep breath -- "is because the Luddites wrote that op-ed calling us a bunch of Know-Nothings ... so we decided to dedefine terms for a while so we could pretend, ya know, that we didn't know what they were talking about." You could see the hope fleeing him.

"But of course nothing can be defined," said TQ ominously; his voice was a deadening tool, lacking pitch, tone or musicality, nulling the air around him. "You see, words require context to have meaning. No context, no meaning. But all contexts are different. Ergo: words have no meaning."

A common groan, frail and despairing. Nominoe whispered to Rackley: "The Pedant strikes ..." Now aloud to TQ, with care: "Including the very words you're uttering?"

TQ lifted a lip to expose a string of lemon pearls. "Precisely."

Nominoe: "... and pairs with The Dumbass! Delicious!" Along with that the groan again, now odd in that it said nothing, just a last noise; low jaws, broken postures, cocktails swallowed whole or set aside: the confab had lost the energy to seem indifferent, and just like that it was gone, its parts set adrift, to be taken up elsewhere.

Nominoe looked the happy look of a trophy-hunter, and a little spent, with a light shine. "I can't even tell them the conversation's been killed because, well, it has been. As for TQ, don't speak to him or he'll do the same to you." He forced a path to a view terrace, where a canoodler was evicted and they went to the long chairs, Velbin at the door.

Muted proceedings behind them, the lighted tower stacks and unseen water before. It was like that for a while; Nominoe was looking at him. "A killed conversation gives out great gouts of dead air. Look! You're covered in it."

Rackley almost looked. "Sorry, I'm ... I was listening to the basin." There at their feet, a quieting sound.

"The babbling brook. Finds something to say irregardless."

"I don't know what to say."

"That's alright, I'm here to tell you. Tonight I think I showed you some adventures and experiences. And I think you took in the sensations well. The colors, sounds. Not much harm done. Maybe it's a knack for you. Now: what did I teach you about art?"

"I'd love to know what you taught me about art."

"I taught you that it is all allowed." Nominoe pulled from his folds the book in question and presented it in two palms like an offering. "Even when it's not. All your darlings. In lambskin. Dead in your hands. It is all allowed."

Two days later. Nominoe rolled in and beached himself on the black daybed he'd bought and placed there for this purpose perhaps. Velbin expertly brought him a comestible from the snack-room fridge. Nominoe: "Look at you." In time this was an instruction, and Rackley did. "You look like someone who cares about his appearance."

"Yes, I do. Care."

"And you should. But you can't look as if you do. Nothing is more unattractive." Finger pointing. "Ugly fat right there."

Impossible. Rackley lifted his buttoned belly-shirt.

"No, I mean put some. Here, finish this." It was one of those phyllo-wrapped sausages that guests eat. Interesting, a three-cheese blend. Nominoe: "Did you ever think about shaving your head and wearing a hairpiece?"

"No I did not."

"And you'll need a gender. You can't go out in public without one. Controls attire, other things. Yes there are people without gender but no one talks to them of course. Obvious. Listen: if anyone asks you your gender say none of your business but then tell them, because you're proud." The hand free of food now lay exhausted on his face. Three words to Velbin and the note passed over: *Same seeking other.*

Rackley thanked Velbin for the card, excused himself and returned with a dabbing-cloth in hand.

"What basin did you use?"

"One of the kitchen ones."

"Was it destroyed in the process?"

The mosaic with the red glass tesserae and lime-green chips. "I would say no. My biles are innocuous."

"You gotta problem with food?"

"No. Not at all. I eat it. All the time."

"Uh-huh."

"Question. Why don't they just make a new cheese out of the three cheeses instead of blending them?"

Nominoe was quiet for a while and the rest of them were carried along, including Collier, and the cleaning team listening from the kitchen. "How was that? That thing you did?"

"Mm ... horrible, regret ... mostly I was thinking of other things."

Nominoe already had another treat in hand. "The art of cookery has been popular for years. Predates religion, speech and fire. Here's the thing: it's never actually been an art. Why not."

Nominoe would commonly ask a question whose premise was more difficult than the question. Anymore Rackley would just hurl himself at it. "Because it came before art. And ... it was too slow to catch up."

"Hm? No." Flecks of vellum-thin bread material were coating his vest. "The obligation of the food maker is to elicit the nasal human mm noise. Nothing more. Or the equivalent noises from pets, babies, feral pigs. Maybe it's the same noise. You have a dog, find out. But the artist must generate emotions. Could just be the dumb ones of course, happiness, unhappy. Better if they're complex and new; best if they confuse and inspire. For example you read a poem and have a hard sonder. From a tune from your youth, klexos pretty much all day. Maybe one of the Impossible Feelings, like the dread fear of being bored. I have a list written down somewhere. Weltschmerz comes to mind. You know that frustrating feeling where no matter how hard you try you can't forget someone's name? No? Try feeling that over your next plate of antipasti. Can't be done."

"No, I had a meal once where I wept."

"Yes when the bill came. I confess I myself saw a soiree where after the clams all the diners smirked as if on cue. Then suddenly a feeling of mortal fear all 'round. I assure you, Rackley, that was not the chef's intention. I had him arrested anyway." He licked his fingers, leaned out and tapped Rackley right on the khakis. "You. Know how to cook? Can you make a crepe?" A bit of a mix-up for a moment blamed on accent. Rackley: "Absolutely not."

"Prove it!" Velbin carried over a pen and pad. "Write the recipe to cook a crepe de chine. Don't cheat and look at devices. Everyone watch him!"

Rackley felt lit up by the common glare, unkind and accusing: performance pressure: where I shine, where I shine. He gave the pen a twirl and then that click that bodes good things. Now then. He knew it was eggs. All recipes have salt. From there he turned to old friend common sense, wise and never-failing; he added a whisper of fresh dill at the end to make it his own. Then blend, bake until done.

Nominoe took and read it with tiny eyes; then once again with care and eyes distended; he showed it to Velbin who did not look. Nominoe: "You are a wonder and an inspiration. A maker of complex emotions. I nominate you for Assistant in Charge of Assigned Tasks. Now go home so I can think."

Next day, and Rackley was up just an hour when Collier appeared with a task on one of Velbin's cards: recipe for Pollo Loco. Oh the burdens. He pulled on his pants and went and splashed himself. Collier seized up his device and had him set up a work station on the card table. He'd kept the click-pen, so it was that plus unmarked paper, water in a clean carafe, natural light to whatever extent. It went well and Collier was gone, and Rackley was left with the rest of his busy day.

Next morning it was Blood Orange Double Crumb Cake. After the third of these he considered out loud if it might make more sense to do these duties in a public space because he was a best-selling author now. Collier had accidentally sat on a pee pad so it was an easy persuade.

The Food Circus, then: covered like an arena and full of the hubble-bubble that bestirs the inspired word; and also how appropriate. Rackley would settle in with a custom beverage and ideate with cold resolve while Collier impounded his device and idled through texts and mail. Each day an easy challenge. Salmon Maillot. Muffin with Currants. Dog's Breakfast. Scrapple, Burgoo -- same recipe interestingly. Celebrity Chef's Boiled Dinner, using a chef of his own choosing. Bouillabaisse, which he had Collier spell a couple times on paper so he could be sure he'd never heard of it. A dozen more along these lines. Beginner's work, beneath him, and so he thought to stretch his skills a little. Form the ground chicken into gay furbelows. Add an inkling of chicken spice. Braise for a thought, then an afterthought, then let rest for as long as it takes to make a memory. Because why shouldn't people who cook enjoy the experience? In the final three days a twist: recipes for glass, concrete and fire. All of this on a carbon pad: sign, date, keep the original for the files, off goes Collier.

The rest of the mornings or so he'd work on a sequel. Who were these mysterious darlings? What if some of them survived? Just outlines for now, the flesh would come when it came.

Soon the summons. The elevator at North Beach suddenly came up one floor short, and Collier had him lead the way. A banging about, obstructed light, a wall had been removed without the benefit of care; everywhere the apparati of light industry, manifolds, louvres, ducts. Bad language, and the air boiled with the entire spectrum of smells. Around a corner a team in smocks was bent over a network of cooktops, sinks, mises en place. Nominoe wore a bib down to his toes, a great spread of sail very much bloody from battle. Rackley: "Are you allowed to do this?"

Nominoe: "Well I own the building." Of course. "So. Sit here. You know celebrity chef Callaway Browning from the television." Ah yes, Boiled Dinner. He had that angry look like when contestants ruin the risotto. Softest handshake ever for an angry one, thumb in palm.

Browning expertly plated something onto a crudités plate. Nominoe: "Take a picture with your device," which Rackley fumbled for. "People who eat prefer their food to be attractive. The least important part of food, but there it is. The reason is because it is the image of wealth about to be squandered. Also because they might be photographed next to it. Now post it online!"

"Alright. People will be curious what it is."

"One of your recipes of course." Reading: "Kibble in a Breast-Milk Braise, with Crusts & Scrapings on a bed of Glucose and Lawn Greens."

"Ah, yes. You know, I don't remember that one."

"What? Oh. Some modifications necessarily. Due to terms, poor usages, transmogrified." He gave his whisk a flourish. "For example: a weary breath of polonium is in fact radioactive gas. And no lighter fluid. We cannot poison diners at this time."

"Well you didn't mention any diners."

"Of course there are diners." Muttering that it makes no sense otherwise. "And in the end, a body of work rich in vim and whimsy. You should be proud." Here he spooned up a spoonful with all the tastes on the crudités plate and directed it into Rackley's mouth which he'd opened with a thumb and forefinger. Now Nominoe adopted a pair of tiny readers and leaned forward, all pores, digging in. Expertly: "Hold it there. Mouth-feel. Flavor-meld. Hit all five tongue parts, sweet sour unagi. Swish." Slowly, in a whisper: "Swish." Rackley breathing through a nose aflare with new experiences.

"And ... expectorate! This isn't some kind of free lunch." Rackley was handed what appeared to be a common kitchen compost pail and let fly. "I --."

"Glad the Cat Died." This to Velbin, writing. Nominoe wiped down his glasses. "Cleanse palate." They'd set up a hose device so Rackley could have a high-pressure cleanse. Browning had the next concoction in the queue. Nominoe: "A spritz of Dry Air drawn from Swiss Cheese Holes on a light capering of Smoked Seasonal Meat and Chives. By law we have to say it's Cigarette Smoke. Post photo!"

"Must there be chives?"

"More chives!" A chive-mincer came, stir-stick in hand, who minced them in before gently suffusing Rackley with the blend to full effect. After, Nominoe: "Shock at an Ugly Baby," Velbin writing.

After the third of these -- "Chocolate Leather Chew in Vinegar Smell, finished with Unflavored Tartare of Beeves who died by mishap or bad decision" -- Rackley took a break for recovery and to find out what was happening to him. Nominoe, a little off-put: "Scientific method, Rackley. Theory, test and fact. You've read about it. These are new flavors and do not allow for prediction. So we rigorously determine the complex emotion created by each flavor dish."

"Absolutely. Curious why."

"Because people want to be told what they'll experience. And we're the ones who do the telling. Comedy. I Laughed and I Cried. Tragedy. Action Thriller for Men. A New Story for a Storied Age. His Blue Period. Smooth Jazz Stylings. A Light-Hearted Look. Derivative, and Unoriginal. Horror. Try the Tiramisu." He found this funny. "Though wait until we have your recipe. Oh, and what if we don't tell them? And they march into the unknown? The word we use then is: Farce."

"This wasn't the sort of thing you could've entrusted to yourself?"

"Well firstly I don't have the full range of human emotions like you do. That's the skill set you bring. So ably, by the way, so ably. Second, no you're the artist." Obvious. Nominoe paused and took off his toque, pans banging around him. "Your vision. Imagine. For the first time, art that one can taste; art for all the senses if you chew loud enough. We have eight more to go and I'm paying these people."

Successful day. Rackley's sleep was a needed sleep infused -- surely a brine infusion, with larding -- with complex emotions, which he'd heard named but could not tell apart. He awoke to find bed-clothes and eye mask flung around the room; also a note left by an intruder, Velbin: *Art casual for formal, 6:00 pm.*

So a morning of exercise stretches and a smoothie, light writing; afternoon was impromptu yoga, constitutional. He pulled down a pair of denims from which he quickly ironed the creases, and added sneakers, ironic dance shirt, bolo and backwards cap at a rakish pitch. Littleberry threw all that away and pulled him into white canvas overalls for which he was an easel as he, Littleberry, stippled it with art sticks from his fanny bag and, when he discovered them with a shriek in Rackley's baby fridge, condiments. Then an eye-patch, which he was allowed to wear high on his forehead for safety; a single bangle, unpretentious; yarmulke; he could keep the sneaks. A long and painful wait for the canvas to dry during which Littleberry covered his eyes but not Collier.

They drove up Baker Drive and suddenly right past the condo.

A kidnapping, then? And Rackley wondered, as one does during this sort of thing, about how much he might fetch, but they pulled up soon enough into a roundabout with beacons and press, a good crowd whose enthusiasms had the whiff of for-hire. Both a public and private event, with security; it was a restaurant opening, The Mills. Stucco pilasters in fool-the-eye flowered vines, fat clay pots with the latest waterproof ferns: mixed greens, a natural look. He was hurried in; at least one of the goons was a mannequin; the guests were mainly socializing with their little plates in a central open floor all across which were gleaming spit buckets manned by boys clad in black-and-white, cats underfoot. He was taken past this up two stairs to a private viewing table and seated.

Nominoe: "Have some absinthe." In a short flute, ornamental. "Don't drink it."

Rackley took it up by the stem. "Even the glass is plastic."

"From our factory in the Andaman Islands. Sparing no expense." He seemed harried, not entirely here; Velbin would not engage. "Right now we're having four more successful openings in some of our better cities. You've improved tasting, Rackley. For all time. Those who taste owe you a debt. Got a plaque planned. See that group?" Something like seven of them, cocktailing. "I know for a fact that they are each spayed or neutered or what is the word, and yet they regularly meet at private homes and do reproductive acts. Evolution must scratch its head." As he did his new growth of chin-beard. "In 10,000 years we will look back at ourselves with curiosity. Sometimes I like the idea of time travel but other times I'm embarrassed."

Nominoe unamused: Rackley did not recognize or like him this way. "Well, in any event it would mean we had arranged for reproduction. That one. She came back from the future for the free drinks."

Nominoe smiled almost certainly. "I thought you were going to say for the sex. But you always know the right thing to say. She's a man, by the way." Rackley snapped his head across so fast he lost his patch. "Remember what you've learned about art: it is all allowed.

The Project -- The Misunderstood Man

And art looks in the mirror and sees life looking back. We live in a time and place now of new tastes propagating beyond all sense: new genders, and gender grades and blends. There's a temptation to judge, or try to make sense of it; I know that you, as an artist, know not to concern yourself with all of that, none of your business. But they do. Concern themselves with all of that. Obvious. Say you wanted to couple. With one or more. You'd want to know what you're getting into. What sort of complex emotions you should anticipate. So yes, for fuck's sake concern yourself. What is the pronoun of the one in the brown hair?"

Yes, nicely-combed, the color of woods, really stood out. Rackley made his way through the mix: turned out to be a Mackenzie by name who had, according to the account, recently been to a clinic in Lucerne and emerged a new man. Rackley turned to run back the news but Nominoe evidently didn't care now if he ever had, palavering on the far side of the floor with the bald one in blond wig or was it blonde.

So he was alone now in the middle of everything: the uneaten repasts, the repartee and the mustardy smell, the women beautiful in boring ways, a distant dance beat; as he made his escape a talking-circle closed around him in which he was noted and praised a bit; he became bound up in some kind of arts parley; the word dialectic was used and his hearing shut down; he nodded until he realized with a shock that he'd become head of the queue. The Manichaean world-view, Rackley, your thoughts or stance, you're the artist here after all.

Heh-heh. He looked back for Nominoe: lost in the general blend. Crap. A rancid taste in his mouth, acid, ferric and with just a whiff of regurge as he cooked up a casual smile -- "Henh." -- and made to crack wise from a cludge of found thoughts. "Oh, you know what they say, Del. There are two types of people: those who aren't good with numbers." Dot the i with a gesture so they know you're not an idiot.

Good one. Around him time began to retard, a quieting effect; the several sets of eyes on him soon began to dull and seek distraction. Of course in the mind where the jest had been made time ran on fire and gangly-legged; the acid taste entered his bloodstream; Rackley tried to pretend he was elsewhere, a beach or some damn thing; a card: *We're not being clever this season.*

Nominoe: "That was okay. I like your use of deadpan towards the end. The soul of comedy. Let the joke be funny without your interference. And also it wasn't original, and we're not doing that either right now. Been done, god knows. Done to death. Just stop it."

Rackley dabbed himself with a stolen napkin. "Those people." Who had left. "They didn't have eyebrows. Were they from the future?"

"Yes, and they're headed back with the bad news: situation unchanged. Ha-ha. Not really. No actually that's a result of some complaints making the rounds. Seems that despite all efforts they were finding themselves seeming surprised. Or impressed and so on, it's all about the eyebrows so off they go. My idea. There's been a little chaos because they're also used for sarcasm. Oh look at yours all agoggly, break out the clippers. No actually I had a plan for this evening. Have you noticed that your efforts all these months at making a good impression have had the opposite effect? No? Interesting. In order for me to make the most of you we need to constantly recalibrate your general esteem, and I was hoping to work on insults. The delicate art of. Diaphanous creatures, easily bruised. Spontaneous if you can manage it. Natural, innocent: a poison feather dropped with care. Laughter in the gallery is a force multiplier." He scanned the room, made a choice and spoke to Velbin. To Rackley: "Alright. Wait for my cue, which will be a nudge and ahem. Hello! Brie, with Sime, of course. What a pretty stage you've prepared. Rackley, Brie did backdrop for us this eve."

"Yes yes, flowers, here and there a fribble." A rusted voice, almost a deathbed voice from someone lost to dissipation. "Bunting's by slave labor in Ghana, which we're against. Oh wait you're Rackley, that's right. I sampled your Inappropriate Laughter. Terribly good. I now understand my friends better. This is my friend Sime."

Sime: "And I had some Hey, you Suck at Sex. Wild, man. I had no idea. Must be awful."

Nominoe: "Sime is more than just a friend, Rackley, he curated the art for this evening and also created it."

"Well I did my best as do we all. Dug deep. Colors mainly. No theory for it yet. Auction later: money raised will defray the cost of acquisition." He gazed around them in that proud and wishful gaze. "Hope you think they suit the event."

A card, and the cue. Rackley cobbled up a mean-mug. "Festive. Inspired me to order some absinthe. (Raise glass.) That's the one that causes blindness." Here he added a short laugh, sharp and inappropriate.

Sime nodded and said to Nominoe, "Perhaps next time you'll deliver my riposte."

Moving on. Nominoe: "Well ... not very insulting. I mean, I wouldn't have felt insulted. Diction okay ... did you know you become slightly sibilant when you're doing badly? No one noticed. But overall too gung ho. Not professional. You won't need that anymore." Velbin plucked the goblet from him and discarded it. "Imagine a surgeon: of course he enjoys his work but he shows no enthusiasms. That's not what you want to see in someone cutting away. At most a sweet smile; a calm, expressive hand; spontaneity of course. Who's this coming?" Cute couple, arms engaged, of matching pants-suits and a mix of ages. "Rintz! Not since the play, hi. Rackley, Rintz translates satire into Aramaic, other languages. Introduce us."

Rintz: "Aramaic and Linear B. They veritably cry out for a lighthearted take on things." He had glasses like ice biscuits; and so much gold on him that why didn't he just buy himself some proper eyes. "My new wife, Ameridia." She was small and attention-getting, a posy for his buttonhole; her bosom had been set up with a generous reveal, and had its own tattoo, a logogram.

Nominoe: "Yes, springtime. The heart yearns. New wives." Indicating the obvious:

"The most noticeable thing in the natural realm, now made more noticeable. Introduce us."

Ameridia: "It's Mandarin. It means wisdom."

The card, and an elbow hard against his own. Rackley read and dropped the card and drew up his conniving bon vivant's smile. "So a one-word oxymoron."

Ameridia had kept her brows, which were carved in the Persian manner; she raised one and reached out with her almondine she-eyes and raked him cap to Keds; Rackley felt his skin burn; in a second he was bled out, a husk of mortified flesh. "Nice bangle," she said, turning toward better company.

Nominoe seemed to get a lift, and Rackley felt a tremor of gladness for that at least. "Ouch, I am collateral damage. Never underestimate the power of wives, Rackley. They define art the same way they define fashion or décor. I always ensure that ArtProjekt has a full complement of wives. Come, you look like you could use some slander. I know I could." Without the bother of a pause he dropped into the parting crowd, Rackley crawling behind; the brave bangle fell to the floor and was never seen again.

"So that's Old Fodge, a prick who, when he acts like a prick, imagines a heavenly pantheon of pricks nodding in approval. You can tell by his skyward cast. Can one ascend to that circle someday, by deeds? One hopes … The man there feigning a false leg is MacTeague. His guiding principle presupposes his superiority to those around him. When I share his company it's all, you know, when-in-Rome … Then again, there's Gel, who refuses on principle to compare himself to others. How noble of him, as he will takes pains to tell you … Minarelle is mainly her garb. And do you know the gag where they ask who are you wearing? Well, here you can address the garment and ask it who's wearing you, and she'll answer on its behalf. Cute means to an introduction … That's Scherli, born Shirley. She can't do accents so she's affected a spelling. I'll send you a text … Bon travail, Browning," passing quickly, ta-ta, off to the loo with a backward look; Rackley had never felt more hated … "You'll notice that surgery has given our menfolk vaguely identical drearily handsome faces. Depending on what you find handsome. Ferler, for example, there with the leading man features and marks, only drinks hempmilk. Because, as he says, it was good enough for Socrates. See, not so handsome all of sudden, eh? ... Ah, Professor Fazicker, hello. Stands here Mills Rackley, the star nay the gas nebula of the evening. Rackley, Fazicker's in the writing game." Fazicker: "For late-night telly. Ad libs and such. All the networks. Ten years Mensa member." Moving on, Nominoe: "You see, I have this theory that only members of Mensa would admit to being members of Mensa. I make a point of talking to Fazicker because it's nice to have my theories confirmed ... Chantrelle here is a master of null-speech, and is worth studying for her techniques. For example, she will describe, during a conversation, a dream in detail; these details are of an experience that never occurred. She will describe, but in no way emulate, that cute noise her baby makes; no cuteness is conveyed. She might describe, with noises, the best tiramisu she's ever had; words and sounds cannot convey olfactory sensations. Oh and sometimes her descriptions are null-minus, a mirror-reflection of meaning. For example she'll say trust me, which of course means don't trust me. Chantrelle speaks constantly but there's no record of her ever having said anything. Can be useful if you need to talk to someone while thinking of other things ... Emory and Rai, a gay couple. Although everyone knows they're not gay, so it's kind of an embarrassing charade. Come on. Just admit it ... In consideration of the old artist's code that says write what you know and do what you're good at, here's Hildt, who only tells lies. By the way, there's an etiquette that's been built up: he hates being disbelieved when he's lying. All that work for nothing. You've wasted an old man's time and skills, and for what reason? Question yourself ... After, you might want a cleansing soak in truths; Asterman will provide. Will he ever. If they handed out awards for stating the obvious, he'd need a bigger mantle. Handy to have around for when you want to have a conversation while thinking of other things ... Thoms, he'll drape you in compliments, but they'll be sarcastic. Don't worry, he's quite good at it, you won't be able to tell. So you feel great, he makes fun of you while at the same time mocking you, and it's wins all 'round ..."

What the hell. Rackley broke in. "Question. Which I guess I meant to ask before. And several weeks ago. Who are these people?"

Nominoe almost smiled. "What? These are your people, Rackley. Your tribe, in which you grow pre-eminent. Arts experts. Rather a lot of them, I know, but the arts by definition generate the most experts. So many ways to become one. Perhaps by general acclaim. Or by highly particular acclaim. One might make some art, always appreciated, or unmake the same with an amusing critique, also appreciated. Probos there, parrying with the salt spoon, became an expert by giving a large gift to ArtProjekt. The gift was in exchange for a small grant, which I approved, which made him another expert. Now he's a double-expert and is to be avoided at all chances --"

"No no no, I misspoke. I don't care who they are, certainly not now that I know. What I think I meant is why? Why are these awful people here?"

Nominoe stopped and turned, the bacchanal lapping at their ankles; he drew up a long pause, to which Rackley assigned a succession of misreadings: rebuke; the foreplay to a jest; epiphany. It turned out to be a species of regret, which the words of which would not quite explicate. "Entertainment of course. Pleasurable time-killing. Kill time with pleasure. And you're wondering why we use pleasure when we kill time, and it's so we don't notice what we're doing. Fatten time until it chokes, so you can watch its face change. Stir metal salts in and burn your time alive with all the bright squander of a national celebration. Hack your time into seconds with your bunka bocho and mix it into your mixed grill." A small pause, or just a part of one. "Poor time. You know, it means well. Loads of potential, of course."

And now a different type of pause, which was not a bridge to the next thing but simply an exeunt to the parking lot, Velbin with a look that warned against pursuit.

Rackley digesting. One of his tribe beside him, drunk on green drink: "Maybe something he ate."

The Project -- The Misunderstood Man

———◉———

A sudden rap on the glass: someone from the home guard making himself indispensable. Rackley lowered the window just enough to avoid eye contact. "Yes."

"Can I help you, sir?"

"I dunno, what are your skills?"

The captain's expression brought the line to delicious fruition. "May I see some kind of identification, sir?"

Rackley thinking. Glock probably. Constable's badge of pure silver with pearl inlays. He dreamed up one of his dark, swollen sighs and pressed it into the glass, a frosted spot in which he placed a thumbprint, a bit of spoor in the fog for the investigator. He touched the thing that raised the window, pausing just a wink as the spiral crossed the officer's line of sight. And the cutter closed with a satisfying and slightly lisping thock and the head of the conversation came down kerplop into his lap, his fine wine belly, his belly full of the best spirits, on which he folded his hands, forgetting this had happened, and remembering.

———◉———

The stanchions grew; clearly stanchions would not do. Ugly or ungainly at best, with evocations of blood and dead flesh, it was surely one of the more mismelodious words in the language, along with such horrors as whinge, shrift, macaque-scrotum. The Dept. of Appellations was tasked with fixing this and in other ways with making the whole matter more interesting, more important-seeming, and frankly more fun, because thus far it was a ratings debacle.

History was consulted, and all its grand cachet, and came up with an old pair of exotica: ganglou, the word for the watch-towers on emperor Qin's crenellated wonder; and kule, which were the stoic fighting-corners of Constantinople's defining walls. These did not test well and anyway history also pointed out that barbarian chiefs had breached these barriers repeatedly, a bad harbinger in a time begging for good ones, men dying like insects, which by itself was a ratings concern.

Let's call them pillars then, like those hewn by Hercules, for who does not admire those strong arms of popular culture. Wait: a reader on the task-force finds that the Pillars of Hercules are in fact a gateway, welcome. Again a messaging problem.

So just sell naming rights to a commercial concern: surely clever people could do better; the windfall might pay a bill. Commerce was contacted and came back with a silence rich in incredulity. A naming contest then, for schools nationwide, all the young imperiled, whose imaginations and promise and impertinent courage would of course find a euphonym or at least a team mascot; free ice sample to the winning Hawks or Monsters. But their attentions had been lost to their devices. Then why not name each edifice after a president, a hero, warships -- which after all had already been successfully named -- or scandal-free stars from entertainment? There were 8,000 of them (edifices) in the plans, and right away the stores ran dry.

All solved in the end by the very teams in the field -- that epoxy of patriots, hirelings and homeless teens -- which were fitting the ungainly things together, who were calling them Pikoes, after the cartoon guardian towers from a hand-held console game -- role-playing multi-shooter -- rolling through the camps. Experts prettified that into piquet -- which they might've started with in the first place -- and it stuck, although there was a final auto-corruption to PK.

So PK 1734, high along the Squamish, in the Canadian Cascades finally pouring down. Thirty meters and going up and up; seen from above, as the ice might see it soon, it seemed to stand in its own tide-pool, with particular whorls of repeated activity at its feet. Not for the squeamish: thirty meters whose spidery lattice had already taken two brace of worker bee. Ten more of same were hard at it *now in the buttresses, wrench and torch, fed by a maternal crane, a day in early winter, snowing as with the other days, and with a white and hidden sky. Now comes from his bungalow young David Ogden, Newarker, just two days on the job, dressed in corpulent winter kit in woodland cammie. He revives his motor-sledge and drives it to the near corner, call it a foreleg, of the triped; alights and leaves it running; quickly up the footing and places a palm on the great fetlock there; then he was gone in a black flurry of gore and green fleece.*

Crack down the canyon and back. The picket drops its white beards; it rocks now like a hemlock on its root ball; and is felled, and takes it with all due dignity, calmly down, spalling the not-quite-dead. Beside these and poor Ogden: a photojournal team here to get the story, which they certainly did; a trencher already nicely half-interred, something about a conduit; two over in crushed quarters who might've been awakened first but for their sake let's agree not.

Like at Hoover Dam, say, or Verdun, the practice along the river was to set the bodies aside and hope for sorting should time ever allow. So they were bagged -- not Ogden, now a slurry of seasonal colors -- and taken away and arranged in file with the ones from before in a stall outside camp. The shelter sheltered nothing of course, no more than the wooden boxes or catafalques which mean nothing to their occupants; who would be kept quiet and cool in enfolding snow, and decorated with pictures and loops of the local flowering hellebores, and eventually as heroes.

The sun goes down and the cold creeps out, and a fog, which under the lamps is a concealing light. Cold night, a perfect cold. Inspection teams worked in frozen sweat and looked for signs of the spark, the electric arc, and the incorrect care and safekeeping of perhaps a kilogram of Semtex-7. At daybreak they suddenly discover the obvious, or actually that they have been numb to it: the sun came up at PK 1671 and Jonathan Sayre, driver, drove to his designated foreleg and embraced it goodbye just before its demise; and at PK 1676, well north where the river was a stream, Abigail

Hammond, in her best Sunday safety yellow, serenaded her end with a long ululation, which at first they thought was an owl. Now let us forget their names; a new player had declared a game.

Majmueat Khasa, or Makh, whose late founders in their teahouse in Torbat-e-Jam had named themselves first in Turkmen, then Kurd and Persian before settling for promotional reasons on the Arabic. An international operation now but still most at home where it was born, the Khorasan provinces and Golestan, the slopes and dry woods of the Aledagh: the broken remains of the Khwaresm Shahs. Its beginnings were Israel of course, that doughty grievance. When necessary its beginnings could be prebegun under the beating hooves of Timur Lang and his black powder, who melted relics and made the mayors of recalcitrant towns swallow molten gold, awful of course but also with all the awful knowledge of its eventual retrieval; or, time allowing, in the galloping steps down the grassland of Chinggis, Hulagu, Ogedei, who might invest a royal city and reap its dead of their dextral ears, then to send them by riders in eight great sacks to the corners of the compass: testimonial, introductory letter, clarifier, all read and received by Makh, and kept in bright memory.

The best of the old grievances spool forward, timeless: the intruder. Who had come of late as traders, with an eye for Khorasan's priceless basalts and feldspars, emeralds and garnets, rare earths and yellowcake, in exchange for which nothing more than modernity: pavers, sewerpipes, spools of copper wire, solar panels, office towers in the latest materials and eventually, when the market was lost to a trans-Himalayan cartel, an appetite for it all but no longer the means. Intruders, in the form of meddlers from the national capital, who imposed on them a regional election including fraud, won by a party, investigated by that party, which was acquitted by that party, soon put down by black powder. Intruders: who of course did not bring about the temblors that smashed the infrastructure just referenced -- that would be god -- but did bring the gifts just after: canvas tents pestilent with mold, two hundred pallets of refuse -- ham and lima beans -- ready to eat, and barrels of plastic water, surely there to help induce vomiting. The intruder had nothing to offer, and even less when he did.

And always Israel, so near to hand, intruder, wound, ovipositor of the West. The communiqué that came just after PK 1676, written in oddly correct and unaccented American English, neither hortatory nor mad in any sense, instructed the reader to quit Israel: its consulates, treaties and affairs; its claims, its soccer teams, its books and films; its aid and recognition. Or the bombs would go on. Plausible enough. And implausible enough to ensure continued warfare. And plausible enough to obscure the fact that these attacks were not a means to an end, they were the end.

Makh were not unknown, were on the radar, in the files, the chatter, referenced in the notes, but still a surprise. They were not the dead-enders as could be found in Maziq or Almultazim; unlike, say, the riflemen of Alsayf or Alramh, they were not gratuitous with their gore; their periodic decretals were not far-fetched with odd allusions or references, as were rendered by the likes of Wusul Tawil ... eventually it's easier to simply state the clever thing that Makh brought which no one else had.

(This is not impossible. If a cult can possibly be clever then surely it's a product of evolution, highly unlikely but also inevitable. Makh was born this way: Makh emerges from the machinations of chance.)

To wit: Makh's hate for the West did not extend to the particular Westerner, and would not deny him his diet, music, his carnalities and sins, certainly not his science. Makh's religion was too precious a thing to be used as a blunt instrument or imposition. Thus were opened their rolls to the whole of the spectrum of ontological belief, however unsavory or new. Anabaptists, Buddhists and on down the list, going to hell of course but aiding the interest of heaven whilst in transit; Makh were happy to embrace even the labor of the godless, who, grasping at their forelegs, could expect no more reward than the flash of ennoblement that might echo on in their stead.

As well, Makh were oddly apolitical given their epic political plan. Asking only the hate held in common, they took in politicals of every caliber and kind, regarding whose persuasions they confessed an entire indifference, the type of apathy that can only accrue in the absolutist, whose capacity for philosophical opinion has already been consumed: who has no room in him for anything but the one thing. Makh were pan-anger, and all the malevolents were made welcome: the men and women against industry of course, with their explosive sabots; fascists, anti-fascists and blends; green fighters, and for the other creeds and colors. Prolife and carniphobe, anarch and apocalypt, irredentist and anti-fluoridian, all the diaspora, the scattered sharps and flats of the anti-Occidental world.

That world was parts of every part of the whole world, all its islands and all the continents in between (note to doubters: a Makh operative at McMurdo Station had been carefully bending the ozone data for years), and of course America, in whose open spaces anti-Americanism is born and thrives, and whose people would not be denied their science; Makh's enemy was not modernity, after all, but moderation. And somewhere along the way a chemist at the lab at Los Alamos grew aggrieved at the nature of his handiwork and conveyed several pounds of it to the enemy of his people, along with its recipe, which I have beside me but will not recite. Tritregonex-30, or T-30 hereafter. A miracle in its field, heaven-sent for murder.

When warmed it becomes a cream, and takes to the skin like an emollient, where when dry it becomes invisible to the senses (except for taste -- on the skin it tastes like toluene -- and also except for the very best dogs). At any point a bolus of the stuff can be added to the alimentary canal as a supplement, take with food. On the fourth day or so a rash forms, but surely by that time the aspirant has managed something better than a rash.

You set it off with a spark as from a watch battery, or that of a device, hearing aid, hidden in a ring, easily contrived. In dry air at sea level the ensuing blast wave -- a moving wall of air harder than an emerald or a garnet -- starts at 13 kilometers per second, faster than your reaction to its passing through you, as fast as Jupiter in its orbit, god of thunder and bringer of jollity; to put it more clearly,

The Project -- The Misunderstood Man

if I were telling you this tale aloud and you were measuring how quickly the words reached your ears, take that number and multiply it by 37. Think of how much time we could save.

The bombs went on, along the Lillooet River, the Toba, the dry valleys between them and their many tributaries, along the lengths of all of which we came to recognize and then anticipate the distant boom, the belly-laugh echoing off the overcast, and then the final toll of fallen metal, the armor clanging around them. New hires -- they came by the twenties on V-22's -- were shunned, debriefed, stripped, accused and eventually put in quarantine, which asyla might themselves erupt in four days or so or when the itch becomes too much: an entire flight of hires dead for those keeping score.

They pressed Giles Bishop for his thoughts, which were organized and platted into orders, and in go the marines, one of whom, a lieutenant, blows up PK 9811, plus his charges. 2nd platoon, nearby, promptly lost unit cohesion, with impressive violence. Sad, understandable.

New arrivals slowed to none, and also the work, or to match the pace of the ice, minus its confidence. A plan was made to maintain morale by constant resupply, and at PK 1420 the C-130 made its drop, came about, gave the triped a broad gralloch across the belly and came burning down on her own pallets of paper mail, dry tack and military vodka, plus those harvesting same, clever.

One stressor did end happily: exploding drones took down a PK on Chum Creek, and a kill team was dispatched and found the operator in a crevasse nearby, under an ice-white canvas, and managed to blow him up before he could. How did he get there? They found snowshoes and a hand-sleigh, with tracks. So he'd walked.

At last there came a screening method, using light in the ultraviolet; devices were installed in mustering stations in northwestern states. These halls, these rooms and auditoria in which naked men came tenuously together, were necessarily closed and windowless, and one could use the principle of reflection in redoubling blast waves. 13 k/s obviates the need for shrapnel of course, especially because now the parties themselves provide it: in particular, the petrous part of the temporal bone, small and dense, shaped a little like a wing. Suffice it to say that at the station in Winthrop, Washington, there was no triage after or the taking of a pulse.

The screens were moved upstream in steps: from the mustering house to a new security house at the gate, rich with hires; to the trams that brought them, where the emergence of the wand with the odd bulb coming down the aisle was the trigger; to recruiting offices, then the security houses at their gates, where in time there were no recruits but always at least a couple of grunts behind a hapless blast wall. The Makh were burying them in the dead.

Advocates came from anywhere, and money, and methods, but the cause came from Khorasan alone, and the plots, the esprit de corps and of course the communiqués, at once lurid and plain-spoken; and, at times, as we now know, shockingly dishonest. Well not shocking. For example, it's clear that, despite their claims to the contrary, these were not, strictly speaking, acts of terror. Makh didn't care if the West were afraid and in fact preferred it otherwise, seeing as the placid die more easily. As well, these unwitting dead all this while were in fact chosen with a conscience and care, limited only to those who would impede the plan, which is to say God's plan and condign wrath, the Great Frozen Flood.

Makh's was a humble hate, not frivolous or full of gestures; bound in service, obedient to auguries and signs as best they could find them. They hoped for good things, and that prayer and deeds would be recompensed with an ice sheet to suffocate America and all her works; hopes and prayers shared by the mullahs who harbored Mahk and held them in awe.

In the ice-proof bunker under the Blue Room, Giles Bishop presided over the weekly crisis panel and man-handled the brief. "Says the Khorasan had earthquakes in recent years, here, and here," smashing the dates on the page with a finger that used to play pro sports. "Were those ours? Can we hit 'em again?"

New Science Minister Dowd's face was made of dough, and he folded it to match the president's, conspiratorial lines, then added regret. "Not at this time."

The Project -- The Misunderstood Man

Bishop nodded, who was here entirely thanks to the arrangements of the man beside him: Bishop had just won his third term, by running as a running mate, then having that man -- let's let history forget him -- it wasn't the man beside him -- win and then resign. Clever play -- not his own, although the president always gets the credit; he spoke now with the confidence of a man with a mandate. "You know what would be cute? Hit 'em with a little gla-ci-a-tion. A bite of their own ice. Now that would be poetic. Poetic."

Now Dowd's face did not move, perhaps not privy to all the possible emotions. "Like a lyric by Dodgson."

Nominoe would sometimes, like now, parse the president's face, and in a trice or two see each of the classical sins, one at a time proudly displayed, which was one; plus some of the newer ones, like open-mindedness, undeserved humility, etc.; also a couple he didn't recognize. To all of these or any one of them he appealed with two documents he placed beside. The first was a prognosis, a ledger of time-lines and place-names read now by presidential finger, depressing facts upon the page. The second was a page of bullet points: recommended actions or perhaps reactions listed in order. The president read them, and read them again in an order of his choosing. He took the paper, reading, into an adjacent safe room; then on a long unscheduled weekend.

He emerged declaring a televised address. There he was, high above his lectern, grim and unreadable, using his learned heldentenor. "Whereas the Islamic Republic of Iran has committed unprovoked acts of war against the government and the people of the United States of America: therefore be it resolved by the Senate and House of Representatives of the United States of America in Congress assembled, that a state of war between the United States and the Islamic Republic of Iran is hereby formally declared; and the President is hereby authorized and directed to employ the entire naval and military forces of the United States and the resources of the government to forthwith initiate Operation Hammerfall: the complete and entire embargo of trade goods leaving or entering the ports of Iran, whether by road, rail, air or sea, and excepting foodstuffs and medical supplies, which embargo to begin immediately upon ratification of this decree by our alliance members and the Security Council of ..."

Just behind Bishop's right shoulder, and before the flag, Nominoe. Rackley had never seen him more unsmiling.

Certain points bear re-emphasis.

When considering the ice and in particular the Oort cloud it helps to imagine Oort as a god in the Greco-Germanic tradition, with moods and faults, quarrelsome and sometimes hard to figure; unseen like all gods (except the spurious or absurd gods), but also needing to be noticed, which is natural. His heaven is the cloud to which we attach his name, made entirely of dirty stones of water ice, 5,000 astronomical units from Earth, which place being his hell, or ours.

We cannot guess at his original motives but we know he's a rascal, which gives us motive enough to explain the following: once upon a time Oort took up several of his precious stones and sent them down on a thousand-year journey, where they lighted here at last at 40 k/s and begat life. Generously we can assume he found this interesting at first; we know for a fact that in time he is horrified, and turns again to the only skill in his quiver -- unlike mortal man, gods cannot learn new ones.

So after the balms come the bombs thereafter: big bangs, biocidal by design (these are not, strictly speaking, acts of terror). Every relatively few years, throw another black flock of stones, nearly succeeding a time or two; but clods of ice are not precision tools, and each effort is followed in due course by explosions of life, water being its predicate, frustrating for a well-meaning god.

The Project -- The Misunderstood Man

Does water have genetic memory? Does it dream of its life in the stars, and its master, whose pleasure it still exists to vivify? Does it think of ice as its natal form? Is ice simply the subtler rendering of Oort's grand plan?

These questions propagate naturally from the great and lasting question of the natural realm: that water, critical biosolvent, is the sine qua non of life, and also its best murderer. Fire feeds the land, lava makes land, tremors make mountains of the land, but ice is more clear. Man had once known and were discovering again that it is the worst thing in the world -- maker of nothing, where the only living things are the worms that the dead require; where nothing can make a home, where nothing grows, and grows.

Surely the worst thing. But it turns out not.

Rackley victorious. Now a period of correction and pause.

Nominoe having a soak in the big sink by the bay doors; the unimmersed parts of him were having a sweat. Tap running: if you keep the inflow going to match the one down the drain, you have a clever cleanse. For all of this Rackley had deputed the tripanel asian screen with geisha. Velbin watched him, showing the odd adenoid.

Nominoe: "Oh and I have good news. The board said yes and I approved the okay. From now on you'll be using just the last name. Rackley."

Surprising, but he'd heard about this sort of thing. For every measure of fame they take a name away. Keeps you humble. "Exciting day." He made some joking sounds. "I suppose now I'll have to rebrand my online presence. Wouldn't want to confuse my fans, ha-ha."

"Correct. Your web blogs, your social accounts. Favorite lists, grievances. Your quip-of-day for inboxes. Breakfast accounts, with images, links. All redesignated in order to reflect your new status. Once you're done with that, you can in proper conscience shut it all down."

Rackley: "And the right time to edit up the old headshot. Lose that moustache. Add ten percent Gaussian blur, suggests the passage of time. You know, in a way it seemed like you said shut it all down."

Splash and a wrestling noise. Nominoe appeared wearing shorts and a smoking jacket, sampling from a platter of flurgonder and pule. "The great age of the internet is in its last decline," he said, sitting. "Sad like any sunset. The promise, the vision, was of a gathering-place of discordant parts, the family of man. A noble thing … with all the flaws attendant: a genius might tinker in silence, but all idiots opine. And did they, until it was nothing but; until even the idiots quit the place, because they didn't want to be associated with such people. I shall miss it."

"Oh my." A little shocking, as was common anymore. "Me too. Aside from my art of course, the internet is my preferred medium for communicating with my public."

Nominoe wiped his mouth on a paper napkin, exposing a smile. "Okay. Ideate."

Yes, and Rackley consulted his notes. "So been considering our food night, and our restaurants -- I saw you gave us an award last week, thanks -- and art enthusiasts, and why putting unsavory flavors in their mouths, with all the incumbent dyspesis, would also cause them to enthuse."

"Rackley, you are asking the question about art which nobody knows what it is. I don't even know what it is, although I know the answer."

"And then so been thinking about tattoos. Dunno why. And applying that same, sound principle. Have it quietly decreed that all new tattoos must include a gruesome misspelling: the phantom apostrophe; their they're there."

Nominoe: "Blood-chilling."

"Any of the classics. Or the technician can have a go. It's easy, I've tried it. If the design is wholly graphical, you just append a little misspelled phrase."

"Imagine their surprise. And if they don't notice, you point it out."

Rackley: "They'd have no choice but to declare it deliberate. As an irony perhaps."

Nominoe clapped. "Here on my body I defy the rules!"

"An act of auto-vandalism. Nothing could be more radical. So soon they think yes, now I kind of like it."

"One would think you'd have to. It's a fucking tattoo."

Rackley triumphal: "Idea: art that forces you to like it. Velbin, make a note of it." Velbin grew still.

Nominoe plopped his palms on the belly newly fed and cleansed. "All wrong. First off, the term erroneous tattoo is a redundancy. And I hate repeat hate redundancies haha. Second: as I said recently on the internet, which apparently you've stopped reading, to your credit: I've lost interest in tattoos. Yes they're out of fashion but that's not it, most things are and anyway I hear that's all the rage now. The point is there are too many. We're all full up. Imagine a world with too many sounds or smells: a world with too many cryptic skin trifles is cacophonous to the eye. Billions of glyphs and block-letter band-names, degrades vision, blinding, causes accidents."

"I had no idea."

"What I have in mind is tasteful tattoo-removal scars. Handsome. Instead of that semi-opaque art on your fat, how much better to appear as if you'd somehow come to your senses."

"Right. I get it."

"We're setting up clinics with surgeons and laser beams. We'll call it Kill your Doodlings, something like that." He waved a finger. "Goes for you too, by the way, my erroneous tutee."

"What? Nonsense. Needles." Rackley stood and rolled up his sleeves.

"Okay. Pink, hairless, no tattoos, just like it says on your birth certificate. A bold statement." Rackley took his shirt off, turning in the light. Nominoe: "Whatever statement you made you are now retracting. In any event, as a role model you will need a removal. No needles involved. Lasers, scalpel. I'll pick something nice from the Mandarin. Spelled correctly. Imagine it boldly removed on your fatty bosom." Which he reached out and tapped. A-cup. "Then I'll post an image of it on the internet, if that'll help. Pipe it right into your search engine."

Rackley reassembled his shirt, the cocktail cuffs, pleated placket and untucked tails, and sat thoughtfully back on his pouffe. "So ... what's your name, then?"

Nominoe contemplating him, that tireless smile, at home in all the feelings; in a far corner Collier put down his puzzle. Rackley, a role model now of course and proud: "Full name. You get to know mine, after all. Seems you even get to design it some. I think I've earned a little fairness. I'll even keep it secret if you like."

"That's quite a tone I'm registering. Magisterial. A bit made up. It's as if you think you're communicating with your public. By the way and I meant to ask: why on earth does one do that?"

"One talks to ones fans so that said fandom might continue and flourish." A good answer he had preconsidered.

"I've always been intrigued by that exchange. You give them a few moments of your time: a quip, perhaps a critique. In return they tell you that you are not worthless. You come away the winner there thanks to their giving nature. So who are these people? Are they mercurial? What is their motivation? You don't know them at all, yet you commend them this terrible power.

"Or, better, you could do it the way I do it. Tell me, are you honest with yourself?"

Rackley: "Yes."

"Yes I'm sure and there's your problem. Here, try my simple method: in order to determine your self-worth, first fashion it as needed. And then there you are. Hoist by your own canard." A short, sharp pause. "Of course it's a lie. But it's my lie. I decide if it's a lie."

Now a laugh. "Actually I lied. My method is I inform society of its opinions, and have them look upon my deeds approvingly. Everybody wins. Alright, I'll tell you my name, my full name. Not because it's fair, which it's not at all even a little. But because evidently I fascinate you. And I want that fascination to continue and flourish. In return, you'll do something for me: you'll give me your assurance that we will never speak of this again." Rackley agreed, and in a moment he had a card in his hand. Progress. Little steps.

He turned the card over: *Nominoe*.

The procedure did not go as planned because Nominoe had set the operation aside in the entire or simply forgotten about it, which was new. At the very bottom of Rackley's relief was a pest of disappointment: surely he'd have been made a captain in the matter; and there'd've been a celebratory event, the likes of which he believed he'd just begun to master. But more than that because of the missed chance for an artist's moment: a Projekt is where ideations are born, shine, and learn to make their own way in the world. Under his proud and guiding gaze. The artist's moment, in time and space, color and sound. Addictive, that, and rich in motivators, and he'd been having good inspirations these days, and would impress them on Nominoe. Sunny day room. Nominoe had called up a course of street fare and was making his way through a tray of fries, left hand guarding. Rackley: "So been having ideas on the fine arts."

"Yes. Paintings, charcoals and the like, the unloved gouaches; cityscape, still life, self-portrait with nude."

"The fixed visuals, which by dint of definition include cartoons, graffiti, and tattoos which I assume you forgot about."

"That's right, though not photographs, which are made by machines, which are these days also made by machines. By the way, historical note, the term fine arts comes from the idea that the other arts are coarse, prone to being performed or otherwise debauched."

Rackley: "So idea: you recall the Accidental Art period?"

"Yes of course. Paintings made of paint, canvas, and then use wind, sneeze, itinerant animals et cetera. Sold for millions, mostly on purpose."

"We patent the process. When actual accidents result in paintings, we would own them."

Nominoe: "And if these accidents also result in death and disfigurement, we'd be held responsible. I'd be obliged to have you arrested. Got anything else?"

"No."

Nominoe nipped a fry like it was a devilkin's finger. "They had a good run. Really left their mark. But their day is done. Paintings are a relic of a simpler time. They just ... they ran out of theories. Especially after the non-theory period." He directed his hand at the cityscape, the low sun and the colors of suspended particulates. "Genghis Khan knew. He declared no art on his adventures. A sunset should suffice. For all of us."

Rackley was reminded of something in his notes, which he consulted. "Okay, so you're an expert in the fine arts and also a fan --"

"Yes, the liar is attracted to the arts, because within that milieu he cannot be proven wrong." All this by rote, perhaps his own.

"-- and yet you've been here all this time yet still no art on the walls." In every room around them, endless eggshell seas.

"Yet still?" Nominoe set the tray aside and with wet fingers wiped salt and starch from his pinafore. "You're new to the arts, and forget how awful it was." His basso now in the lowering tone, hard and made of bad memories. "A man might love art and want the best for it. And then you leave your home and the day greets you with an explosion of pixels far too profuse for you to see; until they have become that frozen and slow-moving stream, all-consuming, of invisible distractions. You cannot look away unless you look straight up into the sky and fall on your face." He gently touched a septum curved like the moon. "Shapes and shades and colors devolve, or contract to the medium of white noise. The stamp, the card, the very tabletop, the Mandarin tat on the back of your hand. The tube stop, the tube itself, every single galoot within. All designed to draw the eye. And drive art into it like a pin. Of course the walls are bare. Off-white, deferent. And quiet."

The Project -- The Misunderstood Man

A shrug of the shoulders, and the weight fell away. "Determining what art to enjoy, and to what extent, was never more needed. Eventually that led to ArtProjekt and that most influential of art movements: Banned Art."

Pen in hand, Rackley thought about it. "Ah, yes. Like the White Album."

"Was it? Well no wonder."

Collier: "No, banned art. With a d." It went on like that a little like from an embarrassing play. Reminiscent of when Rackley'd been told his flat was lined with knotty cedar: he'd heard it as naughty, and there was a small faux pas which he then claimed was a pun, not very well. A palaver kind of the opposite of a conversation-killer, dead but carrying on as with one of Galvani's frogs. Anyway, sometimes Rackley wished things could be more clear.

Rackley: "Say, where is all this banned art?"

Nominoe: "What? How would I know. In some pit somewhere."

"Well how about we gather it together and have a show. Art fans love that sort of affair. We'd bill it as educational. Here's what not to paint."

"Okay, first off the damn things were banned for a reason, make the eyes sting and burn, I'd imagine, never actually looked at any of it and I'm guessing that's why. Also: a gallery full of the stuff isn't exactly banned, is it? That's fraud right there, and a massive lawsuit. " But now Nominoe was up on his elbows, showing strong signs of reconsideration. "No, if we're going to do it it has to make sense. Have integrity." Conjurating now, eyes middle distance, right hand alive and reaching. "Here's how it happens. We commission new paintings from some of the region's most promising young talent and ban them. With all the attendant outrage. Then ... we have our exhibition. Our extravaganza! Comprised of this." He whispered to Velbin, who conveyed the card.

Rackley looked at it, turned it over, and again. Blank.

"Note-cards. In fact we'll call it NoteKardMachine. Each card mounted on foam-core and given the proper light. Emblazoned with a brief biographic of the art in question, along with --"

"Yes!" Rackley interrupting, Nominoe allowing. "Along with the outrageous reason for its bannedness."

"Banishment, perhaps banned state. But yes, the art at this point is superfluous and set aside accordingly, the important thing is it's banned, which people love, can't get enough of. Go home and run a dust-mop over your kitten-caboodle. Package coming."

Ten days of routine, immemorable and possibly twelve, made of mental prep and psychologizing. Then there it was without notice, paintings, a plastic-wrapped pallet of them, his small, hard bed flung aside to make room. Velbin placed a packet of note-cards on the bedside table, with a ball-point. Rackley: "Wait, am I responsible for --"

Nominoe: "Banning is a lot of work and I'm busy. Anyway you're the artist." True. "Have fun with it. Add color swatches to better describe. Spindle if you see fit: this is art, as you know. Upside-down if it's dada. Leave a blank line at the bottom of each card. Let me know when you're done, gala in two days." At the door on the way out: "Look, we charged the artists a fee of course to cover the costs of commission. So they have a lot at stake here. Do them justice."

Rackley waited until it was quiet, took the dog beside and contemplated his burden. Nick the bubble-wrap with half a scissors and send it to the corner where the rubbish goes. He counted twelve frames: yes, a lot of work. He lifted the first: it still had moist oils, which perhaps he had smeared. He fanned them out against the wall; not all the paintings were exactly that, of course: water-color, pen. He did not really recognize their styles or genres, and now had failing confidence that he could ban them effectively.

Each came with a packing slip full of biographics. He started with that, and pulled over and sat on his old milking stool. Okay. Now compose.

"Nerve Net. Artist: Judith Welf. 34 x 28. Four or more overlain pastiches in new tones. Reason for banning: smeared oils."

He read it, gave it a reprieve, read it again. He took the ban to the lav window, where he put it under a finger of natural light. There it lazed on the paper, taking up space. Alright, call it a practice draft. Testing the concept. He went back and tried another.

"Untitled. Artist: Khomar Tork. 42 x 30. Itinerant golden orb with square corners on an orangine cloth. Reason for banning: no title."

Better possibly. The ban had the benefit of being correct but art is not meant to be merely correct ... he was reminded of his rich background in critique -- of which banning is a species -- and the techniques of that craft that he knew. Think with all the senses, all five and then all the rest; step into the mind of the artist and find where it had wandered; if you can say it in fewer words, do.

"Distributed Being. Artist: Charles Baudoin. 40 x 44. Animal form etched in copper with head backwards. Reason for banning: bad form."

Yes, better. Getting it; capturing it -- the exegete's critical role, to illumine art as if by unveiling what had been there all along, beneath our unwillingness to see.

"Decentre. Artist: Lambert Lambert. 28 x 28. Nacre and acrylic pastilles purporting to be a seascape. Reason for banning: nacreous; queer smell."

Now a rush of good bans, albeit in steady steps, as befits confidence, the birthright of any new bloom. Then the edit: comb them out, make them right, which is all that art really wants of us. Before long twelve done. And done.

At the end there were flourishes, all just so; the sun was coming up; he made his bed beside his new objets d'interdite and slept the sleep of the steward of a successful day.

He was delivered to North Beach mid-gala. There was Nominoe, with a flute of Feuillatte and praise. "Everything I expected," he bubbled. "And a little bit more. A proud day for you. No rooms have ever been more embosoming."

Yes, the little spotlit cards, beside each of which, paced out perfectly by someone who'd read the numbers, its empty expanse; a lure, a promise, a luminance, the mystery in the narrative. Quite lovely really, and Rackley basked. "Who knew I had the knack?"

"No one at all! But it was in you all along. Hoping for its chance. How many flowers are kept from flowering by the footfalls of the world?"

Rackley sought the nearest piece -- one of his favorites, Pierre Study #4 (reason for banning: first three missing) -- and eyed the line along the bottom: $12,000.

Nominoe: "I know. But a lot of deep pockets and purses here tonight. I expect them to pay for this champagne. In fact the champagne is here to help with that. Go walk amongst them, collect your accolades."

He did, coursing the eddies. In one circle Sheffield was hard at it. "Art. Even my dog makes art. Took a shit, considered the lines, the te-heh-heh-texture, goes Bau-haHAH HAhaus! BaHAHAAHAUuh-HAUS!" Rackley watched the clapping hand, the dancing right thigh in its beaten sheath of brushed wool, and laughed a natural laugh.

Now a man in glasses and itching beard. "Hullo, we met in Percy that time, the selection?" Yes, the fellow on stage. "Seems like so long ago. I like what you've done here. Look where's that clever wife of yours?"

Rackley turned his head. "Somewhere I'm sure. Always seems to be." He tapped his empty glass with a pen, an alarum for those nearby. "Thank you all for coming tonight. I confess it's a proud day for me. I'd even call it ... a banner day?"

The applause was honest and good. He filled with warm air and was sent aloft.

At the end, in the middle of the cleaning, he found Nominoe unfurled on a deck lounge and asked him for a summary. Nominoe turned up his eyes, that were a blend of pity and blame, underlain by that smile -- a remnant now, worn down by the evening -- and Velbin's hateful gaze, and said: "We didn't sell a single fucking card."

They began their bleary next morning at the new neighborhood Toast 'n Boast. Nominoe raised a slice of cinnamon marble rye. "Alright. Here's to effort. May it never be so trying."

Rackley had spent the overnight amassing theories, and he

played them out now for a time. Also: "And another thing." He lifted his own gobbet of brown raisin bagel. "It's time I had an assistant. I am overworked. And I think I deserve to fire someone."

Thus Cecil. Quite white, and glabrous in the British style. Very nearly unctionless, and could speak easily on all the topics without a hint of authority. Positive but otherwise amenable. Handy with a flowerpot, ate crisps, finished his puzzles for him, was good for the odd firing -- for things like bad form, queer smell -- and, to the point, was a spy.

Nominoe: "Prostitute? I thought you people used porn for that."

"Nothing to be ashamed about," said Rackley, reddening. Now they were at Le Bean Sublime. Velbin did not alter his stare, which made it worse. "I am a man of ordinary habits in that way, by way, if you care. Anyway, it's legal now, everywhere, thank god."

"When she acts like she likes it, that's legal now, everywhere, too … wait, which god was this? I am feeling a surge of religiosity."

"No, she liked it. By the end I could tell. In fact I taught her a couple things. About acting. It's mainly in the eyes."

Nominoe: "A lesson for us all. Was that her compensation? After all you have no money."

"I traded her some of the paintings. All of them."

"Why you little sneak-thief. I will add that to your credits."

Rackley set down his coffee chai. "No, listen, you told me to shove them into a pit. I quote you."

That was funny enough for Nominoe's hard animal laugh. "In 10,000 years we will look back and think: we're not looking back at all because we died out because of your whores and porn. Evolution gives up and shoots herself in the head."

Suddenly it's my fault. "Well what about you then?"

"Children? I honestly don't know. And I'm sure they have their doubts. I do know you are barren. The two of you had one in the docket but she got that offer to host that awards show that summer. I've heard she was quite the vixen with the quip."

Rackley now a pinker hue as he began to blanch. "Also I have a demand. I think I want to be paid."

"Ah. Rackley going through his rebellious period again."

"I have made you millions of dollars. With my new ideas, my hope, and my public behavior. Millions."

Nominoe: "And I have welcomed them every one. My thanks. I, in return -- with my domiciles, garb as befits, free driver, with my coupons, my deliveries of bananas and soy cakes every Wednesday -- have kept you alive all the while. Alive and ideating. Tell you what, do well with that in future, and we'll try to send your way some of the crumpled fivers you so crave." He raised a finger and brought it down like a blade on a block. "Go."

That had gone okay, and Rackley read now from his pad. "So: film. Don't know why I didn't think of it before. Film being the amalgam, the best blend of the artistries. Starts with story of course, the last art to be unimprovable by software. That's where I come in. Then we add a score, and there's --"

"Filmcraft indeed! Surprised I hadn't thought of it. It really is the milieu where the arts can do what they do best. So many forces at work, so many senses. The camera hides the flaws in the plot, the plot hides the flaws in the sound. And there's acting, makeup and hair, those clothes they wear. They all dance around, hiding as needed. What's this story about?"

Rackley nursed a long and delicious reveal. "ArtProjekt."

Smile; the rest of Nominoe's face was left to undecided surprise. "Oh politics then. And probably a part for me."

"Prominently. From your humble beginnings, once we find them out. And likewise we follow ArtProjekt from simple startup to the civic mainstay that we know, all as seen through the eyes of a promising young artist. We'll use fiction as needed to keep from being banned. Heh-heh."

"Politics: religion plus hate and minus beauty."

"Alright. That's one approach. Surely the actors will be attractive."

Nominoe had wandered: "Why politicals are more persuasive than religionists: politics is necessarily adversarial, and hate is more important than love. Republicans; Christians; leaf-blower; shoppers tie the dog outside and let them bark: here, my enemies, I strike you with words. And if they're not there to hear you, well, but so much of our therapy is imagined. Yes, make your movie political. Then somewhere in the story we add that hate leads to idiocy: you owe your enemy nothing, especially not your labor, and reason is wholly labor. And we'll mention that part of hate's appeal is you no longer have to listen. Don't listen: don't learn. And not learning is not thinking I believe. Listen, learn, think. The three taboos. So tell me more."

Rackley boiled with objections and bright ideas. "Yes I will. But surely leaf-blowers are --"

The card was in his hand: *I already said I don't listen.*

If Nominoe didn't listen, neither did he tell, revealing nothing in two ways.

One: even the least-interesting parts of him, or any person, the least resistant to inquiry, were subject to his veil: name, age, fecundity, origins humble or otherwise. For example: one morning Nominoe made a horrible rhoticity, or possibly it was the afternoon and a glottal stop that seemed to go on and on.

Rackley, exasperated: "Accent ... where from?"

Nominoe paused, carefully; taking offense perhaps, or wondering whether to. "Little corner of central Texas."

Rackley was startled. "Wait, but that's where I'm from."

"I'm so good at this."

"No, I meant --"

Velbin passed a card. *You're the one with the accent.*

As well, Nominoe might suddenly issue the odd soliloquy, quite unsolicited, on an abstract to which he'd given obvious care, and which by the end he managed to make impenetrable. Like using words to scrub away troublesome spots of clarity. For example: Rackley began to have, especially after the failure of the film projekt, classic artist's sweats, the terror that informs the artist, in dreams or day-dreams, that his gift has been taken from him: the unexplained gift, akin to telekinesis or flight, a grant from on high, taken from him by his advancing age, his vices, a stupid world. He mentioned this to Nominoe.

Nominoe: "It's not the sort of thing that's spoken of between gentlemen. Yes, I guess you have to be at least a little religious to be an artist. Brilliant minds require a brilliant maker. Nothing else makes sense. Lesser lights are perhaps not the product of a deity. Anyway. Strength. They say it's first among the virtues. Because the rest reside on it; or depend from it like flowering wisteria. Prudence withers without it; hedonism tries to be a virtue but tires easily. Of course they also say it's the first among the virtues to go, the first victim of senescence; and then as the vines fall away they leave the vices to flower; to be embraced because what else is there."

Rackley couldn't guess his age and wouldn't bother. "So does strength require strength?"

A pause, which in time became vexation, communicated nicely as with a virus. The card: *How the hell would I know?*

Other examples:

• Rackley mentioned he'd been progressing nicely with his KMD sequel, with the recent addition of (illegible) author's notes, as well as new characters and a couple of surprise erasures near the end. Nominoe had thoughts on the writer's art: "Right, well, regarding that sort of thing. I know there are a lot of people who are suspicious of the trick. It goes like this: reading is hard work, alone in the arts that way. And the author makes you learn the names of the characters and has you watch them carry on and at the end nothing comes of it. Ah, I get it. Three weeks of work. Well done. You shortened my life by that amount. And if you're wondering why that sort of thing still sells, it's this. Well done. You shortened my life by that amount. Thank you for that."

"Is that why you don't read?" Rackley'd never seen him crack a book.

Now the pause, a mile long, until the stare softened and began to rest; at long last the card: *thank you for that.*

• And then the monograph that didn't trail off but rather trailed in, in a limousine to an event, beginning with a digression on people crossing against the sign, inaudible, that branched and perambulated onto broader transgressions, still inaudible, and that ended with, "Anyway, an example of how we're all growing more stupid."

Rackley, dutifully: "Why do you think that is?"

"Because I can."

• And this, that seemed to come out of nowhere: "Life is an elaborate, celebrated pause prior to becoming worm-food. Example: a man dies at the age of ninety and announces he's trounced his older brother, dead at eighty-five. I took longer to be worm-food -- that's his last bit: at least I took longer. Hence the celebration. And then there's his dead brother shaking his head, incredulous, and says what the hell took you so long."

If art is the anti-science then it is all the things that are opposite science, including hate, lies, idiocy and crazy thinking. Given a little temerity, Rackley felt he could've rightly questioned his choice of mentor -- Nominoe, the embodiment of art, its life and breadth -- if he'd ever actually chosen. But anyway he wasn't rash that way; he certainly had strength enough to make sensible life choices. The most he could muster was a bit of selfish advice: "Perhaps if your pronouncements were not so opaque you would be less misunderstood."

Nominoe: "What? By whom?"

"Me."

Now not a smile, or cast of the eyes or other features; not even a pause, which needs a terminus. By all of which Nominoe said that the status quo was more or less exactly as he'd have it.

The film came to nothing: its flaws were comprehensive and were hidden, each by each, in a complete circle -- call it a quadrille -- of obscuration and so it was perfect just the way it was, at a considerable savings, and no actors acting about; Nominoe promised a good review. Over the next few months there were three more Rackley-inspired projekts:

• Nominoe was running through his harangue on originality. "Tyranny. Hordes of original thinkers. Yes, you have an original tattoo. So does every teenage girl, on her ankle. Common hordes. Original things are the suffocating gray fog of modern life." He acknowledged that this was not an original idea, "refreshingly" so. Rackley had at it for a day and came back with this: "All art is either revolutionary or plagiarism. So let us take plagiarism to a level of high abstraction -- metaplagiarism. Those who find it revolutionary are fools and cannot understand."

"You already stole that idea, something about bold new styles. I think if you steal an idea twice you've effectively given it back." Nominoe grew bored with this or otherwise resistant until he recalled he'd read recently about a forgery that had sold for more than the original because of its notoriety. Of course: a forgery, which is merely a megaplagiarism: simple and unoriginal. He chose as source material the 20th-century masterpiece Piss Christ. "We'll make several, for improved notoriety. Of course, for notoriety nothing tops murder, so we'll arrange a couple. No not actually, Rackley; as I've explained, this is art not reality. What's the word. Rendition. Let's say Samoa. A couple of promising young artists. Promising as in we'll make them promise not to tell, haha. Then we'll need a crack private dick. He uses DNA and breaks the case; then the fakes hit the block. The Piss Christ Forgery Murders!" He pushed the entire pitcher of lemon julep at Rackley. "Drink this."

Heavy headlines, a vigil and a gala; then more or less the whole thing came to an end when Nominoe carted in and dumped the lot into the brass basin in the great room. "You can't get DNA from urine. Perhaps you will do a little science next time you decide to waste our time."

- Rackley casting for a new genre and mentioned architecture. Nominoe: "Not an art. Architectural structures require toilets -- I don't have an objection per se: our first conscious creations go down toilets; they are the cradles of humanity -- and art cannot contain toilets. Not since Magritte's 'Ceci n'est pas une toilette.' Someone had the idea of artistic toilets, but they were always too painful."

Rackley said he knew all that and offered: what about an edifice that was only its toilets? Ideas began to burble: in structural design you always start with the legal requirements ... physics, toilets ... everything else is decoration ... and as we know, in architecture ornament is a crime ...

Plans were drawn up for a three-story mixed-use building that was only its toilets. Would use various wire suspensions. Copper-piped, properly spaced and sexed, but subtly so. Plus catwalks because you have to get to them if you have to go. They began the build in the atrium of Town Hall, and were halfway in when a parentless tourist child evidently pulled a ground floor flush and the dream came crashing down in a cascade of john-water.

Nominoe: "I told you it's not an art." He handed Rackley a mop as he left, tweedling, "To-da-loo."

- Rackley had an idea of branching into the non-arts and ennobling them, and came up with style-chess, in which a win in the great game is given not because you bashed and stumble-bummed your way to a regicide but for the virtues of your play: by the grace, wit and generosity in it, there on the board for all to see and learn from. Right away Nominoe was amenable, asking but why limit it to false battle? Hence style-boxing. Which, to be an art, must describe or at least evoke the human condition: all those virtues, yes, but also folly, falsehood and ill will, without the likes of which the definition of man is incomplete. Victory to the thug who most makes us think; or, better, weep.

One part in this would be Rackley's of course, as the artist. He was given a couple of days to limber up and compose; he would use the principles of dance -- and hope to have an advantage there -- including Balinese hand-dancing. Yes: the sweet science.

The venue was Civic Arena; good crowd, in the few thousands. Rackley, in the blank trunks, was paired against recently unrendited stone sculptor B. K. Prentiss, sporting the tan. At the gong Rackley jaunts, sidles a step and plies a feinting jete-morte, to acclaim, followed by a wise and wandering right roundhouse, with a twist, full of good effect; over the remainder of the frame a flailing Prentiss is docked several demerits for overdone punches and rabbit punches, and Rackley feels the tingle of impending victory. But he cannot rise for the second bell, and Prentiss takes home the prize.

Nominoe wasn't in the locker room, which was fine, his remonstrations already throbbing in Rackley's head, but Cecil was, with styptic swabs, tinctures and gauze, a couple of well-dones, then an envelope. On its face a message in Nominoe's hand: "I prepared these remunerations for you myself. I enjoyed them and I hope you enjoy them too." Inside: fifty rubles.

He gave Cecil the night off and Collier the slip. Wadded in his wallet were coupons for an egg sammy and drink from Thanks-a-Latte, and he used them; he left the rubles for the barista, who'd been kind to him, and added to the gratuity a tale as to their provenance.

Walking home. Is that snow in mid-May?

He skipped the lift, five flights, and went in. Lakme was there -- Lakme, for whom he knew he sometimes didn't have time -- dead by her bowl, no reason for it, bloody-shat the floor beside. He called Nominoe because what else was there; who arrived quickly with a couple of his body men, who loaded her and her bowl into an old beach towel or something they'd pulled out of stowage. Helpless; off she goes. He tried to speak but faltered. Nominoe, not opaque: "What am I your shrink?"

Immediately he was alone, and he did what he always did when he was home, which was to create a home as if she were still there, Noma, in the ether, departed but left her spirit behind; looking down in the kindest way, and he would show her how he remembered: always crack a window at night despite the season; dry the wash in the draft if you can; how to properly open and air a good bottle of red. And how to clean, for example, a blood-stain, boiling water and vinegar, a certain sequence with the cloth; he got on his knees and was careful not to dab in ways that appeared false or performed. As she watched, her pleasure was remade tenfold in him.

Noma in a better place now, although last he'd heard she was teaching at an art camp for women in Michigan or so, so who knows. Probably better. He considered calling her. Her love for the dog had always exceeded his own, perhaps only until now, and surely she would want to know, and of course she had the right. He perseverated on this, dutifully, until it became a bit of absurd theater, with the dialogue, plot devices and pitfalls of a thing he knew he would never do. Finally, drunk on good bottles of pilfered party wine, he called Nominoe and asked for her email. Nominoe: "I already told her. She did say how sad."

Next night. A smothering lack of sound. He couldn't hear his own breathing against it. The window open a crack and he looked for sirens or a domestic matter but nothing, nothing but the smell of his hoodie there wet with vinegar. Was I once lulled to sleep by the meter and timbre of the life beside me? He got up and fumbled for the radio, and music, a numbing agent against the quiet; it too was dead (how sad), and he went to send it crashing at least. He was stopped short.

They say great art is the child of tragedy, and suddenly there it was, stirring, begotten of this new stillness in his life; a blade of grass thrust up from a grave.

He grabbed a pen and sleep is dashed upon the rocks; an idea becomes an opus, which becomes a work of remedial genius.

Rackley: "It's both a work of homage ... and a work of retribution."
Nominoe: "You have my ear."
Rackley put on a show of getting into character: deep breath, stare, look at notes and discard. "1952, Woodstock, New York.

Composer and theorist John Cage, who had already gained renown by his compositions for 12-step scale and prepared sound, introduces to the world a bold, new and seminal way of hearing that world: 4'33". I know you know it."

"Yes in seedy old Maverick Hall. All hell broke loose, if I recall my reading right. Shouting, a shower of gold coins on the stage, demands for a refund, all the earmarks of crazed minds. Sounds like quite a time."

"Great art'll do that." Rackley became pedantic in a way that Nominoe could only admire. "4'33" was silences, some subtle and some infinitely small, strung in a sequence of that duration -- any peripheral non-silences being included as with all music. For what are musical notes without the spaces between them? They, too, have something to say. 4'33" let them speak. Perhaps for the first time."

Nominoe: "A deaf fellow in the gallery signed that Cage got it exactly right."

"Next day fellow composer Igor Stravinsky weighs in. Says he hopes Cage continues writing works in this vein, but of much greater length."

"One of the prettier ripostes of that half-century. You know I knew Stravinsky, back when. Quite a character, good Russian accent. Did you know he couldn't carry a tune? Interesting."

A lie for color, and Rackley left it unremarked. "Stravinsky was a natty hand with a melody, and had some cute ones, but he wasn't a defier. He did not confront the norm and say: I defy you, norm. And as far as his riposte that you love so much, well. Igor? Careful what you wish for."

What pluck! Nominoe's brows to a new height. "You mean ... ?!"

"I do. I introduce you to: 4'34": the Silence has More to Say. And in that extra second we don't hear silence, we hear --"

"Yes! We hear Stravinsky saying ... nothing."

"Correct. What now, Igor? Oh wait, he is long dead. But Cage's silence ..."

Echoes on. They were in the side foyer, a library dressed up

The Project -- The Misunderstood Man

in classics got from a by-the-yard outfit. Nobody reads books of course, but nothing looks better on a wall. They contemplated Cage's silence for a while, with its crunching of finger foods, Cecil's dissipated wheeze. Nominoe: "Well anyway. So --."

Rackley: "I've already set it up. In two weeks, Osburgh Auditorium. Got it catered, and the valet parkers; website pending. All we need now is a pianist, and someone to turn the pages."

Nominoe, both pleased and unsurprised: "Oh for piano we'll go with rising star Eudo LaZouche, Memphis City Philly. Just the right look for the job. As far as page-turner ... well. That's you. Of course it is."

"What? I dunno how to read music."

"I'll teach you. No more difficult than learning, say, algebraic notation. Difference being it's all open to interpretation."

"I could learn that."

Two weeks, then; now premiere night and party. The four of them important in their town car and bar; Rackley, master of tux-casual; Nominoe with some last bolstering words: "Do not look at the audience or acknowledge them in any way. Don't rush the tempo, as your nerves might incline you; imagine old Cage tapping a toe. Take your cues from the instrumentalist: he might emote; you must not. Before taking the stage you'll need to pee: check your fly."

Rackley: "Cecil suddenly has a task." Who smiled, as did Nominoe; whose smile became contemplative. "Music. We cannot avert our hearing. Thrust your feelings into me, like you dipped your finger in holiday gravy and stuck it in my ear. Held it there. And said how's it feel.

"The beauty of 4:34 is people will sit through it. Will they ever. Most modern music they wouldn't, too painful: yes, music is alone in the arts in that it can be used to generate sustained pain. You are wise to know that. And you have done better."

Collier used a credential and let them off by the special entry in the basement. Nominoe: "And here I'm going to leave you to it. Good luck and all that. And look: I want you to know I'm so pleased."

Rackley was touched, and took it with grace and a wink: "Take care should all hell break loose."

Nominoe smiled; now another pause, which would be for Rackley the last of so many; an elaborate pause, made of several different moods strung in series. "I am safe with my scribe beside."

Rackley took the lift up two levels and bumped into LaZouche: not too tall; a sad, distracted artist's cast. One pleasantry apiece seemed about right. He found the lobby and quickly led a corps of hangers-on; he ordered a Galliano with a twist, which he'd read in a men's magazine, and which he then conspicuously put aside. "What I do is drug enough." Quiet kudos and good.

Now a good twenty minutes of first-order mingling, palavers and of course acclaim, for his work and for his wit, and for which he was a vessel of infinite depth; ribbons and garlands that served to strop his repartee. Fazicker: "Yes, I believe it was Daniel Auber who once said, 'Close your eyes and get rid of the words. What's left is music.'"

Rackley: "You forgot to get rid of the words, Edward." Nods and huzzahs, subtle as befit the scene.

Then there was this: a young lady: "Did you miss me?"

"I miss you right now. You are?"

"Amice." She extended a hand; as did Rackley, as if with a sou in it. "We met at the gallery."

"Yes. But I so enjoyed our introduction that I thought we might do it again."

The effortless tease of chide and flattery, the soft lash; so now he was, impossibly, a seductor. And why not. The moment is mine and I'll define it any way I want.

Even Cecil noticed. "You are shining tonight," he said, refining Rackley's creases with a pocket crimper. "Radiant. You are a source of light."

Good hire. Now the sound of the tone, and he hurried backstage and peeked through the curtains. Full house, all hands, good walla. House lights coming down, and with them a hush of expectancy. Now a woman in designer black with an introduction he had not approved and would not acknowledge, humming. One last look at the score -- his score. Tacet; adagio. Two clefs and two two time. No key signature because that didn't really make sense here. He sipped from a secret flask of good red, steadies the hand.

At the cue they came on together, LaZouche crowding ahead but let him if that's what's needed: you preen, I'll perform. Applause, crisp and unpretentious. They took their seats. Deep, swirling breath, exhale and the head is clear. It has all led to this. Begin.

4'34" was a piece of three parts, the first the briefest, the mood-setter; which it did exactly well: contemplative. Second movement: begin.

Suddenly a noise ... actually not quite suddenly, because he didn't believe it at first ... like something you might hear while asleep, the creaking floorboard that makes its way into your dream. A man's voice ... an accent, that braying nasality from the tiny northern states. What the hell is happening.

"-- so I put it on, drop the needle, I'm listening and eventually I'm thinking this is the longest fuckin 4'33" I ever heard. Maybe this is the slow version. Allegro. Instead of the, what is it --"

Adagio. You ASS. Rackley snuck a peek while turning a verso. Somewhere in the dark, left side, an idiot voice, drunk or insane, or just an ass. He'll be arrested in a nonce: now that's an ambient noise worth the price of a ticket.

"-- forgot to turn the tuner on! I go over and get it goin again. I sit down and I'm listenin and wait, it's Pachelbel's Canon. And I'm like I don't remember this part." Remembuh dis paht. "So does the sheet music say piano player sits down, turns on Pachelbel's Canon?"

Around the ass a clod of vulgarians, hooting and bleating. Where the hell are the cops? LaZouche mute and unresponding. Rackley boiled, bladder bursting. Is it Sheffield? The man from Percy? For an encore I will beat him bloody.

"-- bang on the wall and say hey, I'm trying to listen to music here. But then I remember it's about ambient noise. Okay. But then I look at my watch and 4'33" is about to end and I'm thinking if only there's a longer version of 4'33" because Pachelbel is only halfway through --."

Now I have that goddamn melody in my head.

The pride of Microsoft security had returned with a reinforcement, who carried her baton fully upright and ready. Tap-tap.

The car had a moon-roof. He opened it a little and lofted this at them: "If you continue pummeling this vehicle I'll be forced to inform you it's a rental." Good one.

It's said that as you age there is a compression of the future and an elongation of the past, because at the end there is only the past, the present becoming essentially irrelevant. Rackley closed his eyes and thought about the past.

Then he vanished.

Now two ideas, the first ending in a question, the next more confident.

As far as the first idea, I will justify its placement at this point in the narrative by positing that, of all the things Rackley might possibly have been thinking here at the moment of his disappearance (a moment I cannot know but about which I perforce must consider, forever), this idea -- whose description I will try to condense below -- was surely not among them. To wit:

There's a theory that claims to see, in each of the stages of the human project, a synchrony, an agreement in principle, between art and science. To build our theory we start at the beginning -- one of many, sometime after the Permian extinctions, or those of the Cretaceous, and anteceding the last great glaciation -- with filthy animals, feeble and ill-equipped, rags and hacking tools, and fire, at which we would stare in wonder, as we did those in the night sky. This was toward the end of the period of nothing happening, before the invention of the past and of passing time.

But of course there were things happening, enormous things, torments of every shape in nature: tremors and great displacing winds, and water turned against us; eruptions, both around us and above us, that threw down fire; and the rare and indomitable black burning eye in the sky, that might lower the light at midday: the megaphenomena of the natural realm, which formed the foundation of ontological inquiry. And we would shiver by the fire; one day one of us takes up chalk or a bit of coal, raises his hand -- actually let's let him be a she, and imagine it being the female inclination at the start, and all the way along -- one of us draws up her hand against the cave wall and from its outline is derived the first symbol. Mockery at first if that had been invented, then we stared in wonder: a part of the living world had become its idea, but an idea not trapped languishing in the mind but transcribed back to the living and combined with stone. The power to do this passed from the magician into the thing itself; so now an icon, humorless and unswerving, loomed over their affairs.

Several questions. What was happening? Answer: we were responding to our own new and original ontological question: do we have a power of our own, a salve or solution, by which we might understand and even appease the monsters around us? That query is the basis of religion, and of course science: art and science had been born from the same egg.

Also: why that particular glyph? Because the hand is the embodiment of human agency.

Also, and more generally: from whence this spasm of creativity? Evolution of course, from whence all things. As to the matter of the improved fitness that evolution requires (and for those demanding a more robust synchrony): soon after the human hand had gone from tool to idea to icon, a relevant science was born, that of warmaking, which we used to good effect against the Neanderthal, in mankind's longest war, in which we killed them one and all.

So speaks the theory; which also suggests that staring in wonder was our best tool and still is.

We felt well of our invention, which had us suddenly living in modern times, (another invention, modernity, which is used even now) like all the times since; it would be many years before nothing happened again. Now comes the ice, and a great leap of fecundity, as new fonts of courage were called for in the flight across strange country. Art and craft had not yet begun to divaricate -- art is invention, craft its iteration -- and every new image was looked upon as a miracle. Objects of fear -- smilodon, dire wolf, short-faced bear -- predated objects of desire -- stag, boar, peccary -- and of desire: mons pubis, parted pudenda, the males now coming into the game. Humaniforms were rare, perhaps requiring hubris; the famous fertility talismans would wait until the invention of mobiliary art.

During this time a science coalesced, iconology, by which we attempted to understand the things we were making. To understand is to clarify, which is to say condense, and the drawings were now on occasion rendered into shorthand -- circles, stars, squares, other well-proportioned forms -- probably as a result of prayers sometimes needing to be sent in hurry. Anyway, the first abstract art.

Now old Homer, who wrote an epic poem before there was writing, so for whom and for which it had to be invented. They turned to our actors on the cave wall, and what they had become -- A, from the head of an auroch -- and made them into characters of a different kind.

Writing -- both an art and a science -- is unusually plastic, and can be dextrolinear, and incorporate spaces and other obstructions, or not; but all writing requires a linearity. By way of the line, ideas can be watched, on parchment or in stone, as they progress. Or followed, or perhaps the word is entered, or entrained; the written idea can carry the eye, and the mind, changing thought. And so by the letter and the line history was made possible, and its lessons (of which you, now, are a beneficiary); with the line, relentless, as guide, time cast aside its circularity, despite the entreaties of nature.

Irresistible to the eye, the glyphs -- the runes, the majuscules

-- inherited the beauty of the things they described. Polygons, part-circles and connecting bands, they were a gallery of well-proportioned forms, and came to model a new understanding of beauty as being bound up in proportions: the face, the body, just so; the ratios found in the conch, the hornbeam, the ripple, the crystal and the prism, the pyramidal mountain. Man would now remake art in accordance with the rules of the well-proportioned form, in sculpture, portraiture, the science of the well-formed edifice. As well: in frescoes, painted pictures and friezes, the line and the letter allowed man to place his players -- the glyphs returning to their roots -- in a linear manner, heroes, beasts and nemeses moving left to right as would a piece of heroic prose beside. Because of course art is telling a story.

Two particular synchronies of interest: one of us who read and took note was Plato, who then changed thought: out of the ratios he made rationality: for what is reason but one well-proportioned form leading to another; and another man found himself staring at the forms and wondered why they were beautiful, Euclid. Art was making us think.

Next, two developments: the arrival, odd and unexplained, of the Christian god; and the wrath of that god -- by way of the Goth -- which helped him prosper and grow.

In any clash of ideas, first clarify; and the advocates of Jahweh polished their points and directed them at paganism and especially pagan art, the colored walls and statuaries whose stories would not comport with those of the big book at hand (whose cobbled entries had been recently deified), until in time the pagan legends were reduced to a sophism of shards, chips and sweepings (a smash of ideas which would earn the young Christians a visitation of these same crimes at the hands of their future selves).

Not good enough, and he calls in the Goth -- and the Frank, and the Hun, and eventually the Vandal for a more comprehensive wrath; Rome was split end to end, and out spilt the old scrolls, dense and dry, in which reposed all learning, set aside now for fire-starter and toilette.

Suddenly a voyage of undiscovery, a great undertaking in which all knowledge was buried beneath its ruins. We were alexic again after so long, our geometry undevised, reason unknown. The great nomothetes -- Plato, Euclid and all that lot -- tottered and fell away, leaving us with a less circumspect law-giver, who would first break the old ones; language was shattered, and strewn across the continent, where its shards became weeds. Time was broken: no longer a line, certainly not a circle; perhaps a fragment of a line, aching to end with the Second Coming, of unknowable length: perhaps as long as a parenthesis. And even the cradling arms of space itself were corrupted now by a heaven and hell, whose dimensions could never be measured or ascertained, or made a part of all knowledge.

We had mastered letters and numbers; our children were back to scratching at the cave wall. Nothing happening again, not on earth or in heaven or hell, this time by design. How did the arts respond?

By taking up the shard. I imagine someone glancing at the debris of beautiful things -- a display of painted pots and vases toppled by a savage -- and in the sweepings she sees the image of a saint: a mosaic. An old art, forgotten but still and once again beautiful: form from chaos, which describes every living thing; soft focus, as with reverie or epiphany, or when we stop examining; or maybe the secret beauty of it was you cannot smash it with satisfaction.

Also: art at a considerable savings. The Goth had left behind a stockpile of ceramic crud, cullet, odd bits of marble and colored stone, to be recast as points of expression in panels and gallery floors, vaults and ceilings and in particular the spectacles of colored glass that let in only religious light. Now we come to our synchrony: in this post-literate period these expanses of broken space would now become the reliquaries of the old tales (whose scrolls presently kindled the cook-fires), and of course the tellers of them, but in this new way: the presumption of sequence, the prerequisite of logic and literature, is discarded. Our hero might appear here or there and here again in the frozen image, the placement of his chapters subject to the demands of overall design. Sequence is supplaced by simultaneity, the point of the story, or the crux if you like: an approach to tale-telling wholly in accord with a time in which time had become this tiny hyphen of nothing-happening; in which, for most, the principal creative activity was prayer.

So goes the theory. Next: for five hundred years nothing happened, except perhaps waiting in the right way. Then, eventually, and as you know, we would rediscover reason, and all its requirements; then of course unreason.

The armies of El Cid, protectors of the faith but otherwise indistinguishable from the Goth, expelled the heathen Caliphate of Umayyad from northern Spain and took their great barbarian library of Toledo. Perhaps they didn't have a torch handy; or they had an inquiring scribe amongst them, a monk with ink-stained fingers: by some happenstance the likes of which make up history, the archives were cracked open and the obviousities, suspended in vellum or the strange and new paper, were taken up and awakened, exasperated, and repatriated to places that scarcely knew them: Plato's language of logic, which struck some as so much gibbering until he set them straight; Euclid's nubile forms, filling out before our desirous eyes; time moved along his endless line again, as tireless as this march of glyphs across the page.

Learned men had suddenly become like infants learning the link between light and heat, between pain and the sound of crying. The squall of discovery begins here, that continues unabated: the gear, the mill, the machine, the magic of the forge, by all these the obvious things were coaxed out. Leonardo invented the lens, and the camera, and then, having gotten the better of light, covered his canvases in shadow, an obvious thing to do but at the time unknown; he invented the helicopter and imagined taking it above a Tuscan valley, and by that departure the first landscape art was made, hitherto unknown but obvious; in fact he himself, that living synchrony, was an exemplar of a new kind of obviousity being limned out just then by him himself and his peers ... I'll give you clues. Michelangelo's David, clothed in adoration but by some miracle not a saint or son of god; the painter the clear-seeing Giotto, who, born with the gift of perspective, endows his art with it (and us), and now the sight-lines of the art converge upon the viewer, who has become its fulcrum; and then the truly novel idea, Gutenberg's motive type, that gave the everyman a good and new reason to read: the book he might take with him and take in as is his wont ... well, now you'll have guessed it, reader, the greatest obviousity of all time, theretofore unknown: the individual.

Man, newly minted, now made science, which is to say the scientific method, by which any one of us could impinge upon what had been god's privilege, the remaking of nature. The battle between reason and unreason was won, declared the proponents of reason.

Beware your victories. One of Giotto's feature accomplishments was the ellipse: he'd seen a clock's face slightly from the side, and drew it that way, and drew it into the galaxy of singular shapes. A seemingly innocuous corruption of fundamental forms -- a circle cannot be improved upon; an ellipse can be anything, a circle sat on by any common ass -- until Kepler, struggling to make sense of the space that surrounds us, took up the ovoid and used it to reshape the orbits in the night sky: he had made sense of god's universe by stripping it of its perfection: the truth emerges from the unhatched egg. Over the next many years other obviousities -- all of them, actually -- would be in the same way besieged by reason, although they wouldn't be forgotten this time, but simply made wrong.

A man named Manet made art that made no sense: it made nonsense. Careening horizon-lines, figures that only grew as they receded, a table of fruit as seen by four separate and simultaneous sets of eyes. Mockery first, of course, then the awe: by 1915, when the proponents of reason realized that time could slow, that space could bend ... here's a good example: reason had determined that we are entirely made not of matter but of morphic resonating fields; and when the portrait of the lily pond was painted that drew no distinction between the water and what was in it or on it or beside it, the proponents of reason greeted it not with scorn but with gratitude.

The Project -- The Misunderstood Man

We are all filthy animals and crave our colors and shapes. So goes the theory, which can tend to carry on. There's the link between the rise of Rococo and the loss of phlogiston; we were given the languid and draping clock-faces and suddenly discover the mutability of memory; pan-dimensional flux is proposed as a property of space-time, then everyone tries to paint it; and of course there's the uncertainty principle and all its inordinate license ... our theory becomes a bit erudite as you can see, but let's forget that and assume it's true, as an exercise, or at the very least to extend the narrative, as I bring you back to the moment in question. To wit:

What do we call this school, and by what theory, this movement, that describes and explains and makes a synchrony with Rackley's disappearance? By what careful blend -- and at what heat and in what medium -- of reason and unreason, of the individual and his sublimation into the whole, of transfixing visions and their broken parts, were we brought to the vanishing point of this particular tableau? To put it in the simplest way I can think of: if art is transporting, where had Rackley's art taken him?

Not just Rackley of course. Also the robot car -- a kind car, and dutiful, and remembered here -- and the mall cops, the macadam, the incongruous palm and bougainvillea, finally freed of their bafflement; a thousand Lexi, the cast-iron Chihuly, the experimental school for troubled young coders; a protestor, a pair of buskers, a piper cub just above with its gray looky-loos, soaring into gawker's heaven ...

... actually, given that the referent event at eleven oh one Microsoft Circle was atomistic in nature (neutron plus [U-235, U-238, Pu-238] -> fission fragments plus 2n,/3n) (I hope I got that right) (credit here goes to physics, and reason as always), and thus had an unusually long reach across space and time, let us for ease of reading repair to its farthest extent, starting simple and moving in.

(And here I must make an aside about paying attention. There are occasions -- for example in a morgue; the account of your son's death in battle; porn -- in which attentiveness, like a good memory, can do inordinate harm. Advice: train yourself so that, given the appearance of a second sun in the periphery of your vision, you will simply rededicate yourself to your reading and quickly slip behind a low wall.)

A mile north of the event, good King Countiers in their kitchens facing south were spot-blinded. That's the allure of a million billion lumens. A long stride inward, our house-holders were blinded then double-blinded, their eyes flayed from their heads by a storm of flinders -- it's an unremarked quality of window-glass, that provides the view and in the next second takes it. Closer still, we might've been distracted from our blindness by sudden radiation burns, so much worse than ordinary burns in that, should you be lucky enough to heal, you would later unheal, for years, luck no longer helping much; and for those near enough, a light so bright -- call it light in the ultraviolet -- that the blinded are killed in the same instant -- didn't see it coming -- and are spared the trauma of blindness ... and here I'm reminded that by one measure the worst of it was felt by those affected less, by those not simply made to vanish in the entire ...

... actually for ease of reading I'd like to start again, using concentric circles, and with a focus on the topographical: there, up on far-off Nob Hill, a 1904 Craftsman takes a crack in its oculus; now a dislodging of gutters and soffits, weather-vanes all cock-a-hoop, and the oculi have become shards, chips and sweepings; our progress takes us to domiciles marked by signs of battle, trauma and the odd collapse, and the trees have lost their early leaves; another perimeter, where structures have taken a good crushing, smashed and scattered as if by passing ice; the last expanse before the event horizon is black, simmering and greasy, as if the lifting blade of the bomb has pulled back a sheet that shows the filth that underlies a city.

At the center of it all is a void, deep and about the size of a neighborhood, water from broken mains pouring in, like blood rushing to aid an amputation. We're forced to define the void by what isn't in it: Microsoft, as we know; the Pac-N-Sac, Tenorio's Cash Market, Hair Topic, Etc., whose name was made by an odd translation from the Czech; Cham's Chinese and Donut, the much-missed Serenity Wellness Massage; Johnny G's Porterhouse and Chop, Pipe Lion Vape, the Redmond Fire Department of course; Milt's Pit BBQ (about which even today no one has made the quip); Cash Box Pawn, and the concrete pad where the old Sac-N-Pac stood; all of it gone, or rather refined, if you will, to its protons and made ready for re-purpose. New parks someday, play-parks, parks for the rich and for the poor, all on new land; museums and markets, an open-air theater, new electricals, light-rail and future infrastructure, all made better-ready for this sort of thing; more writing, more art, more 4:34 ... even, perhaps, should the fates find an interest, another Rackley someday, who'd been made a part of the ball of pure light where it all began, photons now, first a soft mass of them, then their dissemination, sending a signal, for example to the startled sensors at the base on Mars; even, some four years hence, touching the lenses circling faraway Alpha Centauri, an artist to the last.

I said there'd be a second idea. Here it is.

Arguers are not the worst sort of person necessarily -- for example, Genghis Khan famously hated argument -- so on occasion Nominoe would agree to engage one for the stipend. Not too much previous to the event described above, Dr. Edward Ogden, a known academic and disputationist from the local school, invited him for a friendly stage debate on Israel -- good topic for a turn-out.

Full house, protestors and a festive air. Nominoe had demanded a candy plate in his dressing room as a joke, and there it was, lucky Collier; Rackley was offered a chair in the wings but chose to sit mid-crowd for full immersion.

Ogden opened with a pun on Menachem Begin. Then a quick sift through Jewish history -- Exodus, twelve tribes, the Trials of Shechem -- then its relevancy, which was the harder pull, but he pulled okay: Ogden was free-speaking and fact-ready, the worst kind of arguer. Now a few paragraphs on Israel, its modern place in the world -- here was where Nominoe got that Ogden was laying claim to the For position; fair enough. For a finish the doctor made a demand, his soft-shaven face cast into a cool glower. "So what is it? Israel. For it? Or against? Answer. Sir." Applause.

Nominoe with ten minutes for rebuttal. "How the hell would I know." He bade the moderator turn over the clock.

Murmurs: something of a blunder? The unwritten rules on argument require argument ... actually these are written somewhere. But also one does not simply admit to no opinion. The very passage between child and adult is defined by the taking of position. Hesitation speaks to character, and its fitness for the arena of ideas; maybe Nominoe didn't get that, and Ogden took him to task with all the tricks: the smirk, the dismissing whisk of the hand, the soft and smiling chuckle, timeless techniques refined in fraternity houses dating back to Roman days. And the ad hominem, the tu quoque, the zinger: "As we all know ... oh, wait, apparently not all?" All eyes turning to where the brunt is borne, and Nominoe, never wanting to disappoint, would offer a bruised face, Velbin topping up his water bottle.

Nominoe's counter-rebuttal was a little more fully-formed. "Not only do I not know, Edward, but -- and I know you won't like this -- but neither do you." A nod, and the moderator reset the time.

Sputtering from the gallery, and shouts of rebuke: a bad breach in any debate: the parties in a parley must not be ignorami, or farepayers might mob for their money back. And to finger the fellow naïf by name! Now it was personal, and Ogden angrily referred to himself and his qualifications for holding an opinion, these very much in memory and easily recalled: member of many universities, receiver of grants and awards, Mensan in good standing, and hewer to the virtues, including probity, thrift and most importantly the strong holding of opinions: a curriculum vitae very much exceeding

Nominoe's, which no one knew. For the end he drew up a couple of poncey scoldings -- "How dare you!" and "Shame!" -- from the British catalog, and bitch-slapped the lectern.

Noising and galomphing, like at sports and a set piece; Rackley bobbed in a sea of enthusiasms. Nominoe waited for the noise to tire ... no, not waiting, just another pause, the kind of thing he would carve out for himself from time to time; cut from his allotment. Now the room was quiet, then restive with expectancy, and there was Nominoe, his expression changing as if in response to some distant Brahms. I was there as you know. I don't claim to know everything about him, but I do know his tones; and when he spoke, his voice was proud of course because he had won, but also strangely and ceremoniously sad:

> *"Doctor: you've done your reading.*
> *And you know the story so far, my friend.*
> *But you don't know if you like the story.*
> *Because you don't know.*
> *How. It. Will.*
> *End."*

LAIRD

Laird noticed something in the tree beside him, then the tree. An ironwood, which he knew from its gray-green and broken bark; the ironwood has long and serried leaves like a weeding tool but not this one, anymore, after the blast, and he felt a little remorse and anger maybe. Even the ugliest tree is a thing of beauty. It didn't ask to be born here. From its lower limbs he pulled a long scrap of fabric, a checker pattern in orange and white. Knots of grease on it, and he took off a glove to give it a feel. So it was half a keffiyeh soaked in brains. He went to his armtrac and tied it to the radio mast.

There was a boy's sneakered leg nearby, and he threw it back into the fire: he liked to keep a clean mission: this was not chaos. And as always he had half a company of complainers policing the grounds. They would run to him with found items, identity cards, bits of AK, like rookies at a crime scene; he'd accumulate, wait, feed the fire.

They always fled to find a mosque. Why. To bring Allah into the mix (who can't be troubled to say you're only making it worse). Or maybe if you know you're going to die. Facilitates the related rituals. Anyway it's not my job to give them advice. A better question was why it burned with such enthusiasm. Houses hereabouts were made of brick, concrete, mud mashed with straw. So perhaps a mix of pews, carpets, stacks of sacred texts. Every once in a while a satisfying pop, as with a roast, which could be rounds cooking off. The smell was just the smell of everyday life, yet some of his people wore respirators or durags dipped in gunslick, which he found ludicrous. I'm not afraid of you, mooj. I am sure as shit not afraid of you dead.

The fire gave out, and in came the hazard team with a last look for rads, and now the D-10s, the big bullies, to render the site unfit for use. He would wait to watch them when he could, his favorites. Unpopular with the mooj. They'd bumble up and kill you by the bludgeon of your own home. One time he'd been in one and seen that if you use the blade right you can lift ten meters of mines and drop them into their own trenches, perfect; also driven one, where he had a flame-thrower appended, whose main effect was for morale, theirs and ours. He'd've used them more often but they broke down a lot here, here in the Khorasan where nothing worked well except of course me.

Approaching a town, AT-0235, hoping to receive fire. A fireman wants to fight fire. But no, a crowd comes forward conceding the town, led by a wise and bearded elder. In early days non-combatants would be held at a distance, by way of hose or sound cannon, and herded into holding lots. They're not all bombers, went the credo: they're all bombs. And war is about adapting, and if you can be clever all the better: Tritregonex-30 was brought to life by a particular spark, and science had conjured a beam, something like a magnetic pulse, that swept all before it with just that right sensitivity. Prowlers in wing formation and the occasional EC-130 had flown all over the badlands and washed it with the beam and been rewarded with red and golden plumes all along. Then from science comes a cathode device, the size of a box and fits on a tank, by which you could bathe a captive crowd. If any of them were among the anointed, well, up went the lot, burkas flying like illegal kites.

So T-30 was no longer the drug of choice, and it was back to dynamite vest and plunger. To address that they were now using wahdah, a special unit, sixty locals pressed into service and happy to live to do it. He kept them in the general baggage train in old half-tracks, hand-cuffed and eating the same as everyone, including the ham-and-limas. Haha. They were brought out as needed to clear the non-combatants, women mainly with their children and others (so-called military-age males were not dumb enough to come forward, which is to say that those of them who did come forward were in fact dumb enough). Wahdah would strip them to their underwear but not more than that, and the young and the old could keep their swaddling clothes: we are not barbarians, we are not the Goth or the Hun, we are not you. Dashiki, niqab, hijab, scarves and baggy pants, into a pile and burned. Then he had them sit for a while under the sun to render them down; their own small sun, heaved up on its meridian, hovering there and killing all it could. He called up the trucks and off they went to someone else's purview.

Laird had no real feeling about any of this because this is just what I do for a living. They moved forward. There's a process to reducing a town. First, for safety, knock it off the grid. There'll be a substation or something, fragile as a flower: send in a spec with a whiff of C4 and the whole thing comes apart, a bright and belabored death. Then selected structures, by Laird and his laser, take a beehive round through the window. Wake up in there. If gunners miss the window he makes them do it again, not a bad rebuke. Eventually you pave the paths: napalm or narrow fuel-air strips to set off traps or mines. Mines -- he'd made a wordplay: kill one of mines, cost ten of yours.

Now urban warfare, and for this Laird had in his caravan a tractor-trailer full of the latest expedients. Cartons of kamikaze robots, bloody and insane; spy filaments thinner than a whisker, and drones the size of a bee; army-grade silly string -- shoot it down a dusty hallway and it shows the tripwires; gamma guns for cooking a mooj behind a wall. He used none of it. When he felt friction he took the building down. Couple of methods for that. If he had air -- when they weren't called away or gassed out -- he'd announce a duck-and-cover and use a guided glide bomb or maybe a baby cruise; he also had vehicle-mounted home-wreckers like the Klopfen-2, the Lancet. For taller buildings a team puts thermobaric charges (Laird: thermobarbaric) at the corners. He'd seen a ten-story tower fall like water, like a slip dropped down a body of air. They called the dust pancake makeup. Bullies would come later and grade the remains. Nice work. The Roman ideal was: not one stone upon another. Not practical now or actually then but a lovely thought.

A break for water and power bars; buildings are assigned. The process would continue by the book: wahdah run through to find sneaks or tricks; haz guys sent in to sweep for nukes and nuke parts. Paperwork goes to the spooks, pale and bespectacled, lisping into their devices. Then in go the carrion crows for a quick loot for restitution, defrayment and reprisal; mark the building for demolition. They could do a town in a day.

Laird had two adjutants, Lieutenants Mirou and Nidha; he told Mirou to dress the part, and he put on his house kit, which was mostly just Uncle Walther and a head-lamp. They walked off on their own down a block, and found a building with a hand-painted sign, Ezhar Al-Raisi, a feed and seed store. They listened. Distant sounds of the mission. He broke a window and peeked in.

This is what Laird did for a living, and this was the living part: he blew up the door with a cone charge. That tone in the ear, and he felt a bit concussed. Seems he'd also blown up a service counter and some burlap sacks of brown rice perhaps. Curtains, thin and stiff with rigor, hung like a woman's dress at a hanging. They moved forward and to a back area. There were signs of a quick exit, a money-box, a cup and an open ledger.

He had Mirou turn on her sniffer -- an OA-22, the latest, better than a dog because it never got bored -- which led them to a hatch under a rug. She moved the dial and announced two heartbeats heard. Laird pulled the cover over and said come out, drew his .425 and dropped down a grenade, following after.

A mooj, bound up in the rubble, his right eye gone and that general area. Otherwise unmarked. Wounds could be so oddly particular. He had a little mooj beside him, a fighter, a scrapper, eyes wet with hate, clawing at his father's hand.

The war was over here but the big mooj rallied his broken parts for a last attack. Mirou: "He says you are not a godly man ... you prey upon the weak ... your name will become a curse."

Laird banged together a line from an old Sufi story -- "Al-shattaim al-khassa al-thanaa," your insults are praise -- and shot him in the other eye. Now from the boy a medley of siren sounds, an alarm, help me, his face a little like a clown's, covered in brick dust; he grappled with that strong hand now infinitely soft. Laird: "It must be a comfort for you. To have had a father worth grieving. Ask him how old he is."

Mirou, after an interval: "Nine."

"Tell him I'll come back and kill him when he's old enough. Tell him."

Mirou: "[Wait until he's gone. You'll find water outside.]"

Up the ladder and into the hard air. Mirou: "Have you no children?"

"Not really."

"You are a piece of shit."

He always listened to his people, however briefly; in this case he had to say no, more like an atom of shit. There was trac nearby and she tried to pull down a jerry-can. Laird: "Nope. Your water." He hung there as she peeled off her camelbak and placed it by the door, her face screwed into a weak and conflicted hate, nowhere near as pure as a child's.

Laird was Lieutenant Colonel George Campbell Laird, commanding officer of 1st Battalion, 3rd Armored Division, which meant nothing. 1st of the 3rd, the Thundering Third, with all its entourage of tradition, which can help men fight, and was used for that purpose up to the point of the military imperative, which is success. For that you adjust as needed, the true art of war and of course life. For example, a battalion holds a thousand guys; Laird's carried over five thousand now, or maybe six this week, they kept throwing men at him. In code they called it Deployment Unit 7: something like fifty big guns, in layered and redundant batteries. Platoons for recon, for mortars and missiles, for military police, platoons for psyops, hazard, HQ, medic, an army of platoons. Detachments, that wonderful word without meaning, of marines, engineers, a special forces team with the mooj beards, never-bathed as a constant reminder of I don't care, fuck you. Ten dozen tanks, carriers, other tracked vehicles only vaguely defined; hundreds of trucks, and the men to repair them, then their own trucks; choppers and VSTOL, and various other air. A rampaging supply train, changing the skyline, rolling hills of it for miles behind, ammo fuel and fan mail, and food of course, crud but so much of it, a manna's horn of it, the victuallers are making us fat and lazy on crud. Even a riverine unit, with its rubber bateaux and nothing to do.

He was gravid with war; he was in effect some kind of general officer -- a rank considered too vital to be put at risk, which decree crashing against his own imperative, so here he was at lower pay by his own hand. Managing all this was mainly just a matter of ordering up more majors, and leaving them alone and having them do same.

Now city AT-3106; he was told it was a university town, which baffled him. Grind up the ring road, skirt a saline lake; an overflight of green teal, loud and heading out. Smart. Arty had been carping about underuse, and Laird stopped the process to call up a couple of light howitzers. Move aside, make way. He put out a map, and had them aim at the power plant; his words were like pheromones for an ant farm; and then they laid on him that gape of expectancy, hungry dogs who could not look away. Okay: two fingers like a victory and the guns opened up, barking like loons. War as dumb as we can make it, can't even see what you're killing. A blind man taking photographs. Nidha's commentary was buried under the big talkers, but he knew it was about manhood. He waited until they got that glow and cut it off, calling a lunch: crud cakes, flavor chews and a piss if you must. Moving on.

He was summoned to the front, call code pdq Alpha: seems the van guys had found an anomaly, a specimen not in the catalog, calling for adjustment, someone with that knack. He roared up in a sidecar, klaxon parting the way. There in the middle of the main road, just off a plaza, a ring of protestors, a score perhaps, prone and locked together by what appeared to be concrete casts, elbow-to-elbow. A sergeant: "The same over there and that block, and we've confirmed that they're handcuffed too, which I don't know how they did that." Good trick. Outwait? The buildings beside gave daunting shade. They were canting, something ordinary, and he heard a Dane in the mix; blond, well-shod; and a voice from regional America, a Michigander, will I show her more mercy or less. An odd mob was forming, from doorwells and other side spaces, cautious and amenable. Some held signs, which he told his aides not to translate if possible; and everywhere the phones aloft, and other devices, making history. You stupid fucks. You'll be the first taken up; hope you enjoy your trench-latrines, film that won't you. They wouldn't of course, their devices going to bomb-disposal.

"Waddah all that rabble up. Tell them use batons. Off they go. One hour. And I want two dozers up here right now." Nidha passing it along. The arrestees in the crowd were processed, the rest evaporating, to upper windows by his eye or other overlooks. He ordered some counter-sniper. For the bully-boys he called up a map. "Open space here." A cemetery two streets over. "I want a pit, six feet deep or so by twenty meters." He indicated the ring of disobedients. "I'm a free speech guy. But they can do it just as well over there. Drag it over and drop it in. And this is important, keep them well watered. Treat them better than they would." He stood around during the process and listened; their protests were not at all curtailed. Everybody wins.

A lot of standing around today; Laird grabbed a flash and this time a shot-shell pistol, and dialed up a whoop of door-kickers; he pointed to the main tower on the square, red-brick and looking down with a reek of conspiracy; he proposed a brief campaign. Through the main entry and he was exactly right: another dozen obstructionists, handcuffed along the hall to a gas or possibly steam pipe. Cuffs again for fuck's sake. All handcuffs have a key in common, a universal. Of course they do. Think. He probably had one in his desk; one of this lot here had it hidden in a cheek; probably that one there, pinched and seeming a bit important. He sent the marines ahead and had Nidha ask for an engineer, bring his torch.

More standing around. Laird might put on the conqueror's posture at times like this and screw in a smile; or, like now, he might go with simple disappointment, which has so much more depth: oh look at what you've done; why am I here; really, why are we here exactly. Not one of them met his gaze. Or actually that one, a winsome look, child-like, I'm thirsty. Laird: "Don't ask for pity if you want it." Good line, must learn it in the local tongue.

To the engineer he said tuck a dollop of solder into each keyhole. He went up the front stairs, skipping a couple flights for peace and quiet. The hall was carpeted and clean, dark of course but lit by open doorways. A classroom, whiteboard covered in methodical script. Microbiology. Lots of file boxes for others to explore. Another classroom, chemistry tools in close order, beakers and burners; if they'd meant to leave in a panic they'd not done it well. A small closet for schoolbooks, holding strong but not long for this world.

He smelled smoke; a door just open, which he leaned on with his gun hand. Small room exposed to the west, blinds up and getting good light; a woman at her desk. It was her desk: her familiar way against it, her items arranged around, jar of pens, a caddy for her device and heavy watch; perhaps five pages in a fan in front of her for correction, and other pages in a low pile beside; in a little dish an improbable cigarette, from which she drew. "Why are you here?"

An area accent educated in England. Laird: "You killed my people."

"And you gave smallpox blankets to your people."

Good one. Did I now. "So kept them warm all the while."

Nidha took a seat across from her in a canvas chair, staring. The woman: "I suppose you know you are going to hell."

Laird: "Nice to think about. But probably not."

She was beautiful in the local manner, with the deep black arches; hair a humble black and gray beneath a head scarf. Hijab. He imagined slaves who, freed from their chains, wore them anyway for tradition. She said, "I was dead before, I will be again. This is my in-between time. I spend that time as best I can." She made a show of organizing her papers but didn't actually do anything. "Will you let me tell you my story first?"

"No thanks I know the ending." One shell to the chest, another to change her expression. I spend my time as best I can. From amongst her papers he plucked her cigarette, disgusting thing, might've burned us all down.

That night he moved his team and the rest of headquarters company ten miles south into the desert to get away from the smoke. His trac was set up with an armored cap that would fold away to help you get shot at, like now. Above him he could account for Corvus and Crater, Berenice's Hair. "An Egyptian queen who gave up her hair for the cause." He pointed at her with his utility spoon. "Just like you."

Nidha: "Why are you how you are?"

"No one knows that sort of thing. It's not science."

"You are how you are because of events in your past."

"No one knows that. Nidha. It's not science. Sorry you're upset but not very much. You don't know, I don't know, difference is I don't care."

"The great faiths abjure cruelty, without exception. The most base of the sins. So I guess you are without faith. Nothing undergirds you."

Nidha and Mirou. Foist on him at first, now kept with a measure of affection. Not quite paternal affection, since he endangered them every day, unless it was. Between the two, seven languages; in his own they'd twice his vocabulary. Listening to them, in their lithe and deliberate eastern altos, was like listening to spoken song, and they had no idea.

But of course they didn't: given all that, they were still children, knowing nothing in seven languages. "We can talk about cruelty and sins if you like. Old conversations; if we run out of time you can find them online in the old Greeks. But here's one way to think of it. As long as we are better than them as we reduce them, we are all lifted up, bit by bit. Even they win."

"Better than."

"So you're keeping score. Well, we're not cannibals. No ritual human sacrifice. We don't torture. Not in a gratuitous way. There's no rape in my command."

"I did notice the absence. Perhaps not one of your skills."

Dark in here except for comms lights, to the benefit of the night sky, and he could not much make her out. She did sound quite upset; he aimed a flash at her and yes she was. Laird: "Something you probably never saw in your reading about the Puritans is the case, and this is middle 1600s, of the boy, he was fifteen, who was convicted of criminal fornication, of which there were many types in those days. He was hanged and his head put on a gate-pole, as a take-notice. You didn't read about this? No? Okay. The important part of the anecdote is his romantic interest: a domestic fowl." He almost made a pun. "As an aside, the sad part: the turkey had been made profane, ruined, and was hacked up and thrown on a fire, downwind. Anyway this was their thinking, their message, and mine too: that you would stick your dick in that. The very thought. Brings us all low. And as you know, the weakest link controls the chain; cut it off if you can. If I run into that sort of thing here I guess I wouldn't cut his head off, but I might beat him to death. I do have some skills, after all."

"I know your philosophy tells you crime expiates crime. But in the end there is always the detritus: the criminal, which is you."

"First, what might be a crime to us is not to them. This is how they live. And you have to speak to people in a language they understand. Second, it's not even a crime to us. Not anymore. They even put it in writing; what we're doing is too important. It's all allowed."

"And there are children crying right now because of you." He knew she wouldn't let her composure fail, not here, and he heard her put up barriers against in a brave voice. "Who are not aware of this nicety. They only know that they are suffering and that life is not supposed to be like this."

"Right, you wanted to talk about sin. I bet you have a whole lecture ready." Now one for her. And at times like this he would take on the role, the didact with the don's cap. "The sin is in why you do it. I get no pleasure from this. I don't hate these people. Did Lister hate bacillus? Hate is for idiots. Here, more history." More history, of which he had a complete supply. "Japan conquered Manila and ruled it for four years. Uneasy at times but otherwise an ordinary occupation. In 1945 the Allies landed and the order came down from Tokyo: kill all. Subete korusu. There were recommendations for disposal -- dump them in the bay; hide them in stacks in burning buildings -- but a lot of open-mindedness as to means. Officer's choice. Have at it. Efficiency was the watchword in the Imperial Army, so start with orphanages, hospitals, I believe a monastery, a school for boys. By the way, bayonet when you can, please don't waste ammo in days of privation. As they made their rounds they found recalcitrants, tens of thousands, in cellars and garrets, desperate or not getting it. Kill the men of course; the women too but it's the details that tell the story. Rape, or actually gang-rape, which is different. Then, when they're ready, cut off their tits; not even for prizes, like scalps, but just because, for dog toys or to toss around; put gas in her hair and get it going. With gas running low. All of this for morale. Maybe they knew they were going to die soon: get your joy while you can, here in the Pearl of the Orient, actually a modern western city, that kind of thing for days, no way to count the dead, how would you do that, a slurry of bones. Are you still mad at me? Yeah? Okay.

"The men who did this were not outliers or the mentally ill, they were ordinary products of a time and place. A culture. Whose destruction, then, was necessarily a good thing. Burn their cities, one by one. Imagine a baby in its layette, on the end of a long knife, as a matter of procedure. And for the joy of course, as we just spoke about. So kill all. Might could've done, but I guess we don't do that, so instead we killed their culture, ground it down, exposed it to the elements. Stub it out and start again.

"That's all we're doing here. This is a land of the old books. They'll get it." Will they ever. "I think of my tools as a gardener's tools. I water the soil. I turn the soil. I turn the earth."

"Dig hole with shovel, fill hole with body."

"Seattle: 50,000 dead in a day, and how many of them got a burial. And did you know of course that the Japanese are helping us with this project now, supplies. Children cry for all sorts of reasons, Lieutenant. Inoculation. Broccoli." At this point the orange moon was lighting up her expression. Laird: "Please don't try to shame me. It's beneath you. All right, I'm a bad person. I don't care. That's what bad people do. Not care. I didn't say you could leave."

"You didn't say a lot of things."

She left, surely unappeased and newly wounded. Laird laid his head back and spied on satellites. Job well done. If you ask me for an apology you might be sorry.

Another night. He was rated for helicopters and the V-series and the like, and various small air; not fast movers or the big bummers, anyway too impersonal: now Laird driving his V-26, the single-stick tilt-rotor; spotter, utility, good for spying like now. In the jump-seat beside him he'd put a map guy; they were being sneaks on city 6050, seemed more like a town to his eye. Hanging around the southern hills, getting a feel for the place; optics were really good, could see the rover on the moon if you gave a shit; and too good, he kept having to back out to find his place. Flat and fairly dark outer core of homes and estates; cement plant, houses of worship of course with their minarets and other markers, tenements tailing out like spiral arms.

Some kind of bad light was bollixing his night vision, and he said Eddins put out a drone, which was done. After a minute he dialed in and could look down on town center, government buildings, street market and public garden; now an open acre with maybe two hundred mooj in a grid, packed like a head-count in a camp, before a flickering color screen and the speaker aggrandized on it, ruddy and waving his arms. Laird had the drone tuck in just above, a quiet late-comer: our heldentenor wears a turban, exhorting or maybe excoriating, anyway a classic battle speech; out comes a scimitar made to circle overhead, death to heathens; now comes a slave girl ... and ...

"What am I looking at?"

Eddins: "Bollywood, sir."

Get your joy while you can. "Call up a Kingfisher." A black bird with a bright tail, put out miles above by a circling Spooky. "On my dot," his laser setting the marker; he brought the tilty up to 300 feet for a better look. I suppose I'm paid to understand these people, so now let's learn a thing or two. Set the recordings for high-speed, send a note to satellite command. The bird would slow to a stall over the spot, then drop straight down. There, he saw it coming; they wouldn't, their peepers full of song and dance. At times like this he might count the kilometers -- Klick. Klick. -- then gird for a little science study, an engineering science, crepitology, and he did that now.

Click: it came in nicely center of mass. He watched it live of course but more carefully in its replay. The science had four parts, the first three occurring so quickly in series as to be a slurry of distinct events. The first effect, the primary, was essentially a bubble of cessation of time, which is to say human time, i.e. time so brief as cannot contain sensation; or thought, in fact the dot of acetylcholine cannot even begin its way across the gap. Within this bubble the players do not move, tableau vivant -- this one sleeping through it, this one picking out a bit of khat -- as they are made subject to a blend of static pressures coming just behind the wall of the blast wave: smash them first from the inside, the eyes and ears, the lungs and gassy viscera. Secondary effects are the air itself, normally so innocuous but which when motivated can cut you to scraps: the air and everything in it, the nuts and bolts -- good graphics here -- and indeed the buttons and bones, as those who are destroyed outright are weaponized in turn. Tertiary effects are for those not destroyed outright, who are lifted and carried along to no good end: maybe into a pile of scrap metal; or up hard against the screen, which it seems is a white-washed wall, much pocked now and beflecked, the girl still plying her wares, nothing much coming of it.

The quaternary effect was almost not worth noting, burns and blood loss et cetera. Watch it all again, the little drone doing good work before its end, here take a medal; with simple filters he could warm the reds and yellows.

Laird noticed he felt pleasure.

His hate full of heart. What can I do. I am a man of a certain time and place. Alright I concede, and yes I am capable of concession, a sign of strength -- the most important virtue is strength, all the others virtues rest on it, call it the strongest virtue -- I concede that if this is what I need then I will use it. I don't care. Civilization requires uncivilized men.

Two documents.

Laird full of shit before an artificial fire, made of oil bricks and whatever they could find, out in the desert like a caravansary, telling tales and building morale. Comes a subaltern, DeRoss, with a message, a must-see, which almost never really is.

"This came outta Camp Barbiya." POW camp; he held a single rag of paper like it was radium. "One of the mooj wears a pair of five-hundred dollar kicks, Red Balls. Look brand new. Keels over so one of our guys goes thanks I'll take it. Tries them on and finds this inside."

Laird: "Not touching that."

Someone found a plastic sleeve. Hand-written note; he didn't recognize the runes and gave it to Mirou, who put on her readers and set up proper light. "'All praise to God and his messengers. I don't know what today is. I have asked them every day, and independently they say the same day, which cannot be right. Commander of the camp is … ' probably saying Col. Cavender." Laird knew him, had no opinion. Go on. "'He told us food is coming. They needed a count, and promised us water, so we did file past. 33,771, which I know is wrong because some of us died during the count. With the water they gave us shovels.' Here there is a gap expressed by a slashed line. 'Not far from here they killed and cooked a wild boar. The smell made many of us ill. We have eaten all the grass in the enclosures. Some of us have eaten scraps of clothing, cuffs or pockets, buttons. My friend Tariq al-Sabbah bit his tongue to drink the blood. I think there are two hundred of us left. We can no longer bury the dead. I don't know why I was brought here, perhaps to bear witness, Farisi Avesta, seventeen, I pray my testimony is heard.'"

To the young louie Laird made a face saying prove my indifference wrong.

DeRoss: "Well they're obviously passing notes. So I say dig them up and check their shoes."

"Good, put together a detail and run it yourself. Reports every morning." Off went that one. To Mirou: "Cavender. Scratch his name out." She pulled the message from the sleeve and did so. "Now put mine in. Can you translate like that?"

"I'll just do it in English."

"Do that and take it to Zarley and tell him we have a new psy-op drop." The leaflets that preceded engagements, surrender-or-die etc. "I want a big print run. Tens of thousands, as much as he can. Our new calling card. Sow the fucking ground with it." To that incomprehending look: "What. Just answering a boy's prayers."

Next day or so a couple of spooks came in, with their belly knives and otherwise acting tough, which was more effeminate than simply not being tough. "At the college, that woman, she actually was an author, in fact I recognized her name. This is what she was working on."

A rude pile of pages put on his map-reading. Typed in English, with some pencil corrections. Once again, this country makes no sense.

The Project -- The Misunderstood Man

In a long-ago age very much like our own, and in a land of rolling hills we all would recognize, a traveling artisan, alone except for the blue dog beside that carried his tools and different effects, was surprised on the road by a djinn, who put him in a bottle.

The djinn, in a voice resounding, said, "Rejoice, O traveler, and be of good feeling, for I give you the privilege of aiding me. I have three wishes I am fain you fulfill. Fail me and you will stay shut up therein, stopped over with lead. Succeed and your freedom obtains, as you like it."

The traveler was minded to escape the bottle, but found its mouth made fast with a leaden cap. He looked upon the semblance of the djinn, and marveled with an exceeding marvel. Huge of height, like as to touch the welkin, and burly withal. Hair black of blee, as deepest night-tide; eyes like two coal lamps, smile wide as a cove. What great bother hast betided me, he wondered. "Could you put my dog in? There's room."

"Dog abscondeth," said the djinn, cozeningly, for of very sooth he had taken the dog and hid it. "Now attend my first wish. Give the name of the bird who has a song but does not sing."

The traveler wotted not the meaning of the wish-riddle, but said to himself I am a man to whom providence hath given a passably cunning wit. And he said anon, "The bird who has a song but does not sing is a nervous swallow."

The djinn made an agreeable nod, and smiled with a surpassing smile. "Keenly clever, pilgrim. But now address the second wish I'll have you grant: name the drink that cannot wet the thirst."

"To hear is to obey," quoth the traveler, though again he wotted not the curiosity. But he fell to pondering, until he felt he did haply know. And he said anon, "The drink that cannot wet the thirst is a draught of air."

Now came a sound resounding, of low tremoring, which was the djinn and his laughter in his belly. "Meseemeth thou art well chosen, young boy, young wanderer, but now list: describe the book of fables which has no words. That is my third wish."

"With goodly gree I will," said the traveler, although it be a

bemusing question. So he girt the loins of resolution; and he said anon, "The book of fables which has no words: can't make heads or tales of it."

In little time came from the djinn a mighty cachinnation, that shook the raindrops from the rainclouds. And he stamped a stamp of his foot that nearly clave the ground; and the traveler was loose on the road, the djinn saying, "Whereby I free you and keep my word."

Quoth the traveling artisan, "Could you put me back in the bottle? I've never been this good at anything before."

The djinn said, "Yes, and I have more wishes." With a clap like a thunderclap he --

"Any copies of this?"

"No. I don't know. You shot up all the drives in the room. And then we blew it up."

Laird took the pages outside. A drizzle of gas; he got them going and gave them a stir. You barely existed before; now you never existed at all.

Regardless the day, when you asked them the day they'd say 425, bomb day; who might be digging the rubble, or giving out the shovels, doing bombs of their own. 425, much-tattooed, and tagged on battered walls both home and abroad; the impetus behind the Walther .425, favored side-arm for officers now and others; four-two-five, four-two-five, oft-repeated, a tagline for the matter, or actually more its mantra, meant to soothe, inspire and spiritualize the mass murder, despoliation and other correctives that must needs follow April 25.

Another: fifty thousand dead in a day -- actually more like forty-five (prior to a terror attack you want the toll as low as possible; after, as high as) -- or actually the tiniest part of a day, a trice; a glimmer. And of course the early ledgers were of no account since by the time any daily sum was done it was outdated. All the bad burns, which are so often just a delay; and so many who were caught in collapses, to suffocate or worse; first-responders would add themselves to the tally (and second, and third), as they probed the pit, an abattoir of atomic parts: by week's end the number, whatever it was, was treble. And then there was the matter of the heavy black plume, the counterpane lifted over and onto the bedroom towns just east, Duvall and pretty Carnation and parts beyond. No escaping it, the roads and bridges fouled with abandoned RVs. And no hunkering down, since to a dustfall of strontium-90 your stucco safe-house might as well not be there at all. Beautiful homes full of families, the homes destroyed without a mark.

We are transfixed by the newly dead, for surely life-lessons will derive and make sense of it. 425 was unusually generous and new in that regard: a nuclear ground-burst mid-city, a first, its remedies never considered. How to count those atomized; or to salvage precious orts and iotas from a complication of materials; how to handle remains which are themselves soaked in radioactive ash. And as far as counting as dead those who never showed up where they should've: how do you count them when that place is gone.

Explorers found the soil to be rich in surprising isotopes. Important improvements in safety apparel were asked for. Eventually robot tractors were told to press it all into the pit, which then got a ponderous concrete cap. New sacred ground, not soon to receive flowers.

The communiqué from Makh, the apologia, came in the form of a translation into idiosyncratic English, perhaps by way of German. "A bold and clear defiance ... genocide against us in both form and fact ... we will not practice a sentimental manner of warfare." About the blast: its focus, Microsoft, had been chosen because its applications were central to the banking sanctions and thus the crimes of Hammerfall, crimes analogized to those against the American Indians, which is to say displacement, hunger and death against an innocent people; timed for a board meeting "for maximum revenge." To the list of demands -- basically quit Israel -- was added the end of Hammerfall, including a pecuniary show of atonement.

The message closed with a light note referencing more devices in-country.

April 25, a date not to be forgotten; to live in infamy, though without the consequent war in this case really. Very little actual warcraft being practiced, so perhaps war in name only, but not even that, since it wasn't named that. (The writer who proposed Reprisal War I later claimed to be a humorist. Note: if you're not funny you're not a humorist.) In time the preferred term was simply operations.

President Bishop's consultations also had been bold and clear. From his secure location -- from whatever secret warship, airship, spacecraft, or actually Appalachian bunker -- he and his team had by emergency decree gathered up all of America's military might and dumped it like from a haversack onto the old dry land in question, then to turn away and say have at it, any army's dream.

Phase One -- destroy the enemy -- had been a bit of a bust, hunter-killer teams everywhere confronted with a couple of bombs, tough talk, no wish to engage. Militias simply disappeared, in a residue of abandoned berets and sand-colored tunics, piles of crappy small arms; Makh shaved their beards and hid in lady's habiliments maybe, disappearing forevermore; neighbor states ceded border areas; even the allies knew better than to get underfoot. Kind of embarrassing war stats given all the effort, and best to just go to Phase Two.

Phase Two: search structures for nuclear material; inspect for signs of its recent presence or manufacture; render said structures unfit for these purposes. Important: interpret this order as broadly as possible.

That codicil was key, and made for a more satisfying campaign. Structures: start with towers and office-blocks, government complexes including utilities and schools; shopping centers; barns and silos and so on, not complicated. And homes of course, and their attendant structures. And wait: if you can live in it, it's a home, so off to the crusher went railcars and buses and the like, caravans and trucks. And someone said you can tuck a nuke almost anywhere, so wells and cisterns, and storm-cellars, ossuaries, latrine pits, pools and reservoirs were inspected and filled with concrete. A dammed lake was blown, and all its little pleasure boats. Phase Two kindled creative thinking.

All of this was contrary to the rules. But the rules were American. We made them and could remake them. Knock out a wall, add a room, decorate according to taste; or simply do without. And at this time America decided we might be better served by something else.

As for those who believed that this makes us no better than them: all that lot died in a fire.

So to summarize: unpleasantness; a lack of body counts, or other good measures, and in fact a lack of clear accomplishments or even goals; a corps of embeds somehow left back home this time, fiddling with dispatches: all good reasons not to give the thing a name; the best reason of all was the better war just beside.

America on a war footing, number one and united in fear and rage. Those who could leave left for towns not important enough for terror, Rupert or Elko for examples, and a thousand others, swallowed whole by camper-vans, run dry and ruined, but there are always more towns. Or they broke into Canada, or other places considered safe from the possible warpaths of the plumes, the greasy black clouds coming any day now. Oregon was overrun.

Washington (the other one) locked down and held very still, probably by way of a plan in place, dug up from old bunkers. But certain other cities or regions or parts of them were bled low: Manhattan, Austin and its satellites, Bay Area and Back Bay, Space Coast, all abandoned and sadly also the good homes so assiduously made. The men and women left behind, no less afraid, feasted on these leavings with end-of-days dissipation.

Those who wandered the roads discovered a mystifying cash-only economy, in which the value of any given dollar might turn on the dyspesia of a sales-clerk; this until the banks ran out, rolling to a stop. Now laws are being flouted, including the laws of economics. A krugerrand gets you a gallon of gas. Eventually the Glocks come out.

Bank failures are common enough in history and well-understood; a general failure across an entire polity is not, or not very; a good analogy is a plague. It kills directly but also by killing those who keep us fed and warm, safe from wild dogs. To wit: utilities failed as critical personnel fled their posts. Power is needed to run the pumps, so petrol, so central to modern life (and of course its exodus), ran to a trickle: failed. And of course the gas at the pump gets there by gas, but what doesn't. So marketplaces failed, not having a lot of options, there are no more dray horses. There might've been manpower to help with this but they were busy with their gamma-meters, stopping traffic, kicking in doors. Amazing how one bomb brings the whole building down.

We hate being reminded that we know how to bang out a killer spread-sheet but not how to hunt, fish or forage; that we can't run our cars on wits alone; that we know how to burn trash in the house for heat but not why we shouldn't. Who do we kill for all of this?

Makh of course, for starters, which network was rolled up in the entire, and then some, thanks in part to the new expedient at hand, actually a reissue of an old favorite, torture. (Note: there are those who think torture doesn't work, but of course it does, why else would you do it, it's time-consuming, and taxing if not unpleasant.) I'll have you know I was not a witness to it per se but I was privy to the principles as they were laid out. It started with the idea of America being best at everything, a point of pride; and let's dispense with the old niceties, like leaving a person presentable, or fully functioning. Anyway, success.

Eventually they are husks, exhausted of use, and -- and this would've been August of that year, I remember because of the pun -- the summary executions begin. I was there for the debate, and the winning side was for an emphasis on ease: mess, noise and cost kept to a minimum. In the end they settled on a pulley and a simple length of cable. Then to crematoria, where they provided their own fuel. Even the ash was used to leaven parkland.

Again, to those who say we don't do such things, the riposte is yes we do.

There was also a more organically American violence going on, grass-roots, can-do, rugged individual, not entirely illogical but mostly: Muslims were attacked, in ones and twos at first, and as opportunity allowed; then more comprehensively as the panic hardened and became clear. Windows smashed of course, that old morale-builder; then beatings, houndings. Actual murders were more impersonal, fire-bombs or regular bombs, the car that interrupts the cortege. Domestic Islam advised self-restraint, which was done, of course it was; but then there were those who were only possibly Muslim, like Sikhs and in particular the local Nepalese Gorkhali, who were bloodied and having none of it: and having at it. These redresses were apolitical and closely targeted, based on things like online boasts and other postings, and were quite personal.

For the government's part, all this was only lightly officiated, in the sense of good luck to both sides, let's hope it's wins all around.

Woven into this violence was another, built around American Jewry, standing in for Israel and tied to 425 only in the abstract; and whose consequent dead were not abstract. Their enemies were carriers of the ancient animus, the permanent condition, that sometimes slept but would stir at the lightest touch; who began with broken glass of course, cost-effective and bold. The sons of Irgun had seen this number and did not respond in kind but rather more like by a factor of ten: simple nitrate devices to take out sources, especially in their gatherings, plus print shops and the like. Bloody escalations would involve a helicopter full of tourists, celebrities and famously an entire awards show. All this in the first week.

By all accounts and according to those who claimed to know, the government's part in this was in providing arms to the one side and intel to the other; and/or vice versa. Situation normal then, nothing to see here, now let's find those nukes.

All this while the real war was nowhere near and just beside.

The ice cracking south not far from Iskut and 40 Mile Flats. On its plateau and by its bluff above Telegraph Creek, suddenly a group appears, camera crew in hand, picketing the towers because of the possible harm to ice-worms, that odd and only nominally-edible annelid which might've been found in these glaciations but in fact had not been found very much. Noble cause but turns out it was a ruse, a bit of ironicality put on by a late show; didn't matter, the lot were ensconced in ice brigs and forced to subsist on pemmican for the next few months, how funny is that. I mention this disturbance only because of its anomalous nature now: anomalies had begun to give to way to the humdrum of success.

The events of 425 and after had rallied the workers in the canyons of the Canadian Rockies in two ways. First, of course, a respite or at best an end to the unnatural violence that had stunned and confused the project. As well, 425 had helped animate the wartime analogy. Privations, low pay and no way to spend it; battle-lines and changing fronts; a renewed understanding of logistics as the most important of the war sciences; clarity of purpose. Kill or die.

It was working. Every day or every 500 meters you start again and save the Western world. Ironwrights and tractor-men, and those whose roles enjoined them to keep that lot alive all the while; who would hack out a firebase from the permafrost and Doug firs, the rocky riverbeds and plains; put up a pylon a hundred feet high, heavy on the north side with radiating wires. String it up or down the line as needed, then break camp for another. Every day or whenever you're told: listen to orders, make your complaints innocuous and become a valued part of a machine. Not difficult if you try: machines come from our loins, after all. They embody our ideals. Build or die.

Working: down a bank on the ravine just by PK 3309, the ice crept up with all the guile of a patch of ground cover -- embarrassing how dumb it was. Within yards it begins to falter and disappear, steaming. It spills its guts; the drool becomes a drizzle and eventually an effluence, which finds its way down-valley to a generator, turning a turbine. Cheers, half-astonished, and champagne is pulled from the snow. The press was there, for pictures and reports, which crowded their way into internet heds that week. In America the celebration was by all accounts sincere.

There were live feeds: we watched in glory for several days. The ice has nowhere to go now -- man is once again master of nature -- except up and down. Some of us noticed it was rising, white back heaving, slowly, as if unfolding from a lounge chair. And as it became a tower of its own its weight doubled and redoubled, until it had also become a digging tool, a spade. The term undermining comes to mind. As it tore the earth (and surely here we must note the odd rhythm of water -- freeze, expand, destroy -- which is one of the original rebukes of nature) it slid beneath the concrete dais of 3309 in a classic subduction move.

Eventually we noticed the ice had overtopped its barrier. Now two things happened more or less within a day. The tower, under assault from below, begins to recoil, setting off an emergency; at the upper end the glacier lets go a frozen mass, a great ziggurat, and the tower is crushed along with a work detail. For another day the ice is an angry mother, dropping calves like bombs. Then once again careening more carefully down, drunk with power and as meticulous as a mad surgeon.

Cassiar is abandoned, and all the towers and bases along the length of the line, which the ice would destroy in the softest way. A soft hammer. If you were to simply lay your hand on its face it begins to falter. But it has more time than your hand.

A study was funded. Seems the whole thing should've been built on the ridgelines (where you can't breathe and tractors fail), because glaciers make their way on melt-water and don't climb well. Oh well. At least the project had given us time. Time for what. The president was curious about ways to stimulate volcanic activity in that area; a study was funded. Science argued about when it began and where, and by whose greed or neglect.

Where nothing lives. Where nothing can be built, and where nothing has a home. Where nothing grows. And grows. The ice came down like a theme.

Operations continued in the high basin. Heavy smothering sky; an old drought from before the invention of water; where the sun had begun her day with a vomitus of heat, Laird swimming in it. 140 degrees. How could anyone live here; no one should live here; no ones live here.

Captain Sayre speaking, charged with securing an old mud town evacuated for some hundred years; mud-straw structures are not bound up like regular structures, and might not as readily give up their ground, "So a couple of daisy-cutters, maybe six or eight." When things would not die quite as needed Laird always said yes to air requests but did insist on being asked first.

Sayre: "And we found a cave complex. We have drones going. Setting up for demo but it's taking a while. Thought you might want to come take a look."

"Yeah okay."

So there you have it. Sayre took a congenial turn: "Volunteer?"

Indicating the kaffiyeh tied to Laird's trac. "Didn't have a chance to ask."

"Okay. Yes sir." Unbuttoned a little of his battledress to show a sports tee with the same checker pattern. "Serious, what's the story?"

Middle Tennessee accent. Okay. Never be afraid to learn something new. Laird undid the rag, rotten with road dust, and threw it over. "Brains on it, might do you some good." That's the fucking story.

The cave complex had been badly described: rows of rough sandstone blocks, stacked and weathered together; a stone ramp leading down, made smooth by old footfalls. Lights had been strung into it, but not by his people, who had tied them to a generator. Signage, not too shot up, told the story: this was an archaeological dig.

Operations continued, a body of engineers; Laird standing around. The air was a murderous air. Boiling out of the ground. The wind picked at his tunic like beggars and he headed down. A complex of halls and passages, shaded recesses where the heat could hide. Suddenly to the side a huge placard, a foam-core board, with a citation in four translations, including German and Mandarin.

"As well as his talent as a military leader, Cyrus King of the Four Corners of the World was an engineer. During the design of this citadel, he advised the builders to use new techniques, including cantilever construction, examples of which you will see elsewhere. As well as the vaulted arch, the first in mankind, which you can see above you. "

He looked up. Sure enough. So they'd been making this whole thing ready for the tourist trade. Either fight a war or don't. Around the vaulted arch, det-cord and bits of plastique. Ruins soon to be ruins again. I wonder if a thousand years from now tourists will come stamping through. Spell my name right.

Now a gallery, standing at one end of which a tall piece of graven sandstone, demarcated by a velvet rope and lit like a scene. Unknown glyphs in the stone. The placard read:

"This is a paean to the Zoroastrian god Ohrmazd. It is the earliest known example of script using both spacing techniques and diacriticals. These writing improvements led to advances in trade, jurisprudence and history-keeping."

He picked a figure and drew his finger along its legs and spine, leaving sweat in the furrows. He imagined an old forebear with a chisel and hammering tool, breaking the rock with single purpose.

Mirou was behind him. "We are ready as soon as you like. I have the detonator and will carry it outside."

No you won't: last man carries the detonator. Over his shoulder: "Just put it down. I'll walk it out." He could hear his voice smashing against the walls; then the scrape of her shoes up the tunnel.

What happened next exactly is not recorded. There would've been a great noise of course, and its cessation. Then darkness, immaterial and protracted: nothing undergirding him.

NOMINOE

Laird came awake. Cursing. Now a period of recovery and rest. In time he knew he was in a military hospital, the smell and absurd examining light. He asked as to the disposition of his troops, and was told the war's over for you, you're going home, a nonsense sentence.

He found his right hand bound up like a crab claw; and seems his body now came to an end right around the right knee. With his other hand he examined his face; he forced a mirror from an orderly's hand and said okay, always wanted a beard.

A period of pretty nurses -- aren't they all now, newly unattainable -- helping him to relearn how to do what exactly. Clearly he'd never walk again, with his robot leg -- with its concocted name and immune to rebuke -- doing half the work. And no, he would never do, or endure, the formality of shaking hands again because a hand has five fingers.

Laird was a stoic: I acknowledge and accept my fucking lot. At the same time he could, when they asked him where it hurt, answer where does it not, and mean it, because the pain was that of humiliation, which is a whole-body pain.

Eventually he was moored in a one-room flat, ground floor and picture window; and a toilet, with adjacent area with found furniture and wall art in which to wait between uses. He took down the art because sometimes a sunlit meadow makes it all worse. When he was done with that he for the first time in his life had nothing to do.

If you've never done it you have no skills for it, and Laird turned to what he knew. Humiliation; end of purpose; feeling of failure, which in this case comes from the fact of failure. Pains beside which the pains of his wounds were frankly sad in their cries for attention. And guilt: thousands of men and women adapting to a new command, Gen. Kendall, a dandy and an ass, that moustache. And oh yes I'm a parasite now, hooked to the ugliest tit in the land. And by the way how fitting for a suddenly ugly man.

He'd never been a drinker except as obliged -- and certainly never in a business-like way, with a goal in mind -- but he'd heard good things. So now something to do. He made it to the corner store and from his stipend bought airplane bottles of vodka (as a stoic, he preferred an intoxicant with no false flavors or crafting), too few. More on subsequent visits until too many: liquor proved beyond his governance, leading to excess, morbidity, broken items. Beer then, which made him bloat and encouraged spikes of phantom gout. Pot was a non-starter, makes a man slow and stupid, evidently the whole idea. He settled at last on red boxed wine, Chianti if he cared, which he found he could administer as with a medical drip. The days softened and became uniform; he could sleep now, watch television.

Late in the year the young couple upstairs asked him, as a holiday kindness, to a casual gathering nearby and its means of meeting new people. He recalled it was a houseboat, on the floor of which he was awakened by new people, around him in body armor, weapons drawn. Story was he'd pulled a goose gun out from under a day bed and fired it a couple times, mainly through a window, clearing the place. He had no memory of any of that to enjoy.

Two weeks in lock-up in lieu of bail. Still nothing to do but now not his fault; walls which were the evil opposite of wall art; the turnkeys took his leg, so there was that at least. An attorney pled on his behalf the ravages of post-traumatic stress -- more humiliation -- and he gained his release, conditioned on two years of proven sobriety.

Laird was submitted to group sessions, which didn't work because he didn't have a problem with alcohol and wondered why any fool would. He agreed to be taken on by a psychologist, which effete he figured to bully, cow or just befuddle. Dr. Cathcart served many schools. Laird's dreams were consulted, invented as needed. He crushed the Rorschach. Sexual clichés were invoked, and he enjoyed reddening the doctor.

But then a breakthrough with the next thing: Cathcart had insisted he journal like a schoolgirl, a task started as a farce but suddenly taken to: Laird realized he had nothing to say but a body of experiences which just might. His career in war-making was a history after all, with all the inherent merits, and warranted being put down in biographical form, book length if he had it in him. But of course I do.

He holed up and bent to it; and went to cafes and libraries; he applied his English minor, and his bellyful of Tacitus, Mao, Darwin. His memory was remorseless: all the names and dates, trapped in its ragged grooves. For muse he chose honesty. A hard watchword. For which there is such a need now. He'd seen the news and they knew nothing. It became something like an imperative: tell America the truth about her war. Without heat or euphemism. All the good things being done there.

In ninety days, two hundred pages: 100,000 lapidary words, a good packet of paper. He proofed it twice, hit the print shop and made copies available to each of ArtProjekt's history imprints.

Sadly for Laird honesty is the worst of the virtues, mostly unwelcome and sometimes grotesque. Only one of the eight tenders came back, saying not right for us, seek help. Even Cathcart only pretended to have read it in the entire.

His humiliation grew dense and imperturbable, throbbing from a lodgement behind where the ribs met. Only one thing for that, a stop at the corner store, where he bought a box or two. He slipped away from his obligations, with excuses at first, then by not answering the door for days at a time, until eventually all interested parties thought of him as someone else's problem. He set up a delivery service, with automatic payments; aside from wine, his calories mainly came from canned meat, salt snacks, the occasional octogenarian drink; he turned off the heat and AC to help pay for it.

The Project -- The Misunderstood Man

He got a church to come once a week to do rubbish and laundry, during which visits he would seek the safety of a back patio. He purchased a couch, also war-torn. Now Laird would settle in to peaceably serve out his tour.

Implacable memory, with its private designs, would break his peace, the way gravity breaks a stone. For example: Laird would, aided by his spirits, have waking dreams. In one of them, the people who infected his memory came and apologized, one by one, as he sat quietly, which is the subtlest power over the supplicant; all of this came at the end of the dream, where things are remembered. And when he woke up (possibly not completely) he wondered if that was good enough. The answer was no: he had not accepted the apologies while in the dream, the only place where they existed. To do so while awake would be false, and a lie. Also: sometimes Cathcart would appear in these deliria and demand that he provide an upbringing, a provenance that explained him. Broken family, incident on a ball field, anything. And Laird would be thoughtful in his dream and say not only do I not know, if I had an opinion I wouldn't listen. It's not science. It's not even thinking. It's nothing.

In mornings he would put these thoughts, or find them scrawled, in his book pads, which he hoped to burn soon.

One day he got an odd piece of mail. Professed to be from the government. Seems he was due a medal, with full military ritual. Tried to reach him by phone, which he had disabled, so please call the following number. He set it aside for awhile and eventually put it on the back of the loo, to ensure that at least twice a day he would give it an eyeful, then walk away.

It came again, more eloquent now in emphasizing that the attaboy in question, the Medal of Honor, brought with it a triple-stipend. The man who answered the phone was twee and probably not military but was otherwise friendly; asked some good questions, confirmed the date and said a package was coming by courier.

Which it did. Laird laid out the contents of this strange aside on the orange kitchen lino. Full service uniform, bespoke of course, which would need to see an iron; beret and dress boots. A tagboard of ribbons, medals and badges ready for mounting, which he assumed were correct for him. Chits for a shave and trim, rail fare to and from, lodging. Credentials and a pass. Important: three big uncreased c-notes for cabs or walking around.

He was briefed and given his blocking on the sunny South Lawn. Stand here and here; don't say anything. Brace for praise from a man who's never heard of you. The actual act of bestowment obliges some hands-on time; grit your teeth, warrior.

He found himself set up in a ready room with a carafe of the local water and an unspecified wait to use as best he could, a familiar feeling. The room was as clean as a theme-park, a museum piece, don't put your muddy hands on it. There was a recess with a bust, ah yes, Beaumarchais, champion of the early days … got the nose wrong … a note by his hand that hadn't been there just before. *"Thank you for your service."*

He turned. Two men in formal attire, one of them very much the larger one, who said, "Hello. My name is Nominoe. It were my doings that dreamt up this shindig on your behalf."

Okay. And what the hell. "I'd thank you. But let's see how it goes first."

"Wonderful answer. Blunt and funny. Unexpected. And expectations met. And now I think you'd like to know why all this effort."

Laird was distracted by the accent, which was certainly a hybrid, with an effort at unlearning somewhere, maybe for radio; also by their matching suits, shoes and ties. The little one was a gap-mouth, tongue lolling, who stared at him well past propriety. Laird: "Fuck are you?"

No reaction except by Nominoe, who laughed. "The military man smites his cymbals. This is Velbin, my scribe. Yours too, actually. Speaking of which, question: Dr. Abulafia's tale, did it have a title?"

Huh. "Lost me a couple times there."

"The academic you shot in the face. During your pillage you stole her story and put it to the torch. Burned it to the ground. Wait, I can see I should have mentioned: we are presently polishing your manuscript. Clean, buff to high shine, fix typo -- the editor's art. Lots of good vignettes there, little details. It's the details that make the story. Gonna get you out of First Person. That early-years bit: no one cares. Remove filler, attempts at humor. And to get it right we've been in consultation with your lieutenants, your lieutenant Nidha, and ... let me think ..."

Laird had seen faces like this, the smile that only left under duress, conveying nothing. "You know."

"Mirou, yes, thank you." Pause like he'd lost his place. "Anyway, we were wondering."

A second surprise for Laird, who'd thought himself done with such things; a second strange beneficence, this one coming with a twinge of violation. His words, his history, manhandled; or was it actually just his trash being retrieved. They might've asked his permission, assuming he still had it to give; he might even thank them in return for an apology. "I never looked at it. And if it had a title I'd have made damn sure I forgot it."

"Another excellent answer. Warm and witty, in the classic style. Something we can work with." A handler came in and Nominoe sent her away with some kind of indication. "They'll wait. And here's the next thing, I think you might like it. Can you still fly the tilt-rotor?"

The V-22. Probably meant the G-class. Laird pulled up his pantleg enough to show a couple screws.

Nominoe: "I know about that, I meant aside from."

"Aside from the fact that I can't, of course I can."

"And I knew that too. We'd like to take you on as flyer. We cobbled together a tilt-rotor to suit your particulars. The work would be military. Without the shooting if that's okay. Military with all the ranks, proper pay and all that. No heavy lifting, fresh air."

A third surprise. And the stoic who'd hoped he was done with such things had not much to say. "Now you can tell me." Why all this effort.

"Because right now there are important things needing doing. And you have so many skills. You're a vessel full of them. A bloody cask. Why would I leave you lying there?" Came the handler again, desperate. Nominoe: "Oh ... and we'll be sober in the cockpit?"

Nominoe had bought himself a bit of leeway for that sort of thing. Laird thought about negotiating in a pro forma way, but was too far ahead for the trouble. Get me out of my shitty digs; into a goddamn car. Into the air again; into a fight again if I can find a way.

Laird was sent to Fairchild in the desert northwest. He brought his medal along and let them fondle it, which paid for goodwill and deference. They put him through a test course in a trainer with the mods: a clever single master pedal, with a middle binding for his good foot, which took him a minute to get the better of; a combined cycle-stick and yoke, smart. A ton of money spent on his behalf, which he might've questioned in an earlier life. His first chance aloft he showed off a little, a roll and tail-slide, discomfiting the tower.

First orders came quickly, for a drop-off well up into western Canada. Maybe that glacier matter? Hope so. He watched them strap down the cargo, pretending to supervise: just the one big insulated box, handle with care. Size of a fridge. Why not, keeps food from freezing.

On his way. Quickly ten nautical miles, and below him the cracks and carapaces of the Spokane Floodlands, broken and beautiful, and he set aside the stoic for an hour, the hum of the engines becoming its own kind of calm and quiet.

Now the ice plain, the new and prospering inland sea, not much to look at. Destination near, and he began dialing things down.

From his headset: "Hello again."

"Speaker identify or clear comms over." Nothing. Irritating. Protocol for this sort of thing encouraged improvisation. Okay. Ignore and carry on, how about that. Seemed to work.

Suddenly something behind him, a black mass. Snap around, crash knife out.

The Project -- The Misunderstood Man

It was Nominoe, in a greatcoat and tartan scarf, precarious headset. "No basin in the back for the air-sick traveler?"

"Start talking."

"Really. When did I ever stop." He lowered the jump-seat and settled in. "Daggers down, my friend. I am more than just a part of your parcel, I am captain of this adventure, please see your packet."

Laird pulled up his paperwork and turned to the stuff he never read. Executive authorization: Nominoe, Office of the President. He'd been roped into some kind of cloak-and-dagger bullshit. "Good way to get yourself killed."

"Heard of better. Can you hear me okay? No not you. Give me two clicks if you can hear me. Three if you can't." Which he thought was funny. Laird heard two keys of the mike. "Velbin is safe at home, eating chips evidently and listening in. Also this." Above one earpad, a camera. "Looking in. Imagine if I asked you to smile and wave. Now then." He handed Laird something. Consumer GPS device. "Any idea how to use this?"

"I know where the fuck we are."

Nominoe reading now from a fold of paper that had seen some gravy. "Go to the coordinates."

"Already there." Laird looking for a camp, landing-lights.

"Ascend to 600 meters and maintain hover. Can you do that? Don't make me take the wheel."

Descend. Done. The army man's lot: obey the incompetent, the martinet, the loon. "By the way, that accent. Obvious fake."

"An affectation. Not easy, you try it."

"There's also the option of just using your real voice."

A pause just long enough for a change in smile. "Also an affectation. Say did you ever shoot men in the head?"

So now it's war stories. Much loved by the safe-at-home. Fuck my lot. "Sure, some were."

Nominoe: "For me, shot in head is not the best. Your brains have a second or two to form final thoughts, but they'll be something like upset, apoplexy, unfair. Dumb. And where brain-cells actually abut the slug, it's what the heck is this. Guillotine is not much better, he picks up your head and it's several seconds of embarrassment. You could have your head blown up, but all those individual bits flying around are forming last thoughts which combined are probably not reflective of reality. Worst: dying at home surrounded by friends and family. The lights go dim and your last thoughts are your loved ones suffering, because of you. I'd rather die next to someone who hates me."

Laird found himself unsure as to the expression he might have on his face. "If you say so."

Nominoe: "I rather think I should. So ... shot them why? You must've been upset."

"425." You ass.

"Right. Ah yes. Well then you sure showed them. I don't know if they knew it necessarily but if they did wouldn't that be something. By the way, you probably don't know, that was my project."

Your project. "How's that?"

"Well, for example I had one of my fellows drive it to target. Though he can't drive so you know, escort it. He was happy to. Well ... let me correct. Who knows what people feel. And I wrote the communiqué. Which was read the world round. My most celebrated work. Funny because I got some of the vernacular wrong, I bet you noticed."

Laird the stoic, abiding the sudden acidification of his blood, the acid bath soaking him from the inside. He found he'd stopped breathing: start again, on a pace bound to the throb of the rotorblades. "Did not notice. So how would a person get his hands on something like that?" A bomb like that.

"What? Oh. I bought them. It's interesting, they're treated like treasures, but mostly those who have them don't find them terribly useful. Can't exactly put down a food riot with. By the way, people overreact sometimes, it was a 100K device, I don't think they make them any smaller, kind of a piece of shit as those things go."

Sharp breaths, like razors, keep the thinking clear. "You killed a lot of people."

"Oh? Is that a lot?"

"I'm sure it seemed like it to them."

"Were their lives important? Because their deaths were important." A pause in which he called up prepared thoughts. "Big bright light and the president sees clearly. Good with crowd, not good with existential threat. And you ask why not just nuke the malefactors of the ice campaign in their homes and lands, but no, cannot be justified. Women, children. The perfidy, and loss of sentiment." A pause, almost immediately abandoned. "He needed a good hardening. Had to hurt. Had two kids on the campus, so that would do it." Laird vaguely recalled reading something about that. "Killed his darlings. And ... success. Got the pickets up and humming."

Laird: "How'd that work out?"

Nominoe sighs; he lightens himself by the weight of an honest laugh. "Prove me wrong, that's how I learn. Prove me wrong every time and I learn and learn so that's how I win. I have been wrong so many times that I float above the earth looking down."

Laird raised his right hand and let it hang there like a tilt-rotor. "I could kill you right now with just my thumb and half a fuck-finger."

"A feat almost worth witnessing." Nominoe placed something on the console between them. Laird had seen these by the dozen, a detonator. Safety cover over the clicker, warning light dead red.

Oh. I bought them.

"You probably know the old philosopher's gag, why is there something instead of nothing. Okay, good challenge for an artist. Nothingness is simply the lack of something, so you start with that. Did a little research and it turns out the better question is: why so much of the bloody stuff? Clearly nature adores a vacuum; or, if you like, clearly the great abundance of god's efforts are dedicated to its manufacture. Every cell in you -- your hands, your limbs, your neurons firing away -- every part of you warring each day on your behalf, saying I fight for you, I make and remake you and will fight for your endeavors, and to which you entrust your time and care, are made, frankly speaking, of nothing. This is our tableau, and we are denied a glimpse of it at every turn. That is unjust. Or to say it better: all the parts of this universe which cradles you, however well, are comprised principally of void. Remove the void from this place and what you have is something about the size of a pumpkin. Heavy one I'll grant.

"Or I'll say it even better. Nothing lies before the beginning and after the end, so it describes every story, including this one. Why wouldn't I want to know this great story in its entirety? But of course when I think about it the thoughts get in the way -- they're things after all -- and that's unjust. And you're wondering --"

Laird: "Wondering what's the big hold-up."

Nominoe organized his breathing. "I'm an idea person. Not so good with execution. Anyway I've done nothing to deserve it."

"If you say so."

"And even if you say so." Here Nominoe indicated distant western light and closed his eyes. "Nicely timed for the setting sun." Spoken in newly accentless American English, to Laird almost lovely, a monophony around a single note, continuing. "They say the soul leaves the body upon death. But what if the body leaves first? Imagine the surprise."

Laird pressed the button, and the surprise was not imagined. Brave drops of dopamine killed in their docks. Replaced by a giant ball of pure light, which cannot be seen: starlight a million times brighter than the sun (which of course is so very far away); nuclear fire, both rare to see and a fire we live under night and day. And there was a great bark, crawling along at the speed of sound, and what a sound, that no one remembers, except perhaps as a mishearing of thunder. In an ambit of three miles, and in an instant more or less, the ice was gone as if never there. Streams of boiling vapor flying up like Nominoe's astounded ghosts.

Nothing was harmed that hadn't already been destroyed; or perhaps a migration of petrels, a pair of snowshoe hares hopelessly lost.

The Project -- The Misunderstood Man

I placed an envelope on President Bishop's lucky pillow with some advice inside and a prepared statement, soon delivered: "Two days ago, after careful consideration, and after extensive consultation with my Crisis team, I directed our Strategic Air Command to detonate a low-yield nuclear device several thousand feet above the Canadian province of British Columbia, and more importantly above the ice mass menacing our ..."

That went well, and five more like devices got the imprimatur. The backs of the ice were broken on one hundred and fifteen contiguous mountainsides; stragglers were tracked down and brutally dispatched: fuel-air bombs, napalm, flame tanks, dealer's choice. All that old ice becomes rain of course, pouring down the valleys and river canyons to wash away the pickets, turbines and other misbegotten ideas, best we forget them.

As far as Nominoe. He wanted to know, at the end, and when everything was gone, what was left over, and thus what it was like before the beginning: the quiddity we're not allowed to see. Surely something to behold. And related to this end he'd put together this idea that one's last thought, ideally the one above, carries on, like an echo, or an image frozen at an event horizon. Anyway. I hope he felt nothing, and still does. My dead prince.

And now our tale is at its end, whose moral holds you here in expectancy. I dunno. And it's not that I don't have ideas as far as that, I do. I have all of them. So which one. And if you think I have nothing to offer right now, actually I do, but I would have to know why, and I don't. And of course who am I to give it if I could.

And so on like that. I told you my descriptions have no meaning. Call it my lot: I'm the misunderstood man. The man with nothing to say.

CPSIA information can be obtained
at www.ICGtesting.com
Printed in the USA
BVHW030917140121
597467BV00021B/19/J